"A stinging satire about the hollowness of the suburban dream . . . Withering in its barbed wit, Ball's mordantly penetrating portrait of middle-class malaise teems with infidelity, inequity, mistrust, and disappointment."

—*Booklist*

"Ball's mixture of satire and domestic drama turns contemporary suburban life into a frightening dystopia." —*Kirkus Reviews*

"From Richard Ford to Edward Albee, Rick Moody to John Cheever, the American suburbs have always had a dark core underneath the façade of Levittown homes and perfectly manicured front lawns. Ball gives her own spin on the tribulations of suburban ennui in her aptly named new novel *The Pessimists*. Ball's second novel is no mid-century rehash, however, because *The Pessimists* is very much a suburban gothic for our current American dystopia. The denizens of Connecticut's Gold Coast include Virginia and Trip, the perfect couple, who secretly hoard a cache of basement weapons to survive the apocalypse, as well as the more conventionally despairing Richard and Margot whose trials only include infidelity and mental health crises. Both twistedly dark and wickedly funny, *The Pessimists* updates our narratives of suburban anguish for an age of American decline."

—*The Millions*

"Bethany Ball understands what it is to be a parent—to be a human—in contemporary America. In *The Pessimists*, she brings unsettling news about the way we live now. I loved this book—it made me laugh, thrilled me, and frightened me." —Claire Dederer, author of *Love & Trouble*

"I loved the sharp wit, pointed satire, and gentle compassion of *The Pessimists*. I was drawn in from page one, and read it in one gulp."

—Jane Green, author of *Sister Stardust*

"*The Pessimists* is honest and hilarious—treating suburban angst, marriage, and private school life both seriously and with the humor they're due. Ball writes with the sharpened pen of writers like Meg Wolitzer and Taffy Brodesser-Akner, but with a dangerous edge and a pathos all her own."

—Rebecca Makkai, Pulitzer Prize Finalist
for *The Great Believers*

"As a portrait of a wealthy suburban community and the secret weirdos who inhabit it, this novel was perfection. From the private school where the kids aren't actually learning anything to the dad stockpiling arms for the end of the world, I was with this story. There's plenty of satire here, for sure, but I also genuinely rooted for these people's private worries and hopes, the humanity that was still there under so much nonsense."

—Mary Beth Keane, author of *Ask Again, Yes*

"*The Pessimists* is a sweet-and-sour gimlet of a novel. It goes down easy, with a satirical edge and a knock-out punch. With raw honesty and sympathy, Bethany Ball exposes the foibles, follies, and discomforts of her comfortable suburban characters, shedding light into the dark corners of their inner lives. I've never seen a writer capture the ambush of middle age so well, with such blunt truth and knife-sharp humor. She details the troubles that come for people whose habitual striving has lost purpose—the disappointments small and large, the widening perforations of marriage and family, the disillusionment and indecision, the simmering discontentment—but also the sparks of joy, the salve of love, and the surprising shoots of growth. She is so good, and *The Pessimists* is terrific."

—Lauren Acampora, author of *The Hundred Waters*

"In spare, headlong prose that hums with erotic possibility, *The Pessimists* cozies up to three jaded suburban couples, desperate to return to simpler times. At its center, a private school that oozes the most horrifying impulses of whiteness and privilege. Ball's singular, indelible voice is reminiscent of Joan Didion: probing, wise, and deeply human."

—Jonathan Vatner, author of *Carnegie Hill*

"I read *The Pessimists* in one sitting, ignoring my phone and my family until I'd reached the final page. Bethany Ball is a writer of singular power, urgency, and humor, a master chronicler of middle-class ennui in the vein of Tom Perrotta and Meg Wolitzer. I loved this book."

—Joanna Rakoff, author of *My Salinger Year*

Also by Bethany Ball

What to Do About the Solomons

The Pessimists

A NOVEL

Bethany Ball

Grove Press
New York

Published simultaneously in Canada
Printed in Canada

First Grove Atlantic hardcover edition: October 2021
First Grove Atlantic paperback edition: October 2022

This book is set in 13-pt. Centaur by Alpha Design & Composition of Pittsfield, NH.

Library of Congress Cataloging-in-Publication data is available for this title.

ISBN 978-0-8021-6035-5
eISBN 978-0-8021-5889-5

Grove Press
an imprint of Grove Atlantic
154 West 14th Street
New York, NY 10011

Distributed by Publishers Group West

groveatlantic.com

22 23 24 25 26   10 9 8 7 6 5 4 3 2 1

For the mothers

PART ONE

I need love not some sentimental prison.
—SAM PHILLIPS

Chapter One

New Year's Eve

BEFORE THE GUESTS arrived, Virginia pulled a sequined
silver slip of a dress from the back of her closet. She
hadn't worn the dress in years, not since she'd had Charlotte. Maybe even before she'd married Tripp. She stripped out
of her sweatpants and T-shirt and pulled the dress over her
head. It slid over her body easily and she admired how the dress
showed her deep cleavage and how the sequins set off her hair.
She ran her hands over her body, her fingers finding something
small and hard and steadfast on her chest, an unwieldy part of
her heart perhaps. She decided to wear the dress to the party.

Tripp walked out of the shower to his closet, where he pulled
on his better jeans and a checked button-down shirt he wore
untucked. For a moment they stood side by side and stared at
their reflections in the mirror.

Is that a new dress? Tripp asked.

No, she said. I just haven't worn it in years.

You look good, Ginny, Tripp said. In fact to Tripp she looked just the same as when they'd met. Like not a day had gone by. Tripp reached for her hand and she let him hold it and then he kissed her on the cheek and headed down the stairs to prepare for the party. Virginia watched herself in the mirror another beat. She lifted up her breasts and let them fall. She sighed. Another year. Another party.

The usual guests arrived, a mix of neighbors, friends, parents of their children's friends, and old high school classmates who had either never left their town or, like Tripp, had left and come back.

The music thumped. It was loud. Rap music, profanity. A teenager had hacked the sound system with their phone. People groaned and rolled their eyes. The volume lowered. Someone put on some jazz. They turned back again to one another and their conversations. It was a burden, they knew, to host New Year's. It was a long haul. It involved stamina and good cheer and goodwill. Now a nice din hummed throughout the house. The party had begun.

Gunter was a transplant to their town from the city. He stood on the other side of the living room and pawed at the three Christmas stockings hanging over the fireplace. He reached inside and pulled out a half-melted Hershey's Kiss. Perfectly good. He unwrapped it and popped it into his mouth. He marveled at the fireplace, which was gas and could be turned off and on with a switch. It was so stupid and tasteless. Only an American could invent it. He sidled up to his wife, Rachel, who eyed the little stack of hardcover novels on a bookshelf beside the mantel. She tapped her finger on the spine of one of the books. The book was called *The Moral Character*.

This is Virginia's book, Rachel told her husband.

Who is Virginia?

The blonde, Rachel said. In the silver dress.

Gunter held his glass of whiskey and melted ice in his hand, waved his elbow vaguely at Virginia. That one?

The host, Rachel said. Virginia. You met her last week at the Petra School.

Ah yes, Gunter said. Now I remember. He stared at Virginia and said, Maybe I am more drunk than I realized.

She's always been lovely, Rachel said.

Oh, Gunter said. I don't know. But Gunter—rakish, European, and ignorant of the sell-by date of American women—watched her closely. She was beautiful.

How old is she? Gunter asked.

My age, Rachel said. All my friends back in the day were in love with her.

In the kitchen, Tripp pulled bottles of wine from a wooden crate on the floor. He lined them up on the counter and opened one with a corkscrew. He cracked open a beer for himself on the lip of the countertop and headed to the deck to check on the barbecue.

Margot—Virginia's closest friend in town—opened cupboards and searched for a can of ground coffee. She and Virginia had met through their husbands when Virginia and

Tripp had moved to his hometown. With some effort, she found the coffee. The cabinets, Margot could not help but notice, were a mess. It would take Margot just an hour of work to whip this kitchen into shape. She heaped some coffee into the coffee maker and poured in water from the faucet. And then, because she couldn't help herself, she pulled a sponge from the edge of the sink and began to scrub the countertops.

The smell of coffee filled the kitchen. Virginia walked in. I was just about to start the coffee. You beat me to it. Virginia took the sponge from Margot's hand. Stop, she said. You don't need to clean. I'll do it tomorrow.

Outside, Margot's two older boys played basketball in the driveway with other kids from the neighborhood. Testosterone and adrenaline and rising endorphins kept the kids warm in their T-shirts and loose basketball shorts. They shouted and swore and cheered and rallied. They did layups and alley-oops, broke ankles, shot three-pointers, and burned energy, their actions creating a molecular effect of heat and muscle and height. The basketball hit the house with a thud.

You should have another kid, Virginia, Margot said. It's so selfish to have just one.

Virginia shook her head. Tripp doesn't want any more. And besides, we can only afford Petra School tuition for one.

Yes, Margot said wistfully. But what about a boy? I'll bet Tripp would want a boy.

There are no guarantees of boys, Virginia said, and she smiled.

Rachel walked into the kitchen. She was tiny and dark and cool in a black sheath and heels, like the city was still in her pocket. Can I help? she asked.

No, no, Virginia said. We have it all under control. So glad you guys made it tonight.

Rachel had been a successful digital stylist in the city but had now gone freelance. She held her cup of wine with her pretty, darkly manicured fingers. Gunter is drunk, she said. The Swedes are terrible at drinking. I'm not sure how we'll get home. I barely know how to drive. Rachel rolled her eyes. We can get a cab.

Oh no, Virginia said. No cabs out here. I'm sure someone can give you a ride.

Margot gestured to Rachel and said, How do you two know each other?

We used to work together before kids, Virginia said. And now I'm really happy she's here. Her kids will go to the Petra School with Charlotte.

Virginia used to steal all my boyfriends, Rachel said.

Not true! Virginia said.

Rachel sipped her wine. Very true, she said. Very.

Outside on the back patio, Tripp stood by the grill and stared at the backyard lights that dotted the snow. One of the lights was out. He wondered how long it had been out. He wondered why Virginia hadn't fixed it. Or what it was she did all day. Tripp had never gotten over the fact that stay-at-home mothers stayed at home, even after their kids were old enough to go to school. Whole armies of women across the nation just filled their days with hobbies and workouts. Christ, Tripp said out loud. How many wives does it take to change an outdoor light?

Richard, Tripp's oldest friend, walked through the open French doors to the back porch. What do you say, Tripp? He walked to the barbecue and picked up the tongs. You think I should flip these?

Give 'em to me, Tripp said. I'll do it.

Richard handed the tongs to Tripp and grabbed the neck of his beer bottle. He saluted Tripp with the bottle and tipped it to his mouth and drained it.

Want another?

No, Richard said. I've had too many.

Tell that to that guy Gunter, Tripp said. I think he's wasted.

Richard peered over at Tripp. How's business?

They cut my commission again.

Richard nodded. My portfolio took a hit.

They watched the steaks grill and something unspoken passed between them. Tripp finished his beer and set the bottle down hard on the railing of the back porch. He reached into his front pocket and pulled out a small gun. A pistol. He set it down beside the empty bottle.

What the fuck is this? Richard asked.

Gunter wandered outside, saw the gun, and picked it up. In Gunter's big hands it looked like a toy.

Wow! Gunter said. A thirty-eight. I haven't seen one of these since my army days. Why do you have this? He pointed it toward the backyard and called out: Hands up!

Tripp pulled the gun away from him and shoved it into the waistband of his jeans. Chill, he said. Come on, Tripp said to Gunter and Richard. I want to show you something.

You finished the basement? Richard said as they clambered down the stairs to the dirt floor of the basement. And you didn't tell me?

Tripp pulled keys from his pocket and unlocked a makeshift door made from rough plywood. He pulled on a light with a string cord and shut the door behind them. He locked the door with a deadbolt.

Inside, there were a few small cabinets, nothing more. Tripp unlocked a cabinet and swung the metal doors open to reveal rows of boxes of what looked like ammunition.

What the fuck is this? Richard asked again.

Ammo. Guns are useless without it. I've got three of them stashed in the house. Plus the Beretta and a couple of shotguns. One hunting rifle. A few other things.

Where? Richard asked.

Think I'm telling you?

But why? Gunter asked.

Rough times ahead. The recession is nothing compared to what's coming. Ice caps melting and filling the seas. Superstorms. Massive hurricanes. Poles shifting. Solar flares knocking out the electrical grid.

You can't be serious. Richard laughed. You'd be more persuasive, you know, if you just stuck to one catastrophe.

You Americans are so pessimistic, Gunter said. I just did a building in Beijing a couple of years ago and everyone was

9

so much more optimistic there. Tell me, what does your wife think of all this?

Tripp shut the cabinet and locked it. Virginia doesn't know anything about it.

You can't be serious, Richard said. Margot leaves no stone unturned. There is no way I could keep something like this secret from her.

She is . . . incurious. Lately very preoccupied.

I gotta tell you. This all seems pretty crazy, Tripp, Richard said. I'm perfectly sane, Dick, Tripp said.

Gunter took a look around. I like it, he said. It gives new meaning to . . . what's that expression? Man cave. Gunter picked up the pistol Tripp had left on the rough wood table. Is it loaded? he asked. He put his finger on the trigger and began to squeeze.

Richard shouted. Dude. What the fuck.

Tripp grabbed the gun from Gunter.

Sorry. Gunter's face reddened, and he said. It's my army training. In the army . . .

They heard the door to the basement creak open and Margot poked her face down the stairs. What's going on down there? she called. Why are you boys in the basement?

Richard bristled at his wife's voice. We're coming up!

Please do! Don't be antisocial now, she said. We want to see your faces. Margot shut the door and above them they heard her footsteps creak off and her muffled voice.

Come on, Richard said. He turned to Gunter behind him. You're a real idiot, he said.

What did I do? Gunter said. It's not like I pulled the trigger. Besides which, it is only a very small gun.

Back in the kitchen, Tripp gathered meat from a plate with his hands and spread it on a serving platter. He splattered the homemade meat sauce over the steak. It was perfectly pink in the middle, tan toward the edge, and black around. Cutting the meat was Richard's job. He did this with a knife so sharp it could shave the hair from a child's arm, something Richard liked to demonstrate on the arm of his oldest son.

The table was set full of salads, rice, casseroles, and dishes of potatoes and beets the others had brought. People grabbed forks and plates and exclaimed over the meat. Everyone was half or fully drunk and hungry. Tripp stood in front of the sink and held his bloodied hands in front of him like a surgeon and waited for the water from the sink faucet to warm.

Bundled up outside on the back porch in his sheepskin parka, Gunter was trashed and talking too loudly. My wife is angry with me, he said. She does not know hardship. She has an infantile idea of what constitutes hardship, like most Americans.

People edged away from him. No one knew him well enough to offer much sympathy or cut him any slack. It was like that sometimes, they knew, when you've had too much to drink. And on the other hand it was tiresome.

What do you think of Rachel, Richard said to Tripp. Virginia's friend from the city? *Nice*, right? He whistled softly.

Tripp shook his head. Seems so? Why? Do you like her?

Richard nodded and then shook his head. No, he said. Of course not. But I mean, she's kind of hot, don't you think?

The night waned. Tripp stood behind Virginia, who hovered over the island, clearing empty wine bottles. He buried his nose in her hair. Hey you, he said. He felt Virginia pull slightly away, caught off guard, but Tripp held her tight. Great party, he mumbled into her heavy loose hair, and then he headed back out to the grill to give it a quick scrub and close the lid. It was still too hot to cover. Tripp, Virginia realized, liked to hide behind the grill.

On the other side of the island, Richard's phone rattled in his front jeans pocket. Virginia watched him. Richard pulled the phone out. His eyes glittered. He snuck a glance at the screen. He looked up and caught Virginia's eye.

Video from my mom wishing me happy New Year's, Richard said. They're on a cruise.

Give them my love, Virginia said.

Neil Young's "Harvest Moon" filled the room.

It was eleven forty-five. Gunter now spoke half in Swedish and half in English. I'm ready to go home, he half shouted. Back to the city. Back to Stockholm! Village life is for small, burrowing animals.

Rachel shushed him. Please, Gunter, she said.

No, Gunter scowled. I don't care anymore what these people think. He stood and watched Virginia gather empty wine bottles and plastic cups and thought to himself: I'd like to lay the American woman on a bed and wrap her long legs around my neck like a scarf.

Richard turned on the television in the family room at the back of the house. The ball began to drop. Ten. Nine. Eight. At the end, everyone shouted: Happy New Year! Happy New Year, they said again.

Richard hugged Tripp. We survived twenty twelve. I guess the Mayans were wrong.

Tripp slapped Richard hard on the back. I love you, man, he said.

Richard and Margot gathered up the boys. Gunter and Rachel caught a ride home with them in their minivan, and left their car behind to be picked up in the morning. Everyone agreed the party had been good. There had been just enough drama but not too much.

Virginia loaded the dishwasher and set it to wash. Upstairs, she half carried her daughter, Charlotte, smelling sweetly musky, from the master bedroom into Charlotte's own and deposited her into her messy bed. She stood in front of the floor-length mirror in her bedroom. She looked tired. Her makeup had smudged. The dress she'd worn was ridiculous. What had she been thinking? She brushed her teeth and wiped off her makeup. She left her dress on the floor of the bathroom and climbed into bed while downstairs Tripp washed the rest of the dishes and separated the recycling. Then the house was quiet. The bed was cold but it warmed. Tripp climbed into bed, freshly showered and damp and wearing an old pair of navy-blue gym shorts. The air between them was icy. Her feet stayed cold.

Happy New Year, Ginny, Tripp said. He leaned over and kissed her on the mouth. In minutes he slipped into sleep where he dreamed, twitching, of tracing animals in snow. His heavy arm draped over her. She waited a moment and wiggled free. She climbed from bed and walked across the room, where she pulled a pair of wooly socks from Tripp's drawers. Back in bed, she lay on her back with the blankets pulled to her nose. Someone lit fireworks over the sound. Tripp snored. The feeling of near suffocation, the warmth of her breath dampening the blankets, comforted her. Her feet warmed in Tripp's socks.

But she was not going to fall asleep. There was a current and it pulsed.

She lay in the darkness and thought of Richard. She thought about the video he'd been watching. A girlfriend probably. In a few moments she would get up and pad down the hallway to Charlotte's room, where she would breathe in her scent and crawl into bed beside her and lay awake until the adrenaline of the night drained away and she would grow heavy and fall asleep.

The next morning, New Year's Day, a village police car slowed and stopped outside the house. Virginia walked out onto the small concrete front porch in her slippers and robe. She carried a steaming mug of coffee in one hand and held the robe closed with the other. She blew on the coffee and watched the steam rise in the cold winter air of the first day of the year. The policeman climbed out of his car with his ticket pad in his hands. He was ticketing Gunter Olson's car. The big Mercedes hulked on the side street beside the NO PARKING sign. Hey! she called. Hey! My friends were too drunk to drive last night. I'll call them now. They can be here in two minutes. Can you wait?

He squinted up at her. I waited already, he said.

He had a big mustache and a tight uniform and no coat. Cops wore their uniforms tight. It was a cop fetish.

Virginia sipped her coffee and watched him. He was young. She recognized him. He liked to park by the town tennis courts and wait for speeding cars.

He stared back, his notebook flipped open, pen poised. She moved her arm and her robe fell open. She was naked beneath. Her breast was exposed. The sun warmed her sternum and curdled her nipple. Wind whipped up the road from the sound and Virginia shivered and covered herself.

She pressed her hand to the top of her breast close to her armpit. The left breast, cushioning her heart, carried a secret.

The cop closed his notebook and climbed back into his big blue SUV. Make sure the car's gone within the hour, he said.

Virginia closed her robe tight around herself and gave him a little wave. Will do, she said.

Chapter Two

Tripp's Madeline

After the New Year, Tripp was sent by his company to find a cheaper place to secure financial records they were required by law to keep for twenty years. Take the day off, his boss had said, and check out the place. It's cool. You'll like it.

The facility, and facilities like it, had been built by AT&T in the 1950s to ensure communication up and down the Eastern Seaboard in the event of nuclear war. Now they were used to store millions of financial records from hundreds of companies across the country, if not the world.

Instead of heading into the city that morning, as he normally did, Tripp took the 287, driving over the Tappan Zee Bridge into New Jersey. If he kept going south, he could head close to Scranton to John Monroe's place, where he'd spent his first weekend in survivalist training a couple of months before. He followed a map on his phone that led him off the expressway. The road turned to gravel and then finally dirt. At the end of it, there was a small hut where a man checked his ID, found his name on a list, and waved him through. A concrete building, dirt road, and shrubs. A steel elevator took him six stories underground. The facility was surrounded by four feet of concrete and six inches of steel. The door opened and then he was hit with it. That smell. And everything came back to him. The smell of the lab in Los Alamos where his father worked when Tripp was a teenager. Cold War–era pamphlets were strewn around the waiting room. Tripp picked one up, folded it, and shoved it into his pocket.

A big guy Tripp pegged for an ex-marine ambled heavily toward him and shook Tripp's hand hard. Gary Arnold, he said in a baritone. Was looking at your CV. Stanford, is that right? Gary asked.

Yes, sir.

Went there for a couple of years, Gary said. Got there on a football scholarship. It didn't work out. Went to the military instead.

Marines? Tripp asked.

How'd you know?

My dad was a marine, Tripp said.

Semper fi, motherfucker. You never served?

Tripp shook his head no.

That's all right. I won't hold it against you.

The facility was called the Iron Mountain and Gary gave Tripp the lowdown. There were shock absorbers on every piece of equipment and steel surrounding the place in a Faraday cage that blocked electromagnetic fields and would keep the electricity on. In the event that the power was cut, a jet engine bolted to the wall would power the facility for a hundred years or more.

Funny how humans will be wiped off the face of the earth, but how much money they took out of an ATM on a Thursday in June will live on forever, Tripp said.

Gary stopped walking. He turned to Tripp and leaned in. Tripp noted the gray of Gary's chinos blending into the gray of the concrete floor. He was the type of man who had no choice but to buy his clothing at big and tall stores and probably had a wife clip his hair military style every week. Maybe, Gary said. Maybe not. Gary lowered his voice. I live a mile up the road and I got a key to this place. When it goes down I know where I'll be. I even got a little bunker two floors down and it's stocked with canned goods. I ain't going down with this ship.

Tripp stared at him a full ten seconds. I'm kidding! Gary said. You think they're going to give a key to some lowlife like me? Making forty grand in tape management? Tripp looked down at his loafers and forced a laugh. But you wanna know something about this place? Back in the eighties if the president was in New York City? If a nuclear war went down this is where they would have taken him.

Tripp drove home from the Iron Mountain facility with the smell of disinfectant still in nostrils. Tripp's madeleine, Virginia would have said. Sophomore year of college, Tripp worked for the Los Alamos Lab where his dad had been a physicist. He'd driven back out west from New York in a little

Volkswagen Rabbit and stayed in the backyard casita of a friend of his parents. At the lab, he assisted the chief tester, traveling with him to the barren desert of the Nevada Test Site. The baking heat of the Mohave in summer didn't faze Tripp and he was the only one of them not drenched in sweat when they traveled there. Tripp loved the scene of empty model houses built a few thousand feet away from each site. Because no bombs could be detonated in the atmosphere, or oceans, or outer space, they tested underground in Nye County, a day's drive from Los Alamos. A hole five thousand feet deep had been dug into the ground, and the rack built in Los Alamos and shipped to the site was lowered down on cable harnesses. The bomb itself—they called it the device—was oblong shaped and about a meter long. They used noisy drill pipes that quieted as they ground their way deeper and deeper. In case of venting, helicopters were readied, and ranchers downwind were given evacuation plans. Later, they were given sizable checks for their troubles. The bomb would detonate, and leave a cavity of radioactive dust and stone. Tripp's job was to take the measurements from the blast. They'd send an electric pulse down the cable to the underground bomb and the blast would crush the cable. This was how they measured the size of the blast. Later they'd enter the data into a gymnasium-size mainframe back at the lab. Tripp was granted top secret clearance at the facility. It thrilled him to wear the badge on a lanyard around his neck and to travel with his boss and mentor, John Dolinksy, who was a pal of Tripp's dad's and had been, years ago, one of the principal scientists on the Manhattan Project.

They'd wait—Dolinsky, Tripp, and a half dozen engineers and scientists—with great anticipation miles out at the edge of the test site until the bomb detonated and Tripp was thrown to the ground, at least the first time. By the second time, Tripp had learned to brace himself. Under their feet the ground roiled and undulated like waves.

Dolinksy was one of the few people who worked in Los Alamos not to live near the lab. He lived instead in a trailer in El Rito, New Mexico, an hour from the lab, the trailer set deep into the pink mountains of the region. Dolinksy took Tripp to his trailer one day on their way back from the test site.

The trailer was small and tidy and up a dirt road that wound round a mountain. Doberman pinschers ran around the house. They didn't bark or approach Tripp. Dolinsky told Tripp there were twelve of them and they'd been military trained. They kill on command, Dolinsky said. But they won't make a sound doing it.

I placed the trailer, Dolinksy told Tripp, on the other side of the mountains from the lab. Dolinksy led him through the dark living room, where Tripp could barely make out a black-and-white TV from the fifties and a large chair and dusty sofa. They passed through the kitchen and out a back door partially hidden by short, scrubby piñon trees. Outside was a concrete patio and a short walkway of paver stones that led to stone steps. Tripp followed Dolinsky through a heavily fortified door. He unlocked it with a large skeleton key and pushed it open. Another staircase led deeper still into the bunker. Dolinsky turned on a gas lantern. It took a while for Tripp's eyes to adjust but he noted the large glass water cooler–style bottles stacked to the ceiling in one small room. Burlap bags labeled RICE and FLOUR and BEANS were stacked against the concrete wall.

I won't last long, Dolinksy said. And I wouldn't want to. But it might give me a fighting chance. Dolinksy stopped and turned. He held the lantern up to Tripp's face and studied him. I've been here since the very beginning and ever since the day the first bomb detonated I've known one thing: man has never created anything he has not used.

Tripp's parents, who had left Los Alamos the summer after Tripp's sophomore year in school, settled in Connecticut. His father took a job on Wall Street as a quantitative analyst, where he made five times what he'd made in Los Alamos. Tripp's mother was happier. She drank less and lost weight and bought fashionable clothing and smiled more. They took expensive trips, joined a private tennis and swim club close to Darien. Tripp went to Stanford, like his dad, got married, and returned home. At Stanford, he didn't study physics. He didn't want to be an academic or a quant. He was a legacy student and the large sum his father donated to the school had played some part in his acceptance. Tripp was an impatient, undisciplined student, and when he got out of undergrad he'd moved to New York City, where his dad helped him get a job as a financial consultant. He'd done okay the first few years. His father helped him buy their house. But then the crash of 2008 happened, his firm closed, and he scrambled to find another job. Not long after, his parents died within months of one another. Tripp was devastated to lose them. To make matters worse, they'd left all their money to the Young Republicans. Tripp watched his star fall. He didn't have so much less than his parents had when they were his age, but it felt that way. It took him a while, but Tripp landed on his feet working as a financial consultant, basically a salesman for financial services. He made a decent living but his savings were all but wiped out.

And Tripp for a long time forgot about Los Alamos and the computer tests he'd run and about Dolinksy and his house on the right side of the mountain—the bottles of water in the bunker, the burlap bags of food, and the twelve eerily quiet Doberman pinschers who'd had run of the grounds—until the smell of that disinfectant brought it all home again to him.

The week after his visit to Iron Mountain, Tripp had his annual performance review. No bonuses this year I'm afraid, Tripp's supervisor had said. But Tripp hadn't been counting on any bonus at all. No one had received one since the markets had collapsed. Lately, companies even on his level were working commission only and Tripp's percentage had been slashed almost in half. Still, Tripp hoped for a raise. He'd worked hard too. Came in early and left late. Made cold calls and attended financial conferences. But his sales hadn't gone up.

His boss was a big-boned woman with a model's face and a mane of shampoo model hair. You'll be happy to know we're giving you one and a half percent, she said. She smiled.

Tripp gritted his teeth and smiled back of course. What else was he going to do? He'd never liked her. Felt in his bones she didn't like him either.

The bitch.

No. It didn't help to think that way. Women could always smell it on a man. They had a sixth sense. He closed his eyes. Thank you, he said.

Don't spend it all at once, she said. Things will pick up. Twenty thirteen is supposed to end with a bang.

Tripp nodded.

That night, his Krav Maga class started at 6:00 p.m. sharp. It was around the block from his office on Eighth Avenue. He didn't want to go. Maybe he'd just skip it. He hadn't connected with anyone there. And he was tired and hungry and disappointed from his raise. He felt desperation rise from his chest like vapor.

But once inside, the Krav Maga class was hype. Tripp was amped. In the dressing room, he saw a guy he half recognized. Tripp waited until he was fully dressed and then walked over to him. You're Billy, right? I'm Tripp. Met you at John Monroe. I was the one sleeping in my car.

Yeah, Billy said. That's right. I remember you.

They walked down the stairs to the street below. Billy told Tripp he was heading down to Pennsylvania to a John Monroe weekend in a few days. It was a special weekend Billy said. Billy asked if Tripp was going. Tripp shook his head. He hadn't been told about it. It wasn't on the website. Yeah, Billy said. Billy looked him up and down and said. My gut says I can trust you. It's kind of a word-of-mouth thing. And, Billy said, it's only for people into it hard-core. They stood with their backs to the glass storefront of a Dunkin' Donuts, all of Eighth Avenue a steady stream of people pushing and shoving their way along the sidewalk.

Hard-core what? Tripp asked.

Hard-core prepping.

You mean end-of-the-world stuff.

Oh yeah, Billy said. Exactly like that.

You believe that shit? That red star crap? The Grandmother prophecies?

Billy cocked up an eyebrow and thumped at the glass. If you don't, why you doing all that John Monroe shit? He thumped the glass again. It's not like it's enjoyable. Cooking up roadkill? Digging a hole to crap in. Why bother?

I don't know, Tripp said. I just, I like it.

The light changed and flickered up the avenue and glinted on the windshields of the cars and trucks that roared past. An ambulance slipped by, its lights flashing but the siren silenced.

You got family? Billy asked.

I do.

I feel lucky I'm on my own. Billy stopped and held out his hands. I got to catch the train. Give me your card if you're interested. I'll send you the link tonight.

That night, back at home, Virginia already asleep, Tripp sat down at the computer in the guest room and searched "prepper."

He took an online quiz: Will you survive doomsday? He took another quiz: Will you survive when the SHTF? He took another: What kind of a prepper are you?

The websites asked questions like: Do you have up-to-date maps of your local roads? Have you prepared for bridges out and mudslides? Is your vehicle sufficient to get you out of danger? Can you manually open your garage door if there is no power?

The country was only nine meals from anarchy.

The North Pole had moved sixty kilometers in a period of only fifty years.

The shifting of the rotational axis was due to climate change. Ice melted. Volcanos erupted. Solar flares from the far reaches of the sun threatened to knock out electrical grids. All the stuff he'd been reading about over the last six months.

An email popped into Tripp's mailbox from "William Baldwin." Tripp opened the link and registered for the weekend using his last remaining non-maxed-out credit card, an Amex. Going back to John Monroe would be a good palate cleanser. He'd made mistakes but had learned so much from his first trip.

The first time Tripp had gone to John Monroe, back when he'd first met Billy, he'd driven his car into work rather than take the train. He'd left work early to drive from the city to Route 17, where he pulled into the Campmor camp outfitting store. He had a list and a burst of purpose as he walked in. He bought a sleeping bag, a tent, a sleeping pad. He bought a utensil set, a plate, a bowl, a cup. He bought a water bottle and a flashlight. He bought a shovel and biodegradable toilet paper. He bought biodegradable toothpaste and soap. He bought a small quick-dry towel. He bought a little folding camp chair. He bought a tiny mirror for tick checks. He bought a rain poncho and a wool shirt and a pair of quick-dry sweats and a hat. He bought a wool baseball hat. It was October. It wouldn't be warm. He hadn't camped since he was a child in New Mexico.

But he had swaggered around the store, gathered up his gear and left it in a heap beside the cash register. He paid for everything with the Amex.

Have a good trip! said the guy behind the register, bagging up his stuff. He wore a tie-dyed Phish shirt. That detail followed Tripp all the way out to his car, and it aggravated him. Love, peace, and harmony? he thought.

Maybe in the next world.

Tripp had driven deep into Pennsylvania where he was waved in to an old summer camp by what looked like a 'Nam vet in army fatigues with a clipboard. The land seemed truly barren. Nothing but sandy soil and miserable pine trees all the way to the horizon. Off to the side of the small dirt road where he parked was a Hummer—John Monroe's truck. He sat in his car a long while and wondered if he should leave. He could take Charlotte camping. Virginia too if she wanted. He should bring them here, to John Monroe. Why spend all that money for private tuition at the Petra School when there was so much to be learned here? But just as he was ready to put the car into reverse, another car pulled up behind him and blocked his exit. He turned off the ignition, sighed, and headed out into the brisk air. Ahead of him, a canopy stretched between trees. Under the canopy clustered a small group of people. There was a camping section, wall-to-wall tents with no room between them. He pushed through to the center of the canopy where people milled around. He could see his breath in the open air but it was mid October and it hadn't been that cold that year. It was that warm wet blanket of late fall. Hurricane Sandy, with the twenty inches of rain it would drop on the area, was still two weeks away.

There had been a hush and a murmur and then John Monroe himself walked into the canopy and took his place in front of a whiteboard. He was bearded, rangy, well over six feet tall. He'd been a tracer all his life, worked with police and the FBI for a spell, and he looked battle worn and scarred. He wore a flannel shirt and a down vest with an old pair of Levi's, and he had a cigarette clamped between his teeth. A pack of Camel Lights poked out of his shirt pocket. He told his story, familiar to most, told as though by rote. Of the Grandmother's teaching and all that he'd learned and the cops he'd worked with and the movies he'd consulted on and the books he'd written and how many people had come through John Monroe Tracing Schools. He talked about the coming troubles and how all the enlightened ones would run for the mountains and everyone else would die in the cities and suburbs in the looting and chaos that would ensue. He explained the Prepper Prophecies. He made them pledge to a sacred silence. They all held up their right hands and did so. Tripp looked around wondering if Monroe was taking the piss. But everyone around him was serious.

One of the "professors" walked over and pasted up some hand-drawn diagrams of structures that could be built depen-dent on season and weather. He flashed the John Monroe knife

as he explained that it was the best knife in the world and with
the knife alone, any number of structures could be built, any
manner of game could be killed, stripped of skin and bone
and viscera, and eaten.

There had been no dinner that first night. Tripp's stomach
grumbled. He wondered why he hadn't brought jerky. Some
of the guys ate jerky out of plastic baggies and it made Tripp
wonder if they'd made it themselves, probably from squirrels
and other rodents, or from roadkill. There were some women
there. That surprised Tripp. They were so nubile and healthy and
young that Tripp could weep. He averted his gaze and thought
of Virginia there. She would never come.

He took his tent out of his trunk and found a clearing, but
it was dark and Tripp fumbled with the canvas and nylon ropes
and plastic poles that wouldn't snap together. He regretted not
getting a headlamp. He'd camped only a couple of times in his
life, if it could even be called camping, as a boy. At a Boy Scout
camp in the Sangre de Cristo Mountains, they'd slept in cots
under heavy canvas stretched permanently over concrete bases.
Sometimes there'd be forest fires and they would get smoked
out and head home in big Econoline vans. Now, he sweat and
swore under his breath when the professor who'd last spoke
came to him casually, introduced himself, and told Tripp he
couldn't actually camp there. In the morning it will be a creek,
the man said, a wad of chew stuck between his lip and teeth.
He spit a long brown stream and Tripp wished he had that too.
He used to pack it back when he played baseball, even though
it made him dizzy and sick sometimes. Well, where can I camp?

Tripp asked. The man made like he was looking around. He shrugged. No spots tonight. Check in the morning. Tonight you can sleep in your car. You won't be the only one. As times get crazier, John Monroe Tracing School gets full up.

Tripp had made his way in the dark to his car with his tent and sleeping bag under his arms. He had the Mustang. It would do.

In the morning, Tripp had woken up stiff and cold with a terrible pain in his neck. The sun pierced his windshield through the trees. It was dawn and already he could smell campfire. He climbed out of the car and headed toward the stretched canvas structure. A group crowded around a woman who knelt on the ground and rubbed two sticks together while beside her a couple of men created a small tepee of kindling. She dripped with sweat, her long brown hair had fallen over her face. She grunted when the tinder finally caught, and she held the tiny bundle of tinder and smoke in her hand to her mouth and blew softly until there was finally a flickering flame. Gently she placed the bundle under the kindling. Everyone around her whooped when it caught. John Monroe himself moved through the crowd and stamped it out with his heavy boot. Good, he said. Now we can eat breakfast.

Under the pavilion, they were taught how to filter water with moss, grass, and dirt. Later lunch was brought out, a Styrofoam bowl of a hearty stew that Tripp ate quickly. It was terrible, not just because of the lack of salt. After lunch they learned how to make cordage out of vines and long grass. Then dinner, more unseasoned stew. Tripp talked to a couple of the guys around him. Many were ex-military. He watched them pull out their own little travel salt shakers. Billy had found him in the crowd and offered him a shake of salt. You're a fucking rookie, but we all were once so I'll take pity on you. Billy also shoved over his own tent after dinner, giving Tripp enough room to set up his. He called him a fucking greenhorn and told him he'd better get with the program or he'd be used for trap meat. After the tent was set up, Tripp and Billy hurried over to the pavilion where John Monroe's son, Jack Monroe explained trapping to them, with charts and demonstrations of milk cartons and cardboard boxes and the "cordage" they'd made after lunch. Get some sleep, Jack said. Tomorrow morning we'll be doing some tracing.

Tracing was what they'd all come there for. John Monroe was legendary. He could follow deer and rabbit for miles and catch them with his own hands. Jack Monroe told a story about his father jumping out of the woods, wrestling a buck, and slitting its throat with the very knife Jack Monroe held up. And if you believe that one, Jack said. I got some beachfront property in Scranton to sell you.

Sunday morning, Tripp woke up with a miserable backache. For breakfast they ate hard-boiled eggs and a little cold bacon. Jack Monroe gave a little lecture about walking like a caveman and they practiced around the camp. Arms hung forward, head jutted out slightly, light deliberate footfalls. After that, John Monroe himself came to teach them tracing. He showed them raccoon poop, deer tracks, tufts of rabbit fur, and a tiny nest of field mice. They ate stew again for lunch with hard bread and weak coffee and then they were back to tracing. Tripp felt better. It was the coffee, no doubt. The sun was shining and burned off the cold mist. The trees above were ragged but still glorious in orange, yellow, and red late fall splendor. Tripp hunted around the grounds far from the camp and the others looked for signs of animals when he noticed John Monroe behind him. Hey, John Monroe said. I've been following you. Watching your tracks. Good to see your headache got better.

Someone blew an air horn and everyone headed back to the center of camp, where they practiced making fires with flint and steel. They worked in groups. Tripp was paired with an old grizzled ex–Green Beret who vaguely looked and smelled like Willie Nelson. He'd been to John Monroe many times before and tried to help Tripp get the right angle, the right amount of tinder. They worked a long time. Out of the corner of Tripp's eye, he could see a woman, buff from Iron Man competitions, rubbing out a fast fire. In minutes it was blazing. She beamed. John Monroe walked over and poured the contents of his canteen over her kindling. Do it again, he said.

It's all wet! she cried.

It can be done, John Monroe said. Do it again.

Chapter Three

VIRGINIA POWERS

THE ONCOLOGIST, Edward, was an old boyfriend of Virginia's. She'd hoped at the time that he would marry her when he finished med school. But he did not want to. Virginia, later, hadn't blamed him. Though she was an attractive and brilliant assistant editor at a shelter magazine, it was not to be.

For one thing, she had no interest in pursuing a career as an editor. Virginia was writing a novel. At night after work and early in the mornings, she worked on it furtively without telling her colleagues or any of her friends. Only Edward knew. She'd met him at a book launch for an Irish memoirist. She'd liked him. A literary doctor. It was refreshing to be with a man who didn't want to be either an editor or a writer, and she fell in love with him almost immediately. When Virginia was with Edward she felt like nothing bad could happen to her.

But Virginia, in her mid-twenties, was unstable. She could barely survive off her magazine salary. She felt out of it and lost with her non–Ivy League education and her Southern propensity for saying "ya'll" and "oh my Lord." She'd been tormented by offhand comments about her bargain-basement clothing, her lack of fashion sense and designers, and her beauty—which was extreme. She was occasionally bulimic, often anorexic. Sometimes she skipped meals out of poverty and sometimes from a real body dysmorphia. Girls in New York City were so much thinner than back home. She learned to live, like the other girls, off black coffee and microwave popcorn and Swedish fish. It was the age of heroin chic. She fell into fits of tears, often in the bathroom stalls of the office. She honestly didn't know how to write a callout or a simple photo caption. The other girls swanned around knowingly, newly graduated from their publishing programs and Ivies. Their rents paid by their parents or fiancés or husbands.

And she hadn't behaved well with Edward. She needled all his friends when they would go out. She would call him late at night and rage at him when he needed to catch up on what little sleep he could cram into his brutal week. She had never met his parents, she'd assumed, because she was not Korean. Finally, he'd broken up with her. You are one of the finest and most beautiful women I've ever known, he'd told her, crying with frustration and sadness. But I don't want to be with you anymore.

For years she put him out of her mind and when his face would swim into her consciousness she would burn with shame.

There had been some good moments between them. When they'd first met and sat on the benches in front of the church at St. Mark's Place in cold late October and felt warm and giddy with love. When they'd spent afternoons at the Hungarian Pastry Shop reading the papers or hours at the Coliseum bookstore wandering the stacks before strolling Central Park. And she remembered how he'd cared for her. When the planes had hit the Twin Towers and he'd left his residency on the East Side and walked all the way to her apartment on the Upper West Side before he headed to Ground Zero to help survivors. Later, married to Tripp and with a preschooler, she'd joined Facebook and friended him but had not sent a message. She'd watched his two children be born, a boy and then a girl. Sandy haired with Edward's eyes and mouth. When the technician had found the lump at her annual mammogram, she'd waited a couple of weeks after the biopsy before she called him. She'd dialed his cell phone number from memory. She was shocked when he picked up. Same number after all this time. She'd dropped Charlotte off at school and driven into the city, where she parked in the Sloan Kettering garage. Edward agreed to see her right away, though normally, he told her, he had a long waiting list. And there's another thing, he said over the phone. We don't accept your insurance here. In fact, you are lucky you know me or you wouldn't have been seen here at all.

In his office at Sloan Kettering, Virginia had waited only a few minutes before she was called. The nurse asked her to strip off her shirt and put on a paper robe and take a seat. The doctor would be in shortly, she said.

Waiting, Virginia remembered the first few times she and Edward had sex. Edward's fingers shook as they crossed under the wire of her bra. His arms trembled as he held himself over her. His nervousness made Virginia nervous. She'd lost concentration and she hadn't been able to come. He told her when they first started dating that he thought she was out of his league. She'd thought the same of him. She'd been so shocked when he broke up with her. He married the next girl he dated after Virginia. The announcement had been in the *Times*. The woman was not Korean. She was another doctor about to finish studies in pediatric oncology.

When Edward opened the examining room door, he looked almost the same. As though the last ten years had not existed. He said, I've seen the films of your mammogram and I have the results of the biopsy. The biopsy revealed an infiltrating lesion. He opened her robe with apologies and palpated her breasts and the hard, immovable lump, which by this point had grown larger. It had been two months since the abnormal mammogram and biopsy. At the time, in the radiologist's office she couldn't bear the look on the technician's face and the note written on her chart: *maternal history of breast cancer*—as though they'd already written her fate, written her off, her death certificate. She'd wanted to ignore it, to imagine it was just normal cysts, lumpy breasts, and swelling from her period and for a long while she had.

I want to be optimistic, he said. But your lymph nodes are inflamed and I'm afraid that's bad news. She wanted to cover her ears with her hands. He always had been, almost until the end of their relationship, a good cheerleader. You'll do great things, Ginny, he'd said when they parted finally.

I'll take you on as a patient, he said. It wasn't ethical, he told her, but his survival rate was higher than anyone's at Sloan Kettering and that said a lot. And she was lucky, considering her insurance situation, to know him.

And if I do nothing?

Edward shook his head. Virginia noted that scalp had begun to appear at his temples. It gave her a tiny shiver of pleasure to see it. Let his current wife deal with the trauma of male-pattern baldness. He exhaled loudly. I don't recommend it. You've already lost a couple of months since the biopsy.

He'd like her to get genetic testing. It would be an additional cost but if she carried the BRCAI gene, it was recommended she have a bilateral mastectomy as well as her ovaries removed. This could send her into early menopause but would prolong her life expectancy. Also, it was important for her daughter to know if Virginia carried the gene. Virginia could have her eggs harvested of course but at her age it was possible there were no eggs left to harvest. Virginia had to understand that the prognosis was likely grave. Possibly very grave, Edward said. But she was strong and mostly young. And there were hormone-based chemotherapy treatments that could prolong her life indefinitely and would be as simple as taking a pill every day. She might not even lose her hair! This is not your mother's cancer—

What are my odds? she asked.

Edward stopped fidgeting and looked up. I really can't say. You could live a long time.

Could I live another twenty years? Virginia asked. You have to tell me. You were always straight with me. What are my chances of living another ten or twenty years? Of seeing my daughter graduate high school?

I just can't really—

She leveled her eyes playfully, almost flirtatiously. Edward, she said.

It's serious, Ginny. And you have no more time to waste. If you have financial concerns, Sloan Kettering has many programs. You can apply for insurance assistance or research studies, there are social work groups. I could get you into a protocol—

Virginia blinked back the nettles under her eyelids. The doctor, her ex-lover, looked down at the pen in his hand now finally still. Was there family that could step in and help? Have you heard of crowd-funding sites? GoFundMe or Kickstarter? People use them to raise money for treatments and care. I'm sure you have many friends up in . . . Where are you? Westchester? Greenwich? . . . Who would help you. People have done spaghetti dinners and bingo nights. Refinanced their homes or downsized.

He stopped and buried his head in his hands and then looked up and asked if she had any questions and Virginia said she had just one.

Yes?

Did your parents go to your wedding?

Of course, he said. Why do you ask?

I thought you didn't want to marry me because I'm not Korean.

Edward began to fidget again. No, Ginny. It wasn't that.

That night after Charlotte went to bed, Virginia ran herself a bath. She liked her baths scalding and deep and so she turned the faucet all the way to the left and ran it until it was full. She dipped her hand in it, but the water had run so long the hot water had run out and it was only slightly warm. Virginia was disappointed. She poured in the Epsom salt and baking soda. She dumped in some lavender oil. Too much. It was fine. She stripped down naked, left her clothing in a heap, climbed in.

It was not unpleasantly cold but she missed the shock of hot water that pickled her skin and made her gasp. Hot baths reminded her of the baths her mother used to run her on chilly, damp winter nights in Louisville. Always the baths scalding hot. So hot, she could only dip half a foot over and over again until it was acclimated and inch her way in: a whole foot, an ankle, a calf. Another foot, an ankle, a calf. She'd lower her backside in and then the great paroxysm of shivering, of intense pleasure. An all-powerful full body joy. She willed it again and again, raising and lowering her body, but that pleasure was only at the onset of a bath. In the bath, she'd take the washcloth and soap her mother gave her and she'd drape the washcloth on the edge of the tub and run the soap over it again and again. Its Ivory soap smell clean and caustic to Virginia's nostrils. It was neat how the grain of the fabric changed with each swipe of the soap. And then her mother had come in and gently told her please to stop wasting the soap and just get clean already.

For the first years of Virginia's life, she'd washed her hair with the soap, then lay down in the bath and swished her hair around in the murky-gray sudsy water until it felt clean. When it had, she'd call back her mom, who'd dump a homemade vinegary concoction over it. This will keep the gold in it, her mother had said.

Her mother.

Virginia closed her eyes and sank lower into the bath until the tendrils around her neck were wet. She hadn't washed her hair with Ivory soap ever since her stepmom had moved in with her fancy new bottles from the hair salon. She hadn't used Ivory soap at all since she'd left home. The water cooled around her body. She stretched her legs until her feet rested on the other side of the tub, and she placed her hands on her breasts. She felt with dread the bump, unmovable, her breasts uncared for and unloved. She and Tripp had not had sex for months. She felt her buoyancy. The smoothness of the bathtub, the water around her. She closed her eyes, took a deep breath, exhaled.

A tiny spider smoothly fell from the ceiling on its spindly thread. It hovered a few inches above the water and then seemed to graze the surface. Its tiny legs became entangled beneath the surface of the water and it curled in on itself. Virginia grabbed the small rubber duck on the side of the tub. "St. James London" printed on its side, a hotel they'd visited as a family on vacation two summers ago back when they still traveled. When was the last time they'd traveled anywhere together? She dipped the duck beside the spider. It seemed to cling to the side of the duck. She placed the duck on the side of the tub and watched.

Had the spider been waiting for her, waiting up there on the white tile ceiling for the tub to be filled to drown itself? Virginia had placed those tiles herself. Tripp had grouted them. She remembered how they'd listened to Neil Young over and over again on a little CD player. This was before Charlotte was born. In fact, Virginia thought back, she might have been pregnant then. Was it that summer? The vanity they'd bought was chintzy and already falling apart, though it had looked so nice on the floor, so much like the more expensive vanities they couldn't afford. She reached over and picked up the duck and inspected the spider. It no longer had attributes that were spiderlike. It was just a black speck.

Hey, you little stupid spider, Virginia said, suddenly furious. Why would you waste your one precious life lowering yourself into a bathtub? Hey, you. What the fuck would you lower yourself in a tub of water for?

The water was cold now, pleasantly cold. She'd stayed in much longer than normal. She sat back and let the water lap around her collarbones. Sank a little more until it reached her earlobes, then her ears. She felt her heart thud in the water. That furious muscle. She imagined what it looked like in her chest wall, thrashing around in that violent way. She'd read once that a heart could go on beating for an hour after being torn from its body. How pitiful, Virginia thought.

She unpinned her hair and dunked her head under. Her hair spread around her. I am nymph, I am apsara, she said, I am mermaid, just as she had said when she was a child. An incantation, the words formed bubbles in the water around her and floated to the surface of the bath. Air will always pull you up, she thought. If it can.

She loved her life. It was the only thing that belonged to her in the end and one day she'd have to give that away too. The secret of the lump in her breast was a jewel. It belonged to her alone. It was not anything she wanted to tell anyone about.

She thought about Charlotte, happy in the Petra School. A garden of Eden for children, with freedom of thought and outdoor spaces. She thought about Tripp. How they'd loved each other once. Maybe the connection had been shallow. He was handsome and she had been lovely, lovely enough that someone had seriously offered her a chance to become a catalog model. He'd loved her. She'd loved him. His normal steadiness. How proud he was of her. People would watch them pass by on the street as though they were movie stars. His parents helped them with Charlotte when she was a baby. They gave them money every now and again, and helped them buy their house and with little renovation projects until they'd moved to Florida and died and left all their money to the Young Republicans. His father, Travis Sr., a lovely man, and the kind of man she'd hoped Tripp might grow into being, had read her book just before he slipped away into dementia. Well done, he'd said. A real work of art.

It was hard to know what had happened between them. Maybe it was money and maybe it was boredom. After the hurricane last year, something had changed in Tripp. A kind of stagnation had gripped them like a sidewalk broken up and strangled by an oak's roots. Maybe it was that he thought they would all die in a hailstorm of brimstone, and Virginia was going to die, actually die, chemo-ridden in a hospital bed as her mother had. It was exhausting to try to suss it out. It would require a lifetime and that was what Virginia no longer had.

On the edge of the tub was her phone faceup and rattling with accruing messages. She'd glanced at the first and ignored the rest. Edward. He felt sorry for her and that would not do. It hadn't been fair for her to go to him in the first place. But how was she to know what was there? She knew what was there. She knew what it would be and she knew how dire the prognosis was. She'd known that from the beginning, from the moment her mother was diagnosed, from the moment she'd grown breasts of her own. The inevitableness of it all was a wonder to Virginia. The only thing that surprised her was that she'd always known.

She was shaky and cold when she stepped out of the bath. The phone was silent. She tapped on it and saw the missed texts from Edward and one missed call. A text from Tripp. She deleted Edward's texts. Tripp was staying overnight at the John Monroe Tracing School in Pennsylvania doing a survivalist workshop. His new obsession. He thought his world would end with a bang and that the end would have meaning. Virginia no longer had such illusions.

The touching detritus of the bathroom. Her razor on the tub's edge. A dish of soap she never touched. The shower gel she used. Two toothbrushes in a mug on the edge of the sink. The peeling vinyl wood of the vanity—no one saw it anyway—the rubber duck from a vacation when things had been easier. When there had been more money. When life would go on forever.

She glanced at the rubber duck again, looking for the sad black spot that had been a spider. But it was gone.

Chapter Four

AMERICAN CHILDHOOD

YEARS AGO, the Petra School bought the old Methodist church just off the main drag of the village's downtown. It had a steeple and a bell that rang at noon. Built around the turn of the last century, it was painted bright white on clapboard and overlooked the town. The doors were painted a cheery red. Agnes, the headmistress, whose great-aunt had started the school decades ago, liked to tell the children that their school was a temple of education.

Each morning the children and parents gathered outside the yard in front of the school. School began at 9:30 a.m., a half hour later than the public schools, and it released the children a half hour earlier. It was nice, as Agnes explained, for children and parents to have that extra time together.

Dads in sweatpants, flannel shirts, and heavy down coats and moms in yoga gear, parkas, and furry boots. No au pairs or nannies. Au pairs and nannies were for kids who went to public school. Or the fancy private school in Greenwich. Agnes liked to stand in the window next to the church door. Tall, narrow, and witchy, with a helmet of sleek red hair, Agnes would watch and wait, as she liked to say that first parents' night each year, for the fermentation to begin. For the ripening. The moment when the school became a body. Sometimes, she'd wait until a few minutes after school was to start. She'd watch as the parents got antsy, checked their watches, ready to send their kids off and get on with their day. But Agnes waited.

Then, at the precise moment, Agnes would throw open the door. She wore her long dresses past her ankles and stood as straight and plain as a pioneer and swept the children in, glancing back at the parents as she shut the door, leaving them on the streets. We are on a new frontier of education, she'd tell the parents. Re-education, she'd say. De-education!

Ushering in the children, leaning down and whispering to one stray or errant child, tripping over untied shoelaces and bulky parkas: Aren't you so glad you are on this side of the door? And it was true that some of the children still cried, unconvinced they were better off on this side, magical or otherwise. Some children required more convincing. Agnes was confident she'd have them all. She intoxicated them. She'd learned that from the Empress—her great-aunt who'd founded the school. The Empress had died not long ago. The parents would wave goodbye to Agnes and the children, and turn to their coffees, their workdays, their walks back to their houses and cars that lined

Midway Avenue. And then, for six glorious hours, the children belonged to Agnes. And she was theirs.

Rachel felt lonely on the lawn. She held on to Anders's hand and waited for the school to open. His sister, Lydia, had already found friends at the Soul Creatures group she'd joined during Christmas break and she'd run off in search of them. But Anders was more like Rachel. He was shy and stood very still and close to Rachel. Someone shouted hello!—waving to someone across the street—very close to Rachel's ear and she jumped a little and spilled her coffee down the front of her coat. She wiped it with the back of her mitten.

Rachel and Gunter had joined the Petra School in the middle of the school year. They'd moved to Connecticut right before Christmas. Back in the city, Rachel had grown weary of stepping around heroin addicts and homeless people. She had tired of stepping over vomit on the avenue in the mornings. There was a garbage problem. Days had gone by and the garbage piled and grew more rank. After Hurricane Sandy, their duplex, between Avenues B and C, had barely escaped the flooding on Avenue C. Whole cars on the avenue were swallowed up by the floodwater. And Rachel had been disappointed in the schools. Although they were zoned for a good public school, there had been so much emphasis on standardized tests. Spelling tests for six-year-olds! So much emphasis on academics for such little kids and so little playtime. Recess was a few minutes in what was essentially a parking lot. It broke Rachel's heart. Gunter had not wanted to leave the city and advocated strongly for Stockholm, where his kids from a previous marriage were at university. But Rachel had refused. The compromise was Connecticut. They bought an old ramshackle house built in 1880 that Gunter, an architect, had ambitious plans for. An open floor plan city loft inside a Victorian, Gunter had said. Rachel liked the house just the way it was.

Rachel stood by Anders and felt her toes grow numb. The cold seeped in through her expensive down jacket. She was eager to get on with her day, to go home and unpack, to set up her small studio in the turret of the house, check in with her clients, and maybe later wander through the village.

Rachel sipped her mug of coffee. She glanced at her phone. It must be past school start time, but everyone around her looked calm and relaxed. They had all day. No deadlines and nowhere to be.

She bent down and whispered into the top of his head. After school we'll walk down to the Double Dip and get hot chocolate.

Anders looked up at her. Will Lydia come too?

Well, yes. Rachel said. Of course. Unless Papa is home.

Anders shrugged. If Lydia is there, I don't want to go.

Rachel sighed loudly and willed the doors to open already. She glimpsed a figure in the window beside the door. Agnes. Agnes had interviewed them when they'd applied to the school. Rachel wanted desperately for her to approve of them. To accept them. To stamp them with her special Petra School stamp. Rachel shook her watch down her wrist and checked it. Who ever heard of a school that started late? She was glad Gunter had declined to join them. The lateness would have driven him mad.

Finally, there was a stirring in the small crowd of parents and children. The parents backed away from the children and the doors swung open and the children ran in, and shouted with their loud lusty voices. Lydia—Rachel could see her pink-tasseled hat in the crowd—was swept into the school without a backward glance. Rachel gave Anders a little nudge and then a harder one. Go, she said gently. Go on. She thought, Please for the love of God go to school. He looked up at Rachel with his large and watery eyes. Rachel felt the two impulses that had competed within her since his birth: the desire to shove him forward and the desire to drag him home with her where he would feel safe and happy.

Come on, Anders, she said in a falsely cheerful voice.

Agnes strode down the steps of the school toward them in her direct and purposeful way. Like she had never had a second thought. Rachel felt warmed and intimidated by her approach. Anders pressed into her.

Agnes squatted down. Aren't you Anders?

Anders looked down at the snow and did not answer.

Agnes looked up at Rachel. Lydia is inside?

She is, Rachel said.

Well, then, come with me, Agnes said to Anders. She reached out her hand. Every child is valued here at Petra. If you are not in the classroom, our little experiment fails.

Anders took Agnes's hand. What experiment? he asked. Rachel strained to hear the answer but they'd already gone up the stairs and entered the school.

Bye, Anders, Rachel called. She dumped the rest of her now-cold coffee into a patch of icy grass and started her walk back home. She cursed Gunter. Gunter didn't have to deal with anything kid related unless he was absolutely forced to.

Two weeks later, a group of girls sat in a circle and their parents stood in an awkward clump behind them. Behind each girl two chairs were set up and Miss Hensel stood and invited all the parents to take seats behind their children. Gunter and Rachel sat down in chairs behind Lydia. Lydia turned around and gave Gunter a hard look. She rolled her eyes and turned again to face front. She had just turned five.

Please, Rachel said to Gunter in a whisper. Please don't ruin this for Lydia. She likes Soul Creatures so much. She is so happy here.

Gunter rolled his eyes. What's wrong with the public schools? Gunter whispered furiously. You want to spend our retirement on this twaddle?

Rachel hushed him and sighed. She had already noted Lydia's stiff shoulders. Gunter had never understood whispering. He'd never understood the need to. He never let Rachel forget that in Europe things were different than America. That he was older and America was a terrible place to raise children. And Rachel, who hated winter as a rule, had thought: Sure, if Stockholm was situated on the French Riviera, she'd move there. But it wasn't.

Miss Hensel picked up a small skin drum and beat on it with the little hammer that hung from a cord. *DUM-dum-dum-dum,*

DUM-dum-dum-dum, DUM-dum-dum-dum. The girls beat the rhythm on their knees with their hands. Miss Hensel gestured to the parents with a quick jerk of her head. The parents joined in with varying degrees of participation. Rachel slapped her thighs with hearty enthusiasm and tried to catch Miss Hensel's eye. Beside her, Gunter sat up very straight and crossed his arms over his chest.

The children put on their papier-mâché masks. Lydia was an owl. Though it was hard to tell and when a few days ago Rachel asked her what it was, Lydia's eyes had welled up with tears and that next afternoon Rachel received a note from Miss Hensel that asked her not to interfere with the creative process of the children but rather to let the spirit within Lydia guide her. An eagle was a fine animal for Lydia, Miss Hensel had written, and it wasn't good to be too critical. Rachel felt some weird satisfaction that Miss Hensel got it wrong. It's a fucking owl, she'd written back and then backtracked with her cursor. That was not the impression she wanted to make. Not at all.

Miss Hensel came out and the children sang a song in Norwegian and then a song in ancient Greek and then another song in Basque and they ended with a song in German. Miss Hensel beamed the whole time and when the songs were finished she said, We try to bring a diversity of experience to our children.

Miss Hensel asked the parents to all stand up and create an archway with their hands and she draped a brightly colored parachute cloth over their backs and the children were led under. The parents all craned their necks to see their child pass. Miss

Hensel tapped the children on each shoulder as they were now knighted in the realm of Soul Creatures.

They took their chairs.

Miss Hensel clapped her hands and the chattering quieted and then she asked that one parent please say one thing—more if they had more examples!—about how Soul Creatures had transformed their child in the last couple of weeks.

Gunter loudly exhaled and Rachel pressed her elbow sharply into his side. She leaned over and whispered, I have no idea what to say.

The parents went around and brightly described some small or large behavioral change. Rachel sat very stiff beside Gunter and when it was his turn, he explained how he'd asked Lydia to empty the dishwasher and how she had done it very well, very carefully and without any complaint and that he'd been proud of her and that she had evidently been transformed in some small way that boded well for her future by her participation in Soul Creatures.

Rachel relaxed. As the next parent spoke she looked up at him and gave him a little smile and he squeezed her hand.

The children went around and presented their parents with a little burlap bag of blocks. This, Miss Hensel explained, was *Fröbelgaben* or Froebel gifts. From these blocks you can build anything in the universe, she said. Friedrich Froebel was a German man who made education his special concern. These blocks are the foundation, Miss Hensel said. The foundation of the kindergarten. And they are the foundation of your children's education. Miss Hensel then looked right at Gunter and said, Anders likes these very much in my first-grade classroom.

Gunter's eyes went wide. He leaned over and whispered to Rachel, Well, I'm impressed. Froebel gifts. It is also what architecture is based on. I played with these in my preschool back in Sweden.

That night, Lydia was happy. She wore her little Soul Creatures crown and skipped all over the house and managed not to annoy Anders—or be annoyed by him—and she did in fact empty the dishwasher without being told. Rachel was happy too. She could still see Gunter's face light up beside her when Miss Hensel had mentioned the blocks. But then as she climbed into bed, Gunter's face went dark.

Gunter said to Rachel, Did you see the dolls?

No, Rachel said. What dolls?

The dolls in the classroom. They had no faces!

Rachel had not seen the dolls. She shook her head. Maybe the dolls are still being made. Maybe they are not finished.

Gunter shuddered. It's far too creepy for me. It is the stuff of nightmares!

But they must have a good reason, Rachel said.

Yes. Like the blocks, Gunter said. Fröbelgaben. What memories I have of them. It was extraordinary to see them there.

Chapter Five

MARGOT'S TIDY HOUSE

ARGOT CLEANED the cupboards while water on the stove boiled. It was Tuesday, and Tuesday was cupboard-cleaning day. As soon as the kids went off to school, Margot got to work. She filled a bucket with hot, sudsy water and unwrapped a clean sponge from its plastic. She pulled on bright-yellow rubber gloves and tied her hair back. She pulled everything one by one from the shelves.

When her oldest, Aiden, had gone to kindergarten, Margot had envisioned herself a super engaged classroom mom. She'd joined the PTA. Become the president. She ran the bake sales, the fundraisers, the auctions, the galas, the bingo nights, the bag swaps, and trunk or treat. She'd been class mom every year since Aiden was little and sometimes in multiple classrooms. There were so many things to do. And the schools needed a lot of help. Volunteering had been her gig. It was, besides the boys, what she did.

There had been the baby she'd lost, of course. There'd been more pregnancies and more miscarriages. She was sure all the babies she lost were girls. As though the cosmic fabric of the universe would weave no girl for her. After the last miscarriage, she'd had some kind of breakdown. Those days were hard to remember. The house was a mess—for months! She didn't do laundry for weeks. Poor Richard took to stopping by Target, where he would buy bulk packets of underwear and socks on his way home from work. The dishes in the sink stank and filled the house with an aroma Margot did not object to somehow. Rather, it comforted her. The outside was no longer contained. Her insides had spilled over. The boys had all seemed to get sick at once and had run around with snot-covered wan little faces not daring ask their mother for anything. Well that was a heartbreak wasn't it.

After that last miscarriage, the doctor told her she was likely hormonal from the lost pregnancies and gently told her to stop trying. He gave her some medication and she'd felt better, and when she was stronger, she stopped taking it and returned to her activities like nothing had ever happened. Only the relief on the faces of the household let her know that something had happened, and it had been cataclysmic for them all.

Her last boy, George, entered the public elementary school and her days were free. She felt restless and strong and threw herself fully into the PTA. She volunteered, signed up for committees, organized fund drives, fun days, and field trips, and sought election to the school board. For the first few years it satisfied her. It gratified even. The second year, Margot began to notice things. She noticed how the same moms volunteered and the dads virtually never. The state testing, rolled out in Aiden's fourth year of school, bothered her. The teachers were stressed and unhappy and tied to a curriculum and couldn't teach the things that interested them. The kids didn't seem happy to Margot either. There were no more field trips for Margot to organize or fundraise for. Recess had shrunk. Kids no longer went outside in bad weather. Bad weather could mean rain, snow, too hot, too cold, or sometimes just mud that the school officials didn't want tracked inside. Or weather the teachers and teaching assistants didn't want to stand outside in. Margot petitioned for a plan where kids would move around schools, the so-called Princeton Plan. They'd attend one neighborhood school for grades K–2 and another school across town for grades 3–4, and so on. No one from the mostly all-white school in her neighborhood would bite. Margot was appalled. We like our *neighborhood* schools, her friends had said. That was the last straw. Margot had not sought reelection.

Margot pulled everything out of one cupboard and set these items in the sink. This cupboard was where Margot kept all of her spices. All the spices were clean except for the paprika that had spilled a bit. Tiny red dust particles of paprika clung to the outside of the bottle. Margot retched. For a moment she felt she might vomit. In her pocket she carried a small vial of bitters. She'd made them herself from a recipe her grandmother taught her: cloves, allspice, lavender, orange peels, and Everclear.

She pulled the little blue bottle from her pocket and squirted it into her mouth. This calmed her stomach. When Margot was strong and happy, Margot could not abide any sort of mess, and now Margot was strong and happy.

Margot bleached the insides of the dishwasher, the washing machine, and the dryer. She suspected the bleach was eating away at the rubber seal of the washing machine door.

After Margot cleaned the washing machine, she opened the little tray for the detergent and she filled it with a mixture of vinegar and lavender oil. She threw in the dish sponges and put the machine on the gentlest low-volume cycle and then did the same thing in the dishwasher.

Done with household chores, Margot focused on dinner. It was important to get the proper ratios of carbs, fat, and protein in every meal. From the fridge she took out a plastic-wrapped Styrofoam tray that contained a raw chicken. She scrubbed it in the sink with a special food-grade sponge. She patted the chicken dry with paper towels and seasoned its skin with salt and a tiny shake of pepper and stuffed a lemon up into its insides to disinfect. She sprayed the surface with olive oil spray. The oven dinged its final temperature and Margot placed the chicken carefully on a pan and shoved it into the oven. The oven door shut with a soft click. The water boiled and Margot poured in the macaroni pasta, inspected in the colander for worms or stones. Her mother, who was dead now, never failed to impress on her the necessity of inspecting rice, pasta, and beans for worms or stones. Margot set the timer on the microwave and sat at the kitchen table, very still.

After the New Year, Margot had joined a meditation group at the Petra School. It changed her life. Every Wednesday night she left the boys with a babysitter and she would drive over to the school where she'd meet a group of mostly women in the multipurpose room where they sat cross-legged on the wide-planked antique floors of the school's old church. Agnes, the director of the school, would give a talk beforehand. She read from the Dalai Lama and Thich Nhat Hanh and Kim John Payne and talked about modern stress and the importance of time spent outside and how children were overscheduled and overwhelmed with schoolwork, sports, obligations, and media, not to mention the evils of overmedicating and overstimulating children. She spoke of the simplicity movement and the importance of attachment parenting, and by the end of the talk, Margot was nearly immobilized by panic. Yes. It was all true about her boys. Teddy, for God's sake, was on medication for ADHD and had been since he was eight years old. What a relief it had been—for all of them—when they'd found the right doctor and the right medicine. Aiden was hyper competitive and all of them spent too much time on video games. Margot began to question everything. Every decision. Margot had not, for instance, practiced attachment parenting. The simplicity movement was certainly not what they did. In fact, their days were filled with activities. Margot only had to look up at the calendar she printed out and taped to the fridge to feel utter exhaustion about everywhere she needed to get the boys to on any given day in any given week. It had not occurred to her when her children were babies to keep a family bed or to breastfeed a two-year-old or to not sign them up for every activity their hearts desired or that their other little friends did. And while these concepts of simplicity or attachment were still somewhat foreign to her, they began more and more to make sense. To make happy, whole children, the family would have to sacrifice more.

Margot, during the meditation that came after, panicked about these things. She sat rigid on the floor and tried hard not to show signs of discomfort. Her flanks were sore after five minutes. Her back longed to slump. Her shoulders longed to round. She had no flexibility in her hips and her knees stood up like wings, not flat and graceful like the other girls. A few sat near the side of the room on chairs. Lucky them. She stole glances at the clock. It was torturous not knowing how long the meditation would last. If Agnes had spoken for ten minutes then there were fifty minutes left in the hour. Would they go until the hour was up? Margot felt her bladder. She never should have had coffee. Everyone around her was still as a forest at night. Everyone else was capable of peace and quiet.

This is a journey we're on, Agnes had said. A Road. Meditate every day, Agnes told them. Meditate during all those little moments where you are tempted to run away from yourself. Meditate during those moments when you wish to speak, when you wish to act, when you wish to distract yourself. Rather than check your phone, meditate! Rather than phoning a friend or reaching for a book or a glass of wine, be present! Dishes can wait, laundry can wait, online shopping can—always—wait! Be a clear call for your children's awakening consciousness. You are their richest example. Be present. Be awake. Be alive!

And the next day after the meetings, Margot wondered if perhaps she was calmer as the boys filed in to the kitchen now since she'd started down the Road. She dumped the steaming pasta into the colander and ran cold water to stop it from overcooking. The boys around her were full of goof, full of rage and love and testosterone. They were full of good cheer and aggression. They came through the garage and pushed their way into the kitchen. They dumped their book bags on her clean kitchen floor. Crumbs spilled and ricocheted off the parquet. Water bottles upended and leaked. They wanted snacks. They wanted endless love. They wanted to be heard and to be understood and to be entertained. George begged for another dog. Buster, he said, was too old to play with. Teddy teased him mercilessly until George burst into tears. Aiden, before Margot could stop him, popped open a bag of chips and shoved his hands—dirty from the bus, from using school restrooms without washing them—into the bag and pushed a fistful of neon orange chips into his mouth. Only Teddy pulled open his homework folder and set to work. He squinted through his glasses. Margot squeezed her eyes shut and thought of Agnes. Be present! she hummed to herself. She counted backward and forward as a method to still her mind and she fed them cheese sandwiches on paper plates. She asked about their days and looked each boy in his eyes as she did so, just the way she'd been instructed.

Later for dinner she served the chicken, served the pasta. No, there was no dessert. She was sure they'd had quite enough of it at school. There were snack and soda machines in the middle school and high school!

What a world they lived in.

The other boys did their homework while Margot washed the plates. She leaned against the counter. She counted backward. She counted her breaths. She took a sip of water from a liter bottle. A little alarm she'd set earlier went off on her phone and she picked it up: Be present! it said, and she tried. The boys shoved their homework folders into their book bags and raced from the kitchen. Well, Margot had had it. She'd just had it. It was time to pull the trigger.

Wait, she said but too quietly. Stop. They ignored her. WAIT, she said again.

The boys stopped and stared at her.

We're scaling back on activities.

The boys groaned.

We are going to practice something called the Road. It's going to be fun! As you know, on Wednesdays I've been attending meetings at the Petra School—

We don't go to the Petra School, George said.

It's a school of a bunch of weirdos, Aiden said, barely looking up from his cell phone.

Yes, Margot said. I realize you may think that. But please be open-minded.

The boys rolled their eyes and scattered. Margot sat on a stool with her hands on her lap. She inspected her nails and the thin line of black beneath the tip of each one. She stood up and walked over, opened the drawer, and pulled the nailbrush from the drawer. She ran warm water over it until it was very hot and ran it back and forth, back and forth over her nails until they were raw and burned. She stood a long while and watched out the kitchen window. Richard's car pulled into the driveway. He stepped out of the car, saw her through the window, and gave her a little wave.

Oh, Richard, she said. She was always so relieved when he arrived.

Richard limped in, still in his baseball uniform. He smelled of beer and tobacco. Take off your cleats! Margot called across the kitchen. Do not come in here and muddy my clean floor!

I did. Richard kissed her on the mouth.

Please tell me you had more than a hot dog.

I did. We all went to Maggie's and had steaks. We beat a tough team.

Margot walked over to the foyer and picked up the cleats between her two fingers, took them into the laundry room, scrubbed them with a wire brush, and then set them on a special rack with all the boys' sports shoes to dry. It was a ritual she liked to do for Richard. She knew he appreciated it.

In the morning she would send emails to the children's various teams to let them know they would cut way back on practices and games. Perhaps the kids would have to drop out. She had also resolved she would enroll them in Petra the next year. She just had to think of a way to get Richard to agree. Perhaps her father had some extra money stashed somewhere. Maybe Richard's parents would help. She thought of how happy Agnes would be to have her wonderful boys and how much happier her boys would be. They didn't know it yet but one day they would thank her. She rehearsed what she'd say to her friends and coaches, debated whether to add a note about the epidemic of overscheduled children, a link to simplicity parenting. Richard spent so much of his weekends shuffling the children from one activity to the next, from baseball diamonds to soccer fields to elementary school gymnasiums. She was sure he would love the idea of more time with the children, relaxing with them in the house.

In the morning, she'd take all the blinds down and hose them off in the bathtub. She'd call Virginia and ask them over for dinner. She couldn't wait to tell Virginia about her scheme to get the boys to Petra. She knew Virginia would be so happy to hear it.

Margot's work was finished. Richard snored in front of the Mets game. Margot picked up the bag of chips Aiden had opened. She would have just a few. A reward. But she ate the entire bag. She had to watch her weight. She would start tomorrow. Her metabolism had never been great but it had slowed. How did Virginia stay so thin, Margot wondered. She folded the bag up as tight and small as she could and shoved it deep into the trash can and then headed upstairs to shower.

The next morning, Margot woke to an email. All three of her boys were being seriously considered for the Petra School. Margot felt her pulse race; she was elated. She thought of all the ways her children would be cherished and honored in that school and how it would be nothing like the public school system. More outdoor time, no junk food, no more homework to fight with them over, fewer tests, fewer quizzes, less emphasis on competition, more emphasis on cooperation, whole child instruction, a shorter school day, longer summer recess. And how they would learn to be present, the way Margot learned from Agnes.

And then, at the end of the email: Siblings will be awarded a ten percent reduction in tuition. Her heart sank. She did the math. Impossible unless she went back to work. And how could she go back to work when the school day ended so early with no after-school care? And what would she do anyway for work?

Dear Petra School Parents: Unfortunately lice has run rampant through our communities. We ask that you replace your shampoos and conditioners with neem-based products. We will be selling them in our front office for $30 a bottle. Furthermore, Meg Maxwell has agreed to delice, a hundred dollars a head. Also, please remember that an organic diet is a lice-preventative diet.

Chapter Six

PARENT-TEACHER CONFERENCES

P ARENTS LINED UP for the first parent-teacher night of
the year at the Petra School. The wood-paneled hallways were festive and cheerful and hung with children's
artwork and slogans about mindfulness. Gunter and Rachel
huddled together while others around them greeted one another
with furtive hugs and kisses on the cheek. Rachel felt self-
conscious. She surreptitiously nibbled at a tiny fragment of
Xanax she found in the pocket of her coat. Her phone vibrated.
It was her agent. Rachel was immediately worried. She'd got
the sense her last client, a major car manufacturer, hadn't been
happy with some elements of a job she'd recently completed.
She was tempted to answer or at least listen to the message but
she put her phone away. The school had a strict no-phones

policy. There were signs all over the hallways: NO PHONES THAT HARM OUR BONES!

Virginia stepped forward out of the din and crowd. Hello! she said. She spread open her arms. Isn't it wonderful here? So homey, right? They kissed. Gunter offered Virginia his hand coolly but Virginia ignored it and gave Gunter a little hug. We haven't seen you guys since New Year's, Virginia said. How are you both?

We are great! Rachel said. How are you? We would love to have you guys over for dinner!

But Virginia was far away already. She receded back into the crush. Sure, Virginia said. Of course. Send me a text!

All schools smell the same. The Petra School smelled just like PS 9. Still, it was apparent to Rachel that Petra was special. How happy Virginia had looked. She beamed with true belonging. Ally Sheedy had sent her children there, for a time. Tori Spelling had sent her children for preschool. One member of an Irish megaband had also sent her children there. There was an old-fashioned wood-mounted black chalkboard and there were tiny nineteenth-century desks. They had been brought in from a demolished one-room schoolhouse in Alsace, according to the brochure in the folder each parent was given. Everything was tiny, reassuringly school-like and wholly unmodern. It was the schoolhouse of a Beatrix Potter or Laura Ingalls Wilder book. A Shaker Village schoolhouse with round wooden pegs upon which the children hung their coats. A large tree loomed through iron pane windows of cloudy ancient glass. The parents were led around the building. They poked into classrooms and closets. Rachel watched the other moms surreptitiously. They were stylishly dowdy, without discernible labels or markers of status. They wore comfortable shoes, clogs, and Keen boots. They looked honed but not hungry. They looked like creative people. Like they ate well and were homey and did outdoorsy things and ate organic foods. They mingled easily. As though they'd known each other for years. Rachel tried to look winning or inviting but she wasn't let in. Not yet. Virginia smiled and waved. Tripp joined her. He was a handsome man, Rachel thought, not for the first time, but he gave Rachel an odd feeling. He made her uneasy in the way that big Waspish men made her uneasy. They were so hard to read. Utterly inscrutable to Rachel. *Frat guy*, Rachel thought. Rachel watched a mother, Julie, in one of Anders's classes rush in, last minute with her hair akimbo. Julie was the mother of the boy Anders had been going on about. Rachel gave her a little wave, but Julie didn't see her. Rachel was determined they would be friends.

Agnes entered, dramatic as always, in a long, black dress that shifted spiritedly around her narrow frame. Like a ladder wearing a cape. She was six feet tall at least and lean as a whippet dog. Her legs ended around her armpits. Her arms swept around her as she spoke, like a windmill. Rachel was so in awe of Agnes it took her several minutes to concentrate on what she said. This is where we have astronomy class, Agnes said as she proudly led them into a room. She gestured toward a large antique brass telescope that pointed out a skylight. It's antique, she said.

Parents followed Agnes outside. One star displayed its meager light in the sky. Gunter leaned over and whispered, This is all a little over-the-top, wouldn't you say? This school. It's so precious. Back inside the school, Gunter gestured at the hallway with classrooms on all sides. Give me a school of cinder block, he said. Give me reality.

Rachel nodded but she had fallen in love.

In the largest room of the former clergy house, a fire crackled in the fireplace. The teachers sat in a line of chairs in front of it. Gunter and Rachel took their seats with the rest of the parents, Rachel tried to look friendly and open. Anders's teacher, Miss Hensel, stood up. She was chirpy and slightly false. Rachel loved her for it. This is what a teacher is supposed to be like. Not tired and real. No authenticity for my precious cargo. Leave reality to Gunter and public schools and the city. Rachel wanted lies and fantasy.

We have no plastic toys, no plastic of any kind whatsoever, Miss Hensel was saying. And our children here at Petra School are not afraid to get their hands dirty! Unlike most children these days! Do remember each day to check your children for ticks! The children help us to wash the windows with vinegar and broadsheets. Miss Hensel went on: We clean the old-fashioned way. We press our own apple cider. She looked straight at Rachel and gave her a wide indulgent smile. You might be interested to know, *Anders* has even churned *butter*.

Miss Hensel extolled the wonders of the Petra School: discipline problems were unheard of, the children spent so much time outside that there were no ADHD diagnoses, no ADD, no dyslexia, no learning disabilities of any kind. Children have long recesses. They climb trees and build treehouses. They are outside no matter the weather.

We have a saying here at Petra: There's no bad weather, only bad clothing! So please be sure to send your kids with extra clothing. A little later we will take you to see our chickens and our goat, Shelley. We have some expert goat milkers! The kids spend more time outside than in! Miss Hensel said. And that's been proven helpful for growing tummy bacteria.

Gunter grunted. He leaned over to Rachel. Yes, he said. That's actually true. I read that in the *Times*.

Rachel beamed up at Miss Hensel. She imagined ten mesmerized children in each of the nine classrooms.

Then Agnes stood up and delivered a teary soliloquy for the founder of the school, her great-aunt, who had died over the previous summer. We called her the Empress, Agnes said. Empress Elise. Agnes wiped her eyes with a sweep of her hand. Children loved her, she said. And the Empress loved them like she loved her own. When the Empress died, she was a hundred and four years old, Agnes said in triumph. As if to live so long was proof positive of her goodness.

She gave her all to this school, Agnes said. We are indebted to her.

Rachel whispered to Gunter: I'll bet the Empress was wonderful! I bet no child hates this school. I bet even the teachers like to teach here. We all *hated* school, Rachel said. You and I hated school. Everyone hates school.

School is meant to be hated, Gunter said. How else will children learn to endure hateful things?

The teachers passed out granola cookies and little paper cups of organic apple juice. The woman next to Rachel turned and offered her hand. I'm Angela, she said. How old are your kids?

My son, Anders, is in first grade. My daughter, Lydia, is in kindergarten.

Anders, huh?

Do you know him?

The woman shrugged. I have an eighth grader and I've taught art here every Thursday since she started kindergarten. If you want to know the truth, I'm so glad to finally be out of this school. We're going public for high school. I know your son, she said. He doesn't like to sit still. They don't like children who don't sit still. They don't like boys, really. I mean most of education doesn't. But Petra School especially. The woman looked up. Don't worry! she said and patted Rachel's hand. She had cloudy blue eyes and a frizz of white hair pulled back loosely over her shoulders. Don't believe everything you hear around here. That old woman Empress Elise was a battle-ax!

Infidel, Rachel thought. She said, They will love Anders. They just don't know him yet. Every child is a blessed child at the Petra School.

The woman leaned in close, close enough that Rachel caught her scent, warm and natural. Her hand grazed Rachel's knee. She said, Her husband was a Nazi.

Who?

The Empress.

Rachel glared at her. Oh come on.

The woman nodded. It's true.

Everyone makes mistakes, Rachel said.

They worship her dead corpse in a crypt in the basement, the woman said. It's very culty around here. She pulled her hair from the elastic and piled it high on her head and tied it up again.

Redundant, Rachel thought, barely listening and mentally editing. Dead corpse.

When Gunter and Rachel were called into Miss Hensel's classroom, Rachel was relieved. Good luck, the woman called.

I just LOVE Lydia, Miss Hensel said. She is just a delight in our Soul Creatures group. I think she must take after you, Mr. Olson!

Gunter grunted. I suppose that's so, he said. They perched on child-size chairs around a small table covered in glue and crayon marks while across from them Miss Hensel turned dour.

Anders seems to be settling in more or less nicely, she said.

More or less? Gunter said. Already on the defense, he crossed his arms and rocked back on the chair.

Is he reading a lot? Rachel asked. He started reading last year. I taught him myself.

Miss Hensel recoiled. Oh, heavens no! We don't read in first grade! We don't *push* children in that way.

It's not pushing him if he can already read, Gunter said. Rachel pressed her elbow into his side.

Miss Hensel paused a moment and looked back and forth between the two of them. Children should not be reading at his age, she said again.

He has already turned seven, said Gunter. Rachel pressed her elbow harder.

Miss Hensel turned icy. She straightened her spine. Well if you must know, we don't teach reading to a child until their first tooth falls out.

He's lost two, Gunter said.

Naturally or was there an accident?

Still, Gunter said. Two teeth.

Well, Mr. and Ms. Olson. Some of the children have not *yet* lost *any* teeth and we don't want them to feel behind, do we? That culture of competition is not one we like to promote here at the Petra School. Miss Hensel opened a folder and glanced at handwritten notes. He's not a very *cuddly* child.

Good for him, Gunter said. He's always been a tough kid. Like me. America is a cold nation that pretends to be a warm one. He shrugged. The child reacts normally.

Miss Hensel glared at Gunter benignly. This was all friendly banter to Miss Hensel. In time, her gaze seemed to say, they'd come around. It wasn't just the children that required education.

Miss Hensel continued, We here at the Petra School find that odd. Most of our children are *quite affectionate*. It seems possible, if not probable, that Anders has a disorder of some kind. Perhaps an *attachment* issue. Have you read Dr. Sears? Perhaps there is a high muscle tension issue. Perhaps a gluten or dairy allergy? Is that something you have ever considered? Would you be averse to Anders seeing a specialist? There are very few therapists we like, but we have one who understands our philosophy. You certainly wouldn't want him to fall into the hands of professionals who don't care for him as a *whole* child.

Gunter's smile tightened across his face like a pulled seam. Thank you, Miss Hensel. Let us stick to topics of education. I am glad Anders is doing well here. Please tell us more about his school progress.

Ah well, Miss Hensel said. "Progress" is another word we do not like here. It insinuates that education goes in a straight line from the uneducated to the educated—

Does it not? Gunter asked.

The meeting progressed more or less in similar fashion. Rachel's stomach grew hollow and filled with anxiety. For Anders was having some difficulties. He was acting out occasionally. They said he'd hurt the arm of another little girl roughhousing. Sometimes they had to put him in the hallway for art and music classes. Would Ms. Olson be averse to coming and staying during music class for the next couple of weeks? The school had wonderful success with energetic boys, Miss Hensel said. But it might require a little extra effort on the part of the parent.

Yes, Rachel said. Yes, of course. We will help any way that we can! We are very committed to the Petra School philosophy.

On the way out of the classroom, they ran into Virginia and Tripp in the hallway. Well? Virginia asked excitedly. How was it?

I think it's great, Rachel said. We love it here. Anders loves it here—he just needs some help settling down. But Lydia is doing great. I mean she's the easy one. Rachel laughed nervously.

Oh yes, Virginia said. I could see that. Well, girls *are* easier, aren't they. Don't you think, Tripp?

Tripp shrugged.

Well, Virginia continued. Let's schedule that dinner soon, okay?

The next half hour they spent with Lydia's kindergarten teacher, who had nothing but nice things to say about Lydia. She was quite old and went on and on, and when they left, Gunter turned to Rachel and said, I don't think she even knew who Lydia was!

That's ridiculous, Rachel said. There are only seven children in Lydia's class.

That night after they'd put the children to sleep, Gunter poured wine. They sat on the sofa. Gunter said, I don't know what to think about that school. Did you notice every child's painting in Lydia's classroom was one color? What on earth was that about?

What did you think of the headmistress?

He reflected a moment. The headmistress? She was kind of hot.

Well, I love the school, Rachel said. It's the perfect school. I wish I could have gone to a school like that. I liked Miss Hensel and I know in time she's going to love Anders. And I thought Agnes was kind of a cunt. She could feel her face flush hot reacting to the red wine.

Gunter drained his glass and reached for the bottle. Which one was Agnes?

The headmistress you think is hot. I see her buying enemas sometimes at the health food store.

Well, there's a thought. I rather like that thought.

Later, Gunter walked up into Rachel's studio, where Rachel was hunched over her computer. Interesting project? he asked, his mood pleasant.

This one is not particularly, she said. The client is a pain in the ass.

Sounds dreadful, Gunter said. He picked up Virginia's book from a stack of books that had been piled on her desk since the move.

Did you read it? he asked.

No, she said. She felt a pang. I haven't gotten to it yet.

I read it, Gunter said. He flipped to the back jacket, where Virginia's author photo was. Born in Kentucky, he read. I didn't know that.

You read it? Rachel plucked off her reading glasses and turned to face him. Yeah, she's Southern. I think she got rid of that drawl just about the minute she moved to New York City. Did you really read it?

I did. I read it on my phone. I just finished it. Some parts I skimmed, of course. But I read most of it.

Huh, Rachel said and thought, All this time she'd thought he was looking at European football stats. Did you like it? she asked.

I found it amusing.

Rachel set her glasses back on her nose and turned back to the computer. She was working on a project for Lancôme and had a tight deadline. She picked up her mouse.

Was Virginia ever a prostitute?

Rachel exhaled. I really don't think so, she said.

Oh, I see, Gunter said. Well, in the book she's quite convincing.

Earlier that evening, at home, Tripp marched up the stairs and tore off all his clothing and lay on the bed in his boxer shorts.

We have to go, you know, Virginia said. She padded into the bedroom and stood beside the bed. She turned on the bedside light. I'm sure Agnes will be happy to see you. She probably has projects lined up for you to take on. And that place, she said. It feeds me. I feel happy when I'm there.

I'm tired of doing projects for the Petra School. I just want to eat dinner and veg out in front of the game. Did you make anything for dinner?

We can grab something on the way. You can get a sandwich from the deli. Margot says it's really good.

What will Charlotte eat for dinner?

The babysitter will order Chinese or from the new Thai restaurant. Don't worry about it.

That costs money, you know. Chinese food. The Thai place. Sandwiches from the deli. Babysitters. Do we have to feed the babysitter too?

Probably. Is this really going to be an issue, Tripp?

Maybe I don't need to go, Tripp said. Maybe I can just stay here.

Tripp, please. It's just a couple of times a year.

Yes, Tripp said. I realize. It's just hard anymore to get excited over a school that costs the same as a private college tuition and my eleven-year-old daughter doesn't even seem to know her multiplication tables.

She'll learn them eventually! Virginia said. What's the rush! Come on. Get dressed. You'll feel better about the school if you go and spend some time there. It's a magical place.

The babysitter arrived. Tripp showered and dressed.

As snow began to fall, they pulled into the school parking lot. The school bell rang. Isn't it lovely? Virginia said. She pulled the coat up around her. I love it here. It's just the kind of school I would have liked to have attended when I was a girl. Tripp grunted and trudged through the fresh snow, sorry he had worn his tennis sneakers. He had some boots he wanted to break in. He felt the dampness seep under his soles and he felt heavy and miserable, and dreaded seeing Agnes.

They pushed through into the school. Virginia grabbed Tripp's arm and held it. He looked down at her and she looked up at him and gave him a smile. Hey, she said. It's good to spend the evening with you. Maybe we can get a drink after.

But Tripp was too nervous. In the back of the all-purpose room, he could see Agnes's tall form. She scanned the room and Tripp felt she was looking for him. When she saw him, he looked away. Felt his stomach flutter and wondered if he couldn't make a run for it. Leave Virginia here. Leave them all behind. Take the Mustang and never stop driving, but Agnes was striding toward him. She held on to his other arm, asked, Might we have a minute? Virginia smiled. She no doubt thought Agnes was wrangling Tripp into some volunteer effort. He'd spearheaded most of the work days so far. He was good with his hands. Good with carpentry and masonry and electrical work in a pinch.

Of course, Agnes! Virginia said. She and Agnes kissed on both cheeks and hugged.

So good to see you, Agnes said. You look radiant as always, Virginia. Such a beauty, your wife, Agnes said to Tripp. Beautiful inside and out.

Agnes had Tripp by the arm. How tall she was. Virginia was tall but Agnes was taller than Tripp even with her flat sensible shoes. She was not an attractive woman, Tripp thought. Not exactly. But she had something.

Her office was the former vestry. There were still some purple draperies with gold trim piled on dusty shelves around the small room.

Tripp, Agnes said, not bothering to sit down but standing beside him, still holding his arm. Standing too close. He could smell her breath and it smelled like camphor. I've been trying to get a hold of you as you no doubt know. You are three months behind in your tuition payments. We love Charlotte and we love you and Virginia. I don't honestly know what I'd do without you. You built half the school with your bare hands! She squeezed his forearm. Unconsciously Tripp flexed his muscle. Perhaps we can work something out? Agnes said, hopefully. I know the financial collapse hit everyone hard. We lost half a dozen families over the last few years. But I don't think you really want Charlotte in the public schools. What with the testing and rampant bullying. The competitiveness. The eating disorders. The iPhones! Charlotte is a dear, sensitive girl. I don't want to see her thrown to the wolves!

Come on, Agnes, Tripp said. He sat down in the hard wooden chair. I hardly see the public schools of Somerset, Connecticut, as a den of wolves. We're ranked top three in the county!

You know we can make other arrangements. We are always looking for a head custodian or maintenance. We were thinking of building a new play structure. Maybe you would be interested? We could set up a trade system. You could come here on the weekends or after school. Would that help?

Tripp placed his hands in his lap. No, Agnes. I'm busy most weekends. I'll get the money to you. I'll catch up. I've just had a bit of a setback.

Outside, he found Virginia again. She was talking to Rachel and Gunter. Virginia spotted him and waved him over. He kind of liked Rachel. She was nervous but sexy somehow. Gunter was Gunter. Not a guy you'd want in your foxhole.

They took their seats in a circle around Agnes, who swayed and rotated in the center. She talked about all the school treasures—the students—and said a few biting words about the public school. The kids are active at the Petra School. They spent hours outdoors in all seasons, she said. Why, the children could spend hours digging up worms in the back garden! Something she repeated every time Tripp came to one of these things. Which was wild because it seemed to Tripp the kids at Petra didn't seem to be able to do much of anything. He'd run the work days since Charlotte was in kindergarten and the kids had been all but helpless. In fact, he could use Richard's boys around. They at least knew their way around a table saw and a hammer and would do what you asked of them.

Soon Tripp and Virginia were ushered into the teacher's room. Her name was Eleanor and she was the parent of one of the girls in the class. She worked there for the break in tuition. That was how they got you, Tripp realized. In fact, the more he thought about it, the more he realized the entire school was run by an army of parent volunteers.

Charlotte was doing well. Charlotte was doing fantastically well. She was a wonderful writer, just like her mom. They just had to be careful with her. She was constantly trying to get books on a level that the school felt was too high for her. I don't believe she's ready for Judy Blume, for instance. Such grown-up concepts! We mustn't push them, Eleanor said. We don't want her to get ideas that are too grown-up and sophisticated.

This sounded like bullshit to Tripp but Virginia nodded her head and said, You are so right. You are so absolutely right! She turned to Tripp. This place is so wonderful. Don't you agree?

Eleanor placed her hand over Virginia's. We love you guys as much as we love Charlotte. Tripp's wonderful handiwork is all over the school! And the way she looked at Tripp made him wonder if she knew about the missed tuition payments.

They headed out ten minutes later. Tripp wanted to go home. He certainly did not want to see Agnes again. Or any of the others in the school. All those smug dads in their Patagonia fleece and Gore-Tex hiking boots. Most of whom Tripp knew for a fact did not pay the tuition themselves. Many grandparents were writing checks to these private schools. Tripp could do the math. He knew what people did for a living and he could figure out what their salaries were and who among them had an extra thirty or forty grand a year lying around for private school tuition.

Dear Petra School Parents: Tuesday is the third anniversary of Empress Elise's death. In honor of her life, we ask all the children to dress up as kings and queens. Lindsay Allen will be selling gold-dipped crowns made from recycled cardboard. Crowns are $50 payable through PayPal or by check. All proceeds from sales will go to the Federation of the Whole Child.

Chapter Seven

THE PESSIMIST

THE WEEK AFTER parents' night at the school, Tripp returned home late after work. It was almost ten at night before he rolled into the driveway. He'd taken his Krav Maga class in the city. And because he had a monthly unlimited he took a second one. Billy was there and they talked about the weekend they'd had at John Monroe Tracing School down in Pennsylvania. See you at the next one, Billy said, but Tripp was already moving forward. He wanted to consider next steps beyond John Monroe. Virginia was already in bed—probably reading, maybe writing, possibly sleeping—when he finally walked in the front door. He showered in the downstairs guest bathroom shower so as not to disturb her. Inside of him a rage percolated.

Had he really wanted to give up his best years as a worker drone? To retire like his father and die two years later, six months after his wife? He at least should have a dog for God's sake. Some testosterone somewhere. Someone he could talk to. Someone he could relate to. He soaped himself, washed his hair, rinsed off, and stepped out of the shower.

He thought back to those two awful weeks after Hurricane Sandy. The lines around the block for gas. The noise of the generator out on the deck ran night and day. The empty grocery store shelves. The price gouging everywhere and the feeling that everyone was out for himself. Like the hurricane had swept away all sense of community and revealed something ugly and previously unknown and unknowable. Hurricanes were only getting stronger. Would the next one flood the entire metro area? Would their house still stand?

He settled damp on the sofa with his laptop and a beer, fielding a text from Richard asking if he wanted to meet some of the other guys at the pub. There'd probably be a band, Richard said, and hungry divorcées at the bar. Busy, Tripp typed.

On the internet, Tripp searched for "automatic weapons." He had his concealed weapon permit folded up in his wallet. It filled him with a feeling as yet undefined. Hope or power. Love of life. He searched "gun shows in Pennsylvania." Pennsylvania was only three short hours away.

He had already begun ordering ammunition online. There were so many varieties of ammunition and for the first time— maybe in Tripp's entire life—Tripp felt happy. He could spend all day looking at the beautiful silver- and gold-tipped bullets. All sizes and makes.

Tripp felt fulfilled.

On the prepper message boards Tripp frequented, he called himself the Pessimist. Prepchan, his favorite of the boards, trafficked in rumors: The North Koreans would set off an electrical pulse and wipe out the grid and all electronic devices. Even battery-powered devices would be rendered useless. The Russians had moved into Crimea. They would break into power grids remotely. Pandemics made in labs in far-flung places. Tripp combed through threads about shifting plates, tsunamis, earthquakes that would crack California like a plate hitting the floor. He read about the recent disasters in his hometown, Los Alamos. Plutonium rods. Uranium ore in buckets in the Grand Canyon museum. Buckets of enriched uranium in Japan.

He toggled back to the website. There was a gun show in Philadelphia the following weekend. If he paid cash he could bring back as many guns as he liked. They never checked his ID, or if they did, it was with a wink. He could even drive over to John Monroe and maybe take an afternoon workshop.

An email pinged into his inbox. Something from Sloan Kettering. Unpaid bill perhaps or a scam. He deleted it without opening it. One day all debts and scores would be settled.

Back to guns. The ones he was really wet for: the Glock, the AR-15, others. He needed Kevlar vests and tactical armor. Night-vision goggles. He opened the John Monroe website, ordered another two-hundred-dollar hunting knife with the Amex he was no longer sure he could pay down. Tripp knew it was ridiculous and that he couldn't afford it and yet he couldn't help himself. He wanted what John Monroe had, which was *security*. He typed in his address, then circled back on the website and added a second one. He thought about giving one to Richard. Not that Richard would know what to do with it.

An unfamiliar email address in his spam folder. Tripp's cursor hovered over it. He hesitated. A fucking virus probably. The subject line said, The Homestead. Tripp opened it.

Hello SHTFr!
Your email has been given to us by an ally. As the world becomes less and less stable, smart actors such as Elon Musk of Tesla and Steve Huffman of Reddit and preppers all over the world look to solutions for end of the world times. We are currently looking for investors for a property already near completion. Please message us on WhatsApp at EagleScout666. We will provide further instructions.

Bingo, Tripp thought.

Virginia came down the stairs quietly, the creaking wood gave away her footsteps. Hey, she said softly. You coming to bed?

I think I'll stay up a little while longer, Tripp said. You want me to sleep in the guest room so I don't wake you up?

That would be great, she said.

A week later, Tripp followed EagleScout666's directions up to the Homestead, five hours north in the Catskills, to spend Saturday night. Technology, it seemed, might one day save humanity. Or at least a select few. A high-efficiency stove could burn a cord of wood that would heat all four main buildings for two days and leave only a cup of ash. The electricity was solar and the garden, in various stages of planting, could feed twenty families until the end of time. There were stockpiles of rice and dried beans and seeds buried in airtight packages under the barn with guns and ammunition. He'd need to pay membership dues right away—a thousand dollars a month. That would cut into the Petra School payment until the refinance of the house went through but he was already saving nearly a thousand a month from cutting their health insurance payments. As the man who showed Tripp around said, security in the coming times was priceless. It wasn't one of those bullshit luxury bunkers underground with flat-screen TVs for windows.

Tripp wasn't going underground. He wasn't a fucking mole; he was a man.

He had spent the majority of Sunday in the garden, planting seeds, removing rocks and weeds. Then he'd been pulled out of the garden to help build a stone fence around the border. He'd worked with the other men. They discussed waterless johns and revolvers versus pistols and where to get vacuum-packed ten-pound bags of rice—Costco, as it turned out. Cans of sardines were best for protein, cans of beets, cans of beans, cans of tuna fish.

How long will these cans last anyway, Tripp asked Bart, an ex-felon covered in tattoos.

Well that depends, Bart said. Ten years usually. After ten years it might be great or you might open it and a botulism Smurf will run out.

Tripp felt at the Homestead he would get out of this alive, whatever *this* looked like. On the car ride back, Tripp felt the grit of the weekend ground deep in his skin. He glanced down at his hands on the wheel, his fingers grimy. Fingernails black. His palms felt raw on the steering wheel. It had felt good to work. If he could have done it all differently—if he could have chosen his fate instead of following the script of his father and his peers —he would have lived off the land, lived off nothing. He would have lived without the false security of paychecks and health insurance and tuition payments and mortgages. He would have said fuck it to the whole thing. But he'd been a good boy and a good man.

Now he'd be a better one.

Tripp listened to an audio recording of *Annals of the Apocalypse*: The shift of a plate, the rise of the ocean floor, simple tectonics, geothermal dynamics . . . Tripp spaced out. He imagined he was back at the Homestead, harvesting wheat or corn. The audiobook continued: Just too much water that needs someplace to go, not even a Category 5 hurricane, not even a perfect storm . . . possible alien contact would be dangerous . . . superflu that wipes out 99 percent of the world's population . . .

Tripp stomped on his brakes and honked at a car that cut in front of him. The driver stuck his hand out of his window with his middle finger up. Fuck you! Tripp shouted. Fuck you! Tripp could kill him. He could kill anyone. When end times came he'd be able to exercise that right if necessary. It was a basic right of a man, one of John Monroe's instructors had said, to kill another man who aggrieves him. Civilization, he'd said, died with the duel.

Tripp imagined his life there if he gave up everything down-state. He would spend his days at the Homestead hunting deer and rabbit and catching fish in the stream. He could skin a rabbit and smoke it too, cutting it into strips, and the meat would last for ages. Prepare the hide and make a load of beef jerky. He'd killed and eaten a squirrel too. Not his choice, maybe, but the wilderness was not a buffet.

He thought of Virginia. Virginia wanted to go to the beach. Virginia wanted to do yoga retreats. Virginia sent their daughter to the Petra School, that fruity, hippie-dippie, bullshit school. She wanted to write books that no one read. Virginia won-dered if they shouldn't go into couple's therapy. She wanted to know where they would spend August. A few weeks ago she'd asked if they could refinance their home so she could redecorate the house or redo the kitchen. Some bullshit like that. Absolutely not, he'd said. They would not mortgage away their future he'd told her. Not for a kitchen redo. Their future was the Homestead.

Oh Ginny, he thought, pulling into the driveway of their house. In some Freudian way, I've always been enraged by you.

Dear Petra School Parents: It has come to our attention that a man in a blue van stopped a group of our high school students to ask directions at 4:00 p.m. this past January 4th. NO CHILDREN WERE ABDUCTED but we turned over the license plate number, make, and model to the police, who are investigating.

Chapter Eight

Virginia Travels

Virginia let Charlotte sleep in that morning, fed her breakfast late, and then settled onto the sofa with a mug of coffee and her laptop. Today. Today was the day she would finally call Edward. He'd left messages. She'd tell him—she didn't know what she'd tell him. She'd tell him she would submit to his testing. She'd tell him she'd like to go quietly into that good night of surgeries and chemo. She'd start a GoFundMe. She'd—

An email landed in her inbox. Virginia clicked it:

Dear Miss Roberts,
Your stepmother, Rhonda Hinckley Roberts, passed away this early morning. You are listed as next of kin. Please kindly call when you receive this message at your earliest convenience. Our condolenses.

She chuckled darkly at the misspelled word and then felt so homesick she ached.

It was easy enough to find a flight from JFK to Louisville. She would go tomorrow. She put in her credit card information and sat a long minute, the cursor hovered over Purchase. It seemed like a miserable waste of whatever time she had left. To see a woman she had not seen in years, who anyway herself was now dead. Virginia closed her eyes and pressed Purchase.

When she opened her eyes again she saw that her payment had been declined. She punched in the numbers again and double-checked them. The numbers on the card were so tiny, but then again, she needed reading glasses. Again, declined. Never mind. She'd call Tripp about that later. She found another card in her wallet, a debit card, and punched those numbers in. Again, declined. What in the world? Virginia said out loud. In her dresser she kept the Amex for emergencies. She fetched it and went to work typing those numbers in. But the reservation had vanished and she had to do it all over again. This card went through. She stood up from her desk to go find Charlotte curled up on the sofa with a Big Nate book, and she climbed under the throw blanket with her and half dozed until Tripp came home.

Tripp seethed as he entered the kitchen from the garage. He opened and shut cabinet doors with a bang.

I'll order something, Virginia called into the kitchen from the living room sofa.

Tripp stood in the doorway. His face in shadow. She could not see his expression. You sick? Tripp asked.

No, Virginia said. She and Charlotte were still in their pajamas.

Charlotte sick?

No.

She didn't go to school today?

Virginia shook her head. She thought to ask about the credit cards. Better to ask him when he was in a better mood.

Tripp stared but said nothing. There was no conversation Tripp would agree to be involved in if there was a chance that he would lose his shit. How fragile he was. He turned and walked back through the kitchen and up the stairs to his study.

Charlotte looked up from her book. Is Daddy mad?

No honey.

Is he mad I didn't go to school?

Maybe a little, Virginia said. But not at you. Don't worry.

Virginia sat back on the sofa. Charlotte announced her hunger. I'll order a burrito from Harry's but it will take a little while, Virginia said.

Virginia climbed the stairs to the bedroom and opened the door. Tripp was sprawled out on the bed. He stared at his phone. Yeah? he said.

Listen, she said. I don't want to fight but I need to fly down to Kentucky to bury my stepmother.

She died?

Virginia blinked at him. I leave tomorrow.

What about Charlotte? Will you take her?

No, Virginia said. She'll stay with you.

What time does she get off the bus? Tripp asked.

She gets off the bus at three forty-five. Come home from work early. You haven't taken any time off in months. Virginia shifted her weight onto her other leg and crossed her arms under her breasts, hitching them up a little.

Have you lost weight?

A little.

Tripp stood up and walked to her. He put his arms around her and pulled her into his chest. Virginia sank a little there, into him. She opened her mouth. She wanted to tell him everything but he pushed her slightly and moved away. I'll take care of Charlotte. Don't worry.

Tripp, she said. Her eyes burned. She'd spent too many hours in the house. She should have gone outside, taken Charlotte for a walk. Tripp, please be nice to Charlotte when I'm not around. And please see what's going on with the credit cards. Have you been paying them?

Yes! Tripp said defensively. Don't worry. I'll call and see what the issue is, Tripp said. I will take care of things. I promise. I'll keep you all safe.

Virginia padded into her bedroom and turned to the mirror over her dresser. She felt weirdly happy to go back home. It would be warmer down there. A full moon shone through her bedroom window. I love this human body, Virginia said. I am so happy to be here right now. Downstairs she could hear Tripp move through the kitchen. He opened cabinets, the fridge, making Charlotte a jelly sandwich while they waited for the burritos to be delivered.

The next morning when the town car arrived in the driveway, Charlotte wrapped her arms around Virginia and wept. Charlotte held her breath and rubbed her wet face into Virginia's shoulder. She knelt down. Be very brave for Mommy while you're here with Daddy, and I'll be very brave for you while I'm away.

But I'd like to see my grandmother too, Charlotte said. I never met her.

Step-grandmother, Virginia said. But don't worry. I'll be back. And in the meantime, you and Daddy will have a lot of fun. She shot a pointed look at Tripp. I know Daddy has loads of fun things planned for the two of you to do.

Charlotte looked up. Really?

Yes, Tripp said. Of course. He bent down toward Charlotte and unwound her from Virginia. Be good, Tripp said to Virginia. His mouth grazed her right ear. Charlotte sniffled and Virginia wheeled her suitcase out the front door to the town car waiting for her.

Bye, Mommy! Charlotte called through tears, Bye! Bye!

Bye, girl, Virginia said quietly but she did not turn around. Shut the door, Tripp, she mouthed to the park and the bluff across their road. She steadied herself for half a second against the car door.

The driver took her suitcase from her. *Shut the door, Tripp,* she said silently. And then he did.

Chapter Nine

JULIE AND SAGE

RACHEL MADE HERSELF A CUP of coffee and she made Julie a cup of tea. Julie's son, Sage, had already thrown his coat to the floor and bound up the stairs to Anders's room. Julie's older daughter, Delphine, stood very soberly by the table, bored and annoyed. Sage and Anders had recently announced they were the best of friends. Rachel was thrilled.

Sorry we're late, Julie said. I needed to finish up a few things at school and then I got into a conversation with Agnes. Delphie, Julie said to the girl. Why don't you run upstairs and see what Lydia is up to.

Delphine rolled her eyes. She's in kindergarten, she said.

Never mind! Julie said. I'm sure you'll find something to do.

Rachel pulled out a babka and cut hefty wedges on a cutting board. She placed it on the table between them. I can't eat too much of this but it's really good, Rachel said. It's from

Russ and Daughters, in the city. I've gained so much weight since I moved up here.

Oh really? Julie asked. Have you tried the new upside-down yoga? Or there's a great new barre class downtown. Or have you tried walking?

Rachel shook her head. Walking in the city had been enough exercise for her but walking around the village and the parks around Somerset she found bored her. The same stores. The same trees. The same corners. The same squirrels. The same vaguely familiar faces. The somewhat frightening deer that spooked Rachel somehow. Have some, Rachel said. She pushed the cutting board closer to Julie. It's delicious.

Oh! Julie said. I can't eat any of it at all I'm afraid. I'm on a cleanse. No sugar. No dairy. No eggs. No corn. No meat. No grains at all.

My God, Rachel said. What do you eat?

Julie shrugged. Yams. Avocados.

Beans?

Oh no! Julie said. Those are the worst.

Julie was Rachel's first friend at Petra besides Virginia. Rachel liked Julie because she was honest and sincere about her own failings and misgivings about being a parent. It made Rachel feel better about herself. In the right mood, Julie gossiped about the school. This comforted Rachel. And she liked Julie because Julie was the first person to reach out to her at Petra. She saw Virginia from time to time, but their children were in different grades and rarely crossed paths.

Well, Julie said. She sipped her tea. Sanders and Isolde got in a wild wrestling match and Isolde bit Sanders's ear. And the Delanos are pulling their kids out of the school because the twins are in fifth grade and don't know the first thing about multiplication! I mean, they'll catch up! What's the rush? It's not like they'll never learn!

Ha, Rachel said. I barely know mine. I mean, soon enough we're swallowed by life and life's expectations.

I know, Julie said. Right? So glad you guys are at Petra. She looked around. I feel like this is a good house. A house I can trust. And you furnished it so modern! And big. You can almost see the sound from here.

Yes, we love it here, Rachel said. She swirled the sugar crystals in the bottom of her mug. Agnes is great though, right?

Julie looked up. She tipped her head to one side. Yeah, Julie said. Of course. Julie scrunched up her nose. Why? What do you think?

Of Agnes? Rachel walked over to her garbage can and opened it with her foot. She dumped the crumbs from her finished babka. I don't know. We've only been there a couple of months but she seems great. She runs the ship, Rachel said carefully. Lydia is very happy.

I'm glad to hear that, Julie said. Agnes is definitely not some-one to cross. She has our children as hostages, after all.

Hostages! Rachel said. That's quite a metaphor.

Julie shook her head and didn't smile. It's not a metaphor. Not at all.

Rachel longed to invite them for dinner but she only had pasta she'd made earlier that day and Julie was on a cleanse anyway. Gunter was working late in the city again. Rachel had hoped they would stay longer. She kicked herself for not making something gluten-free. She didn't like the lonely spookiness of night in the suburbs.

Lydia, who had played quietly in her room, came down, to Rachel's consternation, and climbed on Rachel's lap. Now they couldn't talk as freely. Rachel put on her public voice and asked Lydia very sweetly if she didn't want to go back upstairs and play a little more or find out what Delphine was up to.

Mommy is having a playdate, Rachel said in a voice that let Lydia know she wasn't fooling around. But Julie was already rocking in her place on the armchair. Clucking around and saying, I think it's time we get out of your hair! And: Lydia is such a good girl to play all by herself for so long! None of my children would. Oh! I spent hours on the floor with them. It was *exhausting* but so rewarding.

Yes, Rachel said. Wasn't it? But Rachel felt a pang of guilt. She'd almost never gotten down on the floor and really played with them.

They chatted a bit more, their tones soft and grown-up for Lydia's sake. Julie dropped her voice and said, Agnes says—

But an eruption from above them crashed down the stairs. Delphine came fast down and whispered into Julie's ear.

Rachel rolled her eyes in Julie's direction, but Julie had jumped to her feet.

With her mouth in a thin line, Julie called upstairs: Sage! Sage. Come down. Sage came down dutifully with teary eyes. Julie bent over him. Are you all right? Are you sure? She grabbed their coats off the back of their chairs. We need to go, Julie said tightly. It's late.

Rachel stood. Oh, she said. Is everything all right? Did something happen? Maybe we should talk to the boys! Anders! she called. Come down!

That's okay, Julie said with a final tone. She would not meet Rachel's eyes. And then, in a strangely formal voice she said, It is unnecessary. See you at school.

They left in a hurry. The door slammed behind them. Lydia looked up at Rachel from the sofa with her big watery eyes. What happened? Lydia asked.

I don't know, Rachel said.

Anders came down. I'm hungry, he said. What's for dinner?

What happened? Rachel asked. Did you hit Sage?

Yeah, he said. So?

So, you can't hit him. You can't hit other children! That is unacceptable.

Mom. We were playing a game. He hit me a hundred other times. Anders turned around and lifted up his shirt. Do I have a bruise?

In fact, he did. It was enormous, along the lower right side of his back. As big as Rachel's hand. Oh my God, Rachel said. What happened?

Anders shrugged. We were just goofing around. Sage shoved me really hard into my desk. He started throwing toilet paper

97

all over the room and I got mad and told him to stop and he shoved me. I pushed him back and that's when Delphine ran down to tell on me.

Rachel stood up and walked into the kitchen. She didn't know what to say to him. She didn't know what to believe and she wasn't altogether sure why it mattered or why Julie had acted so strange. Weren't boys supposed to roughhouse? Hadn't Sage been as rough as Anders? Well, she said finally. Why don't you go upstairs and straighten your room while I get dinner on the stove.

Anders stopped in the kitchen entryway. It's pretty bad up there. I think I'm going to need your help.

Rachel held her breath and then exhaled. I'll help you clean up after dinner.

Later, after they'd eaten the pasta, Rachel asked the kids to help clean the table and load the dishes. They moaned and complained, Lydia half in tears. Finally, the kitchen was clean. The dishwasher loaded. Rachel took the two kids upstairs. She turned the bath on for Lydia. The old iron bathtub took ages to fill. She wiped up the spilled toothpaste from the sink. Threw away a tissue. Flushed the toilet. She called out, Who leaves this in the toilet? Honestly! Hung up a towel. Lydia's room was neat as a pin. A careful spread of books on the floor. A bunch of stuffed animals arranged in a circle.

I was playing Soul Creatures, Lydia said.

I see that! Rachel said in her best mom voice.

She gasped when she saw Anders's room. Toilet paper hung like ghostly white wisteria from the light fixtures, around his desk, his bed, the floor. Everywhere. Not one roll but the package of twelve Rachel had just the day before shoved into the bathroom closet. My God, she said.

Anders nodded sagely. I know. That's what I said. Sage was acting crazy. I told him to stop but he wouldn't.

But you should have come down and said something to me if he wouldn't stop.

Anders shook his head. Grown-ups never help, he said. Whenever grown-ups get involved, they only make things worse. He began to cry.

Anders! Rachel said. It's okay! It's not that big a deal. We can have it cleaned up in just a few minutes.

I just have a feeling Sage isn't going to come over anymore, he said between gulps and messy tears. And he is my first best friend.

Later that night, after the kids had gone to bed, Rachel sat with her book and tried to read. She scrolled through social media sites for a long while and then forced herself to stop. She had emails from some clients and former colleagues. She picked up a book from the coffee table and set it down again.

Her phone rang. It was Julie. Rachel filled her chest with air and exhaled. It was so strange how being a mother could take you right back to middle school. That same feeling that she didn't know the rules or who was on her side or if anyone was at all. But no. It was okay. Julie apologized for rushing out. She'd gotten scared, that was all. Delphine had seen something. She thought she'd seen Anders hit Sage, but no. Sage had explained to Julie that it was all part of a game, that in fact Anders hadn't hurt Sage at all. I'm sorry, Julie said again. Sometimes that school makes me crazy.

Rachel hung up. She was relieved. She got up, poured herself a glass of wine, and turned on the TV. And then a prick of paranoia set in. What did Julie mean the school made her crazy? What did the school have to do with Anders and Sage's playdate? What did Anders mean when he said grown-ups make everything worse?

After ten minutes the wine started to do its thing. Rachel drowsed on the sofa with the TV on, a warm, comfortable feeling. She felt a tiny glow of optimism. Things will surely get easier. It can't always be this anxiety provoking and stressful. This. Modern life, middle age, two small children. Something would give. She'd find a group of friends. International people. Everyone here was so white. Sort of Waspish, besides Richard, but it seemed to Rachel he'd been in the suburbs too long. She didn't understand Wasp suburban language or its rules. She realized she couldn't figure out Julie at all. It had to get easier. Marriage. This life with children. Otherwise why would anyone sign up for this?

Dear Petra School Parents: Tonight we will showcase the film *No Activities Equals Stronger Children*. This film IS mandatory and only a note from your doctor or homeopath will excuse you. It is NOT for children. We repeat: do not bring your children. Screens are never appropriate for the developing brains of our eighteen-and-unders.

Chapter Ten

MARGOT'S BABY GIRL

B Y THE second month after the birth, the baby had been gone longer than she'd been alive. That fact was so awful Margot thought it would bury her.

It had taken Margot two years to get pregnant and finally, after treatment, she had. She'd been delighted to have a girl. She wouldn't have known, she'd said back then, what to do with boys. They'd bought the house in the suburbs back where Richard had grown up where the public schools were good and the taxes weren't terribly high. Margot knew perfectly well she could do everything in the house herself. In fact, she'd never felt better. She'd spent hours at the shops in Greenwich and the fancy malls of Westchester—places she would otherwise never go to much, much less afford—where she'd scoured Bonpoint and Petit Bateau for onesies and dresses and blankets and tiny black patent leather shoes. Richard's mother had said it was superstitious to buy anything before the baby was born. Margot couldn't help herself.

They'd brought the baby home but she hadn't thrived. Margot stayed awake with her for two days and two nights and the baby slept and slept and would not eat. Something's wrong with her, she'd said to Richard, but Richard said Lily was fine. He told Margot about a friend of his from the office who'd called paramedics when their baby wouldn't stop crying only to be told the crying was due to colic. Margot, Richard had said. Can you imagine what they thought of them? The doctors and nurses? Let's not be like them okay? Let's be reasonable.

Her name was Lily Pea for Peabody, for Margot's maiden name, and Margot called her Lily Peanut. Lily Peanut, she'd whisper. Please latch on. Please drink the milk. Please.

But Lily would not.

On the third day, she sent Richard out for formula and a bottle. Make sure, Margot said, teary and exhausted and frightened, that the bottles are the right kind of plastic. And make sure that the nipples you purchase are the right size. The wrong size will let in too much air and Lily will get gas.

Intestinal gas and teething were supposed to be their biggest fear as new parents. They'd watched over those two years that Margot couldn't get pregnant while their friends contended with the dreaded gas, colic, teething, eczema, and allergies. One friend hung up a rope from his ceiling and swung a baby car seat back and forth and back and forth until their baby stopped crying. Others drove their babies around in their cars or took endless walks. They gave them baby Tylenol, amber teething beads, baby massage, drops of sugar water, rum smeared on gums, homeopathic remedies from Whole Foods. One mom claimed she put the baby down in his room, shut the door, and tiptoed around the house wearing both earplugs and noise-canceling headphones for as long as she could stand it, before finally checking in to find her baby asleep or even, sometimes, quietly playing with her toes.

How cruel, Margot told Richard.

They weren't going to be like that. They were going to be good calm reasonable parents. They weren't going to freak out, like Richard's coworkers had. They wouldn't run to the pediatrician for every little thing like they'd watched the Walters family do. Or be utterly laissez-faire like the Coopers. They weren't going to worry so much about organic and inorganic matters like the Saads but nor would they feed them cupcakes and Coke like the Edwards. They weren't going to co-sleep until the child was eight years old. What do you call co-sleeping parents? Divorced, Richard's mom had said, calling in from Florida. Or breastfeed more than a year or so. They had ideas. They had books. They'd talked to other parents and they'd made up their minds about some things.

For everyone had had babies of course but no one would do it as well as Margot. There was nothing she didn't do well. It had been like this since always. Back in Illinois, where she'd grown up, she carried a perfect grade-point average all through elementary school and junior and senior high school, and perfect attendance too. She'd scored a near perfect score on the SATs and ACTs and had won a scholarship to the University of Hartford. There, she'd been on the dean's list, editor of the newspaper, then off to a fully funded graduate program in children's literature at Bloomington, where she'd met Richard. He had just finished up a master's in modernist poetry but was ready to get a serious job now. She never finished her master's. She moved with him to the city straightaway and married him a few years later. She had told him she wanted to have a small ballet company. Not one boy? he'd asked. Couldn't you make an exception? he teased. Fine, she compromised. If not a corps de ballet then a baseball team. But she saw herself surrounded in pink tulle and satin. She'd decorated their house in tulle and flowers, painted Lily's room pink, her bathroom pink. All her maternity clothing was flowery shirts and big dresses from Anthropologie. Flowers everywhere. Now: the tiny precious pearl of a baby girl Lily Pea who would be perfect, perfect, perfect. There was no reason not to think so.

After Lily was gone, Margot had sat stunned in the pink-painted room. Beside her was the enormous stuffed giraffe that one of her sorority sisters had sent over and left in the new crib while Margot prepared to bring Lily home from the hospital.

For a week, Margot lived off the soup and the six-pack of Guinness that Virginia—at the time not quite a friend, just the wife of her husband's best friend—had brought over "to make your milk come in," until it was gone and then Lily was gone and she didn't eat anymore.

What she had of Lily was a perfect tiny lock of hair tied with a red thread and kept in a Ziploc sandwich bag in her bedside table.

She didn't eat anything much for a long, long time.

I'm perfect, she said to Richard at night when he'd come home from work. I'm perfect, she'd said. I live off air.

And I eat men like air, Richard had said.

I'm sorry?

That's the poem. The Sylvia Plath poem. Something like, *Out of the ash I rise, and I eat men like air.*

Right, Margot said, not understanding. She'd barely listened.

It had been hard for Richard to get time off work after Lily was born but he managed. He came home early and left for work late. She was a perfectly formed little being. Even Richard had to admit she was not squishy or odd like so many other newborns Richard had seen and lied about—as one does to the parents of the newborn—saying: She's beautiful. Or: He's so handsome. But really, they looked as though birth had squashed all the beauty out of them and it remained to be seen if they would regain any of their previous in utero beauty, such as it was. Not Lily. Lily was perfect.

But after Lily was gone, Richard didn't want to be home. He'd stayed home the whole week while he dealt with insurance, funeral costs, the heartbreak of a tiny coffin lined in pink satin. Margot, sallow and thin and so terribly sad. They'd decided not to have a funeral. They'd told their parents not to come. They had a sense they'd done something wrong and it was best to try and forget and move forward. His feeling that Margot blamed him and that maybe she was right to. And this being America, the suburbs where they'd only just bought their house a few months before, everyone, for the most part, left them alone to their sadness.

It was the fact of their aloneness that made Richard angry. He could see how the neighbors nodded to him and waved courteously, blandly, banally. He understood they didn't want to get involved, didn't know what to say, didn't know how to act. It was as though the fact of the baby's newness negated her existence. It was easy enough for people to pretend so. Richard could hardly look at Tripp, who had the language of competition, of razzing, of lusting after girls but no language for compassion or sympathy. Virginia and Tripp had not yet had kids. Virginia was busy with her book and it was like neither one of them could understand how anyone could be broken after losing something so new. It was like everyone wanted to pretend they hadn't seen the pink balloons tied to the mailbox or the way they'd struggled home with the car seat. A minivan because Margot had said she wanted half a dozen kids at least. Though Richard had grown up there, they'd left, and he'd brought a wife who'd grown up elsewhere, in the Midwest or maybe it was California. Women created attachments, community, social life, and Margot hadn't had the chance to. Only Anne, their across-the-street neighbor who Richard secretly called the Church Lady, had come with her religious tracts and a tin of homemade Chex mix and told Margot very matter-of-factly about her two miscarriages and one stillborn. Anne told Margot that the girl's spirit watched them and could be seen as a blue orb. If Margot looked hard she could see it herself. Richard had hidden out in his study listening while he grew more and more angry until he'd finally burst out of the room and ushered Anne the Church Lady out. Anne, twisted around to call over her shoulder, get to work you two! You have time and youth and beauty on your side.

One night, Margot came to Richard. She was wearing a little outfit she'd bought at the lingerie shop downtown and a pair of tiny mules with poufy, feathery things on the toes. She'd dropped the baby weight so quickly it was like she'd never been pregnant. She came to him and she pushed him down on the bed. Richard counted the weeks. Six, exactly. The precise amount of time the doctor had told him he'd have to wait before they could have sex. To the day.

She could be so seductive when she wanted to be. He remembered the first time they'd had sex. She lived in a shared house off campus where she shared a room. Her roommate had been asleep, or "asleep," as they'd joked after. It had made it hotter. He'd fucked Margot so quietly, to make sure the bed hadn't squeaked. He'd thought maybe she was a virgin but she'd never said so one way or the other. Wasn't it strange Richard couldn't ask? It had seemed like something she'd do. Very practical Margot, she hadn't wanted to make a fuss about her virginity. But no, she'd had an orgasm. An orgasm he could actually feel. She pulsed all around him and her eyes rolled back in her head and he'd thought he'd never loved anyone more and he would never love anyone else after. And for a long time that was true.

Now, she straddled him, it was six weeks to the day, and Richard searched her face for that look in her eyes. But when he looked at her he could still see pain in her eyes. After a while, even that turned him on.

Chapter Eleven

RACHEL IN CAPTIVITY

RACHEL CHECKED her email, called her agent, replied to an email from a rep at Estée Lauder, which had swallowed yet another niche brand. They wanted to expand the brand, the email said, while keeping its "nicheness." Jenna Lyons requested she style some photos for her Instagram. Could she possibly go pick up some footstools from ABC Carpet? Rachel wanted to get back to work and jump into projects and yet she didn't. She liked the details. She liked the jobs. She liked the brands. She loved the outcome. But she hated the pressure, the ten men in a boardroom who signed off on her creativity, such as it was. Village life had sedated her it seemed. It was a place where it felt acceptable to do nothing at all.

She was lonely. That was what. In the city, she could have called ten friends for lunch if she'd wanted to. Or gone to a yoga class. Or maybe even taken a job in-house somewhere and had actual coworkers again. But here in the suburbs, Rachel felt out of sorts. For one thing, she couldn't drive yet. She had a license but she'd almost never used it. She had a car, but she was afraid of it. She'd have to learn to drive, of course. Getting into the city by train and bus was more of a pain than she'd considered. And she'd wanted to make certain the kids were settled. Finding some kind of social life—for all of them—was first and foremost on her to-do list. She'd thought about calling Margot, except she'd sent Margot a message New Year's Day to thank her for the ride home and apologize for Gunter (who'd puked out the Cohens' window and down the side of their car) but she'd only received a terse message back. It was so hard to know, up here, what anyone meant. For one thing, many of them had grown up in the area and Rachel didn't really speak the language. Everyone was polite but never direct. It was difficult for Rachel to decipher. Maybe New York City was the only language she spoke. She should invite people over. She should join a gym or attend those Wednesday evening meditation classes at Petra. Agnes pushed them hard. She had insinuated to the parents that they were mandatory. There was an earnestness at Petra that Rachel had a hard time with. Maybe earnestness was the name of the language Rachel did not speak.

Rachel called Virginia and left a message but Virginia didn't call back for a couple of hours. They talked a few minutes. Virginia wasn't terribly friendly nor was she unfriendly. Rachel asked Virginia if she was doing all right.

It was good at least to work, to stay busy. She had a half-day project in the Cloisters tomorrow and she looked forward to it. Now that Lydia was in school full-time, Rachel could work more with less guilt. But then again, she couldn't work too much because she needed to be back in time to get the kids from school. It was a conundrum. Perhaps she needed to work less, be with the kids more, spend more time at home, the way she imagined Margot did. Rachel tried to imagine what her life would look like if she didn't work at all. Perhaps she'd knit or cook or try needlepoint or cross-stitch. She thought maybe she'd sign up for a triathlon or Iron Man. Perhaps she could be a sign language translator or study a second language. Perhaps she could go back to work full-time and hire an au pair. Maybe they shouldn't have moved to the suburbs. Maybe it was a mistake to leave the city. For the first time since they'd moved, Rachel wondered if it was. Rachel, after all, had never lived anywhere else.

Henry is nearly as tall as the teacher, Anders said one night as Rachel and Gunter prepared dinner.

Really? Were they held back? Gunter said. Isn't that an American thing? To hold back kids?

Yes, Rachel said. It is. It's called redshirting.

Henry told me I'm short because I'm a Jew.

That's not true, Gunter said. You will grow! Besides. You are not a Jew. You are a Swede.

A Swedish Jew, Rachel said pointedly.

Gunter gave a look. On the wrong side, he said. Not really Jewish.

It's the right side if I say it is, Rachel said.

Anders looked between them and said, Henry told me the Nazis weren't all bad.

Really! Rachel said. Her mouth fell open. And what did Miss Hensel say?

Miss Hensel said to look for the helpers.

Well, Gunter said. That sounds very reasonable.

Anders played with his fork. They won't let Sage and me play together anymore.

What do you mean? Rachel asked.

Anders shrugged. I don't know. Every time I start to play with Sage, Miss Hensel or Agnes comes to tell me to go find someone else to play with.

What? Gunter said. That can't be true.

Well it is, Anders said. It is true.

Rachel felt her blood pulse in her fingertips. She pounded out the empanada dough while Lydia filled the circles and pressed the edges closed with a fork.

Rachel waited until Anders wandered off and then turned to Gunter, Why would they separate Anders and Sage? Why would they do such a thing?

Let it go, Gunter said. Anders is happy. You don't know what's going on in the school. Maybe this Sage kid doesn't want to play with Anders. You cannot be so fickle. Please let's not talk about the school anymore. Let it be. Let Anders find his own way.

But that can't be true, Rachel thought to herself. Sage begged her for a playdate every time he saw her in the yard after school. It was Julie who begged them off. Next weekend, Julie said. Or maybe next week.

Meanwhile, notes came home from Anders's school. Miss Hensel called frequently, early in the morning and sometimes late at night. Anders was a problem. Anders had fallen down. Anders bumped his head. Anders had wrestled another child who had bumped *her* head. He'd squeezed a little girl's arm and left a red mark. Anders had pushed down Henry. There was some lurid anecdote about the children. They'd shouted, "Suck on my milk bottle." No one knew from whom it came or if it was meant to be sexual. Anders had come up with the phrase, it was reported but not confirmed.

Still, Anders was strongly suspected.

Anders spent most of his time in school in the hallway. He refused to go to school on days when they had music. He refused to go to school on days when they had art. He was halfway through the Lemony Snicket books when they were confiscated. They were too *negative*. Ditto the Roald Dahl he relished. Miss Hensel sent a note home. Dr. Seuss books were more suitable for him. He could make up his own picture books with drawings alone. The other children had not learned to read yet and they didn't want Anders to make the other children feel bad.

There's a very nice public school here, Gunter said. Right down the street. There is a bus that will even come and pick them up. There are even after-school programs. It starts at a normal time. You could go back to work in the city if you wanted! Our taxes pay for it.

It's growing pains, Rachel said. They know what's best for children. Every child is blessed there. But Rachel was growing less sure.

In the meantime, she turned to cooking. She cooked pastas and ragus. Lasagna, chili, shepherd's pie, chicken in the oven, stews, roasts, pork chops, matza ball soup, and lemon meringue pies. She made brisket and baked cakes, brownies, cookies, snickerdoodles, lemon bars, and strudel for Gunter. She even made a ham. She made pudding from a box and ate it straight from the bowl. Sometimes Lydia pulled up a stool and helped. Mostly she sat under Rachel's feet and played with her dolls.

Rachel grilled. She baked. She chopped vegetables. She considered cooking school. Maybe she'd go to massage school or become a yoga teacher. Something less stressful, less tied to the city. Gunter ate her lasagna, nibbled on her cookies, admired her perfect cappuccinos, and called her a proper hausfrau.

Meanwhile her agent called with jobs, good jobs, with good brands, blue-chip, top-notch, lux, and well-paying brands. In fact, if she wanted to, she'd have more work than she could handle. But Rachel found she no longer had the same ambition. Maybe she was going through something. A kind of lull or chronic fatigue. Maybe, God forbid, she had Lyme disease. Everyone around her it seemed had Lyme disease, and on Facebook it was discussed exhaustively. Meanwhile, during the day, she fretted about Anders and fielded calls from his teacher, Miss Hensel, and the headmistress, Agnes. There were so many half days and days off. So many more than the public school. With no after care, the school day ended so early. Rachel wondered how she would get back to work after all. Jobs took up so much of her days and nights after the kids had gone to bed.

One day, the day before her project was due, school was cancelled for the day. Agnes called Rachel herself. New York was experiencing flooding, she'd said.

But this is Connecticut?

Yes but one of our teachers couldn't make it in! And besides, isn't it wonderful to have the day off? Agnes said. You all can stay home and bake cookies!

She'd have to find a babysitter. Everyone in the city had a babysitter or a good day care with extended hours if not a nanny. Surely in the public schools, mothers worked. Surely in Petra School there were working mothers! She'd find her tribe eventually. Meanwhile Rachel could not get into a groove and instead fell into free-floating anxious fretting. Besides the days off there was housework—cleaning the big house so much more labor intensive than their smaller and more manageable apartment. There was laundry—no wash-and-fold to pick it up from. There were doctors and dentists to see. There were field trips to volunteer for. Could she possibly, Miss Hensel wondered, spare a few hours a week in Lydia's classroom? Anders would surely benefit from having his mom in the class with him.

One afternoon Anders came home and said, I'm the worst kid in the whole class.

What do you mean? Rachel stood at the kitchen counter up to her arms in cookie batter.

Miss Hensel told Sage that he was almost as bad as me today.

Is that what she said?

He nodded.

*   *   *

115

Gunter came home one night vibrating with stress from a project at work. There was a glitch. The city was giving him trouble with permits. The feds with taxes. In his office, the employees were mutinying. His receptionist and assistant had run off together to start their own firm.

Gunter and Rachel split a Xanax and a bottle of wine. Something had gone off with the furnace. The kids slept in cold rooms in sleeping bags with their comforters piled on top.

Let's fuck, Gunter said.

They undressed and climbed into bed and lay facing one another. Gunter rubbed Rachel's arms and shoulders, her belly, her breasts. He touched her face. He combed her hair back with his fingers.

Relax, Gunter said.

Rachel knew she'd need something stronger than a Xanax and a half bottle of wine to relax. She needed electroshock therapy, eye movement therapy, or an acupuncturist. She needed psilocybin or Molly or Horse or Special K. A week in Canyon Ranch or a lobotomy. She needed antidepressant meds, antipsychotic meds, anticonvulsants. She needed to stop drinking coffee and take up artisanal green teas. She needed to give up gluten, sugar, and dairy. Her agent had called and asked if she wanted to take an official break or what. Between her legs she was numb, all the sensation of her body locked up with the march of thoughts across her furrowed brow. Gunter kissed her on her forehead and rolled off. He stroked himself until he was hard.

Down the hall, Rachel could hear Lydia whimper in her sleep.

Do you think she's cold, Rachel asked. Do you think I should go to Home Depot and buy a space heater? Her room is so drafty. I wish there was a super to call. Maybe Lydia should come and sleep in our bed. One of the moms at Petra told me about co-sleeping, like the hunter-gatherer tribes. Miss Hensel said there were societies where children's feet don't touch the ground until they are five years old—

Bullshit, he said. He kissed Rachel a long time and rubbed up against her leg. The wine on his breath reminded her of all those drunken horny teenage escapades in someone's apartment whose parents were out of town. Drunk in a cab, in the subway. Drunk and horny in Central Park, at a club. He pulled down her underwear, cotton, utilitarian. He'd always hated her underwear. Her mismatched bras and graying panties. She'd always been too lazy and daunted by the challenges of properly sorted laundry. He poised over her on his elbows and looked into her eyes. She felt his soft hardness against her.

Mommy?

Gunter jumped off of her, pulling the blanket around him. Fuck! Gunter shouted. Anders cowered beside the bed. Anders began to cry.

Rachel pulled her shirt over her head and led Anders back to his room by his hand. She tucked him back into his bed. She lay beside him a good twenty minutes. His wide-open eyes caught the reflection of the streetlights. Mommy?

Yes, Anders.

I thought Daddy was going to kill me.

Daddy wouldn't kill you. Daddies don't do that.

Lion daddies do, he said. Lion daddies kill their children and they eat them.

He turned to look at her, his eyes falling closed. It fascinated Rachel that children would hold their eyes open as long as they could when Rachel would give anything to fall asleep so easily.

Rachel climbed back into their bed. She'd hoped Gunter would be sleeping but he was awake. He vibrated coarse anger. He said, I'll be so old by the time Lydia is out of the house.

Rachel turned over in bed.

I'll probably be dead, she said.

You won't be dead. But if you are dead then I'll find someone who desires me, he whispered. And then he rolled to his side of the bed and began to snore.

It was while they were still in the city that Rachel had grown tired of her vibrator. Or perhaps it had grown tired of her. It had certainly stopped packing the punch it once had. She'd found it in one of those boutique hotel shops where one could reliably find Commes des Garçons coin purses and interesting and overpriced jewelry and candles. And always vibrators. Battery-powered vibrators had never done much for Rachel. But the one she'd found and consequently fallen in love with was small and tongue-like. It sat on a small plastic throne and could be conveniently plugged into her computer via a USB port. It was pink and soft and Rachel charged it dutifully. Sometimes, her work break was to traipse into the bedroom, remove her pants and shirt and climb into bed in her bra and panties, with her laptop and small charging vibrator.

But after a couple of years, the small, chic vibrator began to conk out. It did not seem to have its initial intensity. None of the vibrators she'd recently purchased seemed to have held their initial intensity. Or was it her? Was it her hormones gone kaput? She'd looked that up too, of course, and it was entirely possible. Orgasms after a certain age were less intense and more difficult to attain. Rachel imagined she'd find one of those early vibrators with an engine as big and strong as a Cadillac on eBay and it would be the thing that finally, in the end, killed her.

She'd read an article recently about orgasms and vibrators. How they diminished the orgasm, how the orgasms attained with a vibrator were less whole body or some other nonsense. She'd filed the article under myths made to make women even more miserable, like how wine and hair dye would kill you. But now that her vibrator was dying its sad death, she was left quite hanging. The female equivalent of blue balls. She thought maybe it was time to go back to old-fashioned, manually based methods.

Only it wasn't that easy.

It took much longer and generally at some point she fell asleep before she finished.

Once she'd gotten off watching other women masturbate. She loved the look on their faces. She'd never liked straight porn. It disgusted her, all those body fluids, the women who faked orgasms or distress or pleasure. She couldn't bear their bare pubic areas that looked red and raw and rashy. Rachel liked watching the faces of men coming and straight porn seemed to find this repulsive. They rarely showed men's faces at all. Gay porn was marginally better. At least the men enjoyed themselves. For a while she got off on men who inhaled poppers and had sex with blow-up dolls. She didn't really know what that was all about but their faces twisted in spasms of pleasure made Rachel crazy. They certainly seemed to be having fun.

Gunter was no doubt proud of his erection, which was rock steady but too quick on the draw. Whereas when they'd first started fucking, they'd fuck several times in a row or ten. He'd pressed into her and grind against her the way she liked and she'd always come and sometimes multiple times. There was something about Gunter that drove Rachel crazy back then. His age, his stubborn maleness, his Swedishness and the way he pronounced things finally and dominantly, and she was certain it would always be that way. He'd always get her off. It was one of the reasons she'd agreed to marry him (the other was that she needed stability and health insurance; she was freelanced at the time after her layoff from *Martha Stewart Living*, the COBRA payments had almost killed her financially, and he needed a green card to stay in the country). She was sure she wouldn't ever get sick of him the way she'd gotten sick of other boyfriends. Isn't that finally why you married someone? Certainty that they could get you off? Certainty that you wouldn't get sick of them?

Eventually he tired of being asked to perform multiple times at one go. Just because I have a hard-on, he told her, doesn't mean I'm turned on. Then he complained she was bruising his pubic bone, which couldn't be possible, could it? What, was he made of glass? They had less and less sex and then when they did have sex it was over in seconds. He no longer ground against her. She no longer came. For a while she faked it, so he wouldn't feel bad. Later she was angry. Sometimes she got so angry she twisted his nipple or pinched him. Ouch! he'd cry and then she'd feel sorry and it would take him ages to come and she'd roll over and seethe while beside her, he snored. Then the kids came.

After her vibrator stopped doing its job she thought she'd try and give it a go with Gunter again. They only really fucked on their anniversary or his birthday or Father's Day. On her birthday or on Mother's Day, as a gift to her, he left her alone.

She thought she probably just needed to get properly laid.

After a dinner of sushi and wine and after the kids were bathed and in bed, she sidled up to him. He sat with his laptop on the sofa, a soccer game on mute on the television. She felt for him under his trousers. She rubbed him until he stiffened and then she unzipped and exposed him. In his husky accent, he yelped, The kids! And Rachel felt herself grow aroused. She'd given up on the vibrator. She no longer touched herself. It was too tedious and took too long. No. What she needed was a good fuck. She slid to her knees in front of him she pumped her hand around him until he was hard. Oh, he groaned as she took him in her mouth. Rachel had forgotten the grotesque sounds a blow job could make. The slurping and sucking and within minutes he announced he was coming. She moved off him and he came on his belly and said, an old joke between them, I thought Jewish girls swallowed.

Only half, she'd said. She let her eyes twinkle seductively. Come on. Let's do it. He looked perplexed. Rachel rolled her eyes. My turn, she said.

Okay, he said. Give me a second to collect myself. Would you mind getting me a glass of water?

By the time she'd returned, taking a few minutes to gargle with mouthwash, he was snoring on the couch. Rachel stood over him disgusted and then grabbed her keys. She drove to the twenty-four-hour pharmacy. She refilled her Xanax prescription and bought some eye drops and a little bag of chocolate caramels. The vibrators were in the aisle with electric footbaths, canes, and toilet seats for the disabled. It was on a high shelf and Rachel, who was all of five feet two, had to stretch to reach it.

She read aloud the box as she slapped it onto the counter with the rest of her things: Braun.

A name you can trust, she said, and handed the cashier her credit card.

When Rachel woke up the next morning, Gunter was gone. She made breakfast, packed lunches and schoolbags. We'll be late! Anders said, fretting, holding Rachel's hand and pulling her out the front door. I don't want to get in trouble! he said. His palm was sweaty. Lydia began to weep.

Where's Daddy? she asked.

I don't know, Rachel said. Her head throbbed from the wine. I don't know where Daddy is. He's probably at work. He probably caught the early train into the city.

They were late. Lydia ran off eagerly to the kindergarten classroom but Anders stayed close to Rachel, holding her hand. Rachel walked him to his classroom. Agnes greeted them on the steps and Anders burst into tears.

Oh dear! Agnes said. Poor Anders. Poor, poor Anders. How do you feel? You must feel terrible to be so late. Why don't you go in and snuggle up with Miss Hensel and tell her how you feel.

Rachel became very cold and still with anger. Is that all really necessary? she asked.

What do you mean, necessary? Agnes asked with a small tilt of her chin. Do you mean are a child's emotions necessary or do you mean is it necessary to acknowledge a child's emotions?

I mean, we were just a little late, Rachel said. He doesn't need therapy for it.

Let me tend to his emotions during school hours, Ms. Olson, Agnes said. Rachel bristled. They stood for a beat in the hallway and Rachel then understood she was fighting a battle in a war she hadn't known until that moment had been declared.

Later that morning, Agnes called Rachel. Rachel was in the kitchen waiting for the oven timer to go off. Anders has been acting up more than usual, Agnes said. Perhaps he has picked up some tension in your home. We'd like you to come in and observe him during music and art class.

When is that? she asked. She nervously eyed the cake in the oven. It needed another twenty minutes.

It starts in ten minutes. Can you get here by then?

Can I come another day? she asked. There was the oven but there was also an ad edit due that she'd put off.

What exactly is important to you, Ms. Olson?

Rachel walked up Midway Avenue to the school. Agnes stood at the front door and ushered her in. Rachel noted Agnes's wanness. There was a burning, devouring look in her eyes. Had she lost weight? Rachel wondered. Or was she preparing for battle? Her fingertips bore into Rachel's arm all the way up the two flights of stairs to the classroom. The low din of school roared in her ears as soon as the door was opened. Miss Hensel was backed into a corner and saying, Children! Children! in a singsong tone. Set-tle do-own! The saccharine timbre of her voice was grating to Rachel. On the top of a desk, a gold paper crown on his head, stood Anders. He held a ruler in his hand like a scepter. The children rallied around him. Rachel recoiled. Agnes gripped Rachel's arm and hissed into her ear: He has a big heart but emotional problems. Have you perhaps been buying him too much Legos? Has he eaten too many sweets? Perhaps too much red meat? Are you entirely organic? Farm raised? Have you tried raw milk or going dairy-free? Perhaps fish oil? I understand he watches soccer. Is that not quite violent? Hadn't Gunter mentioned he'd been in the army? We understand from Gunter that Anders was quite energetic as a baby? Has he been vaccinated?

Rachel was already across the room. She yanked Anders down off the desk before she could think. What are you doing? Rachel said to him. His head hung ashamed and his crown slid to the floor. Her throat strangled her voice. Rachel wanted to howl at him. Miss Hensel charged at Rachel and pulled Anders away from her.

Rachel sat back down and slumped into a child-size wooden chair.

That is *not* how we deal with things here at Petra, Ms. Olson!

Anders will leave school early today, Rachel said. She stood and grabbed Anders's hand and headed out of the classroom and down the stairs to the street.

They walked back toward downtown, Anders's hand firmly in Rachel's. At the suburban outpost of Two Boots, the film *Casablanca* broadcast over one of the red leather booths. They slid into a booth and Anders watched Ingrid Bergman play across the television. Humphrey Bogart's mournful face. Ingrid's hysterical movements.

She's beautiful, Anders said.

Their order was called and Anders ran to grab the slices from off the counter but Rachel realized she wasn't hungry. Her pizza untouched on the plate in front of her. It congealed as it cooled. She called Gunter. Anders watched the television with rapt attention. Rachel whispered into her cell phone: He's such a good boy. Such a sweet, good boy. No one at his other school said anything about behavioral problems. *No one.*

Well, Gunter said. He sighed, distracted. This was not his area of expertise his tone seemed to say. It was a mother's job to deal with schools and teachers and their interpretation of his son. He's older now, Gunter said. He has more problems now. No one would ever confuse Anders with an angel.

He's just a boy! He's a boy who needs limits. I don't know if it's a real school, Rachel said. I don't know what it is. He was standing on the desk! I think maybe you have been right all along. I think maybe we should move him—

Now you want to move him? After you move him you'll change your mind, again! I think until the end of the year he should stay put, Gunter said. He will simply have to learn to behave.

Rachel pushed her phone into her pocket. She picked a piece off the crust and nibbled at it while beside her Anders watched the movie. His mouth hung open. A string of cheese caught on his lip and strung like a suspension bridge to the slice of pizza he held in his hand. How did he not notice the cheese was there? Another fine string of cheese hung from his chin.

Rachel thought about how he still couldn't tie his shoes. How he couldn't tell time. She thought about how he clung to her. How he was afraid at night to go to bed. How hard it was for him to make new friends. How he hated birthday parties.

She'd noticed how he was often impatient with his sister. He tripped her once on purpose. He thumped her when he thought his parents weren't watching. She remembered Sage's last playdate and the way Julie had rushed out the door. Was it possible Julie was avoiding her?

Rachel noticed how his mouth gaped open. How unaware he was of his body. How he could bang into something and not really feel it. How hard he wanted her to scratch his back at night with her fingernails until she was afraid she would break the skin.

Rachel set her napkin over the untouched slice of pizza. It was nonsense, she thought. He is a completely normal boy.

Come on, Anders, she said. Let's go get your sister.

But Anders didn't budge and after a while Rachel got sucked into the drama and high stakes of the film. Anders sat entranced by the images of the muted film. She read the subtitles to herself and felt a warm glow in her chest. She loved him. She loved her funny kid. Boys were so often vilified. In the public school there had been boys much wilder than Anders. Anders had never been a problem. They'd said he was an angel. A good boy. She was suddenly nostalgic for the public school. For the order and quiet and rows of desks. She thought of how Miss Hensel had cowered in the corner. There were ten children in the classroom for God's sake! Why could she not control *ten* kids! She thought about her last conversation with her friend Yael from the city. How she missed her. They'd been friends since their oldest kids were infants. How warm and funny she was. How close they were without being overly intimate. How Yael could see through bullshit. I'll call her, she thought. I'll go to the city and visit her.

The booths filled around them and light dimmed on the street. It was nice to sit with him when he was so still. They'd be late picking up Lydia from the after-school Soul Creatures class. Miss Hensel would no doubt be furious.

Dear Petra School Parents: Our lovely goat Shelley has, sadly, passed away. We will be holding a memorial service Friday night. Please note that for the benefit of all children fifteen and under this will be a "moving-up ceremony" and the youngers will be told that Shelley is going to a service farm.

PART TWO

Marriage is a death cult.
—KATHLEEN ROONEY

Chapter Twelve

THE PESSIMISTS

THERE WAS NO SEX. This was a given. Some gave themselves up to internet porn. They bribed their wives with what could only be considered the opposite of the push present: the fuck present. Extra points for filthy talk and blow jobs and extra, extra points for both. Diamond earrings could be had for access to the "small hole." Transgressions forgiven. Ruffled feathers smoothed. Shopping trips wiped off the ledger. There were women who longed for their husbands. Their neediness was a turnoff.

There were transgressions, of course. Sucky-sucky in a massage parlor or for a hundred dollars more there was fucky-fucky. Rich men had escorts or "girlfriends" they met in fancy hotels or college students they could support, reliving their youth in Bed-Stuy walk-ups. Occasionally the men would rub up together, for warmth and comfort and ejaculation. Not really. Of course not.

Wink.

One husband happily took his Prozac every morning with his espresso and Red Bull. It amped him up, like an amphetamine. And it rendered him as sexless in thought and deed as a eunuch. At night there were no pesky erections, no sex thoughts, and no sex. There was no angle to his dangle. There was no choice but the bliss of choicelessness. His wife could not deny what his body had already disabled. He was not angry when he was asked to stop leaving his coffee cup around. He was not angry when he was asked to walk the dog. Or to attend soccer matches and baseball games. His wife described their marriage as perhaps dull but otherwise perfect.

No, she didn't think discontinuing his medication was a good idea. The last time he'd done that he'd gotten in bed the day after Thanksgiving and did not get out until just before Christmas.

There was one husband who routinely threw back half bottles and whole bottles of whiskey and bourbon. Then with the booze buoying up his rib cage, he'd take up tickling whatever male or female happened to be nearby. It was terrifying to feel his long strong fingers digging into ribs and kneecaps. But for him, it was release. He hoped someone would lay their hands on him, for any reason, any reason at all. If only just for a moment.

The husbands dressed in stocky blocks of khaki and denim and button-down shirts. They smoked reasonably priced cigars and they drank expensive bourbon and they secretly and not-so-secretly saw their wives as "the bitches" and they acted and reacted accordingly. How they really saw their wives was something more akin to "mom." They loved them and they were loved but they weren't loved enough. No one was.

They beat off. They beat off and they beat off and they beat off.

They developed new appreciation for hand lotion. They bought the hand lotion and they hoarded it. They took the body lotions from hotels. Tiny bottles in bedside drawers. In office desks. In their cars' glove compartments.

There were new levels of excitement. There were new levels of titillation. The old levels did not work as well. New porn sites were sought. How odd a thing could get one off but also how banal. They longed for the old and the lack of choice. Choice could kill you. Choice made them miserable. Playboy pinups with natural breasts and the big bushes of yore.

The bushes of yore.

Good name for a band.

They tindered and bumbled, grindered and okcupid'd. Swiping, dreaming, fantasizing, scheming of an exit but the lawyer's fees were so high. The alimony so high. The children's tuition payments so high.

Maybe it was easier to stay married.

They shuddered thinking of their pals spending weekends alone entertaining little kids, then writhed in envy on alternate weekends as those same pals dated girls in their thirties. Then gloated when these same pals remarried, started a second family, began the whole cycle again.

They lusted after wives and friends' wives and coworkers and teachers. They lusted after sisters-in-law and ex-girlfriends and girls they'd wished had been their girlfriends who still looked hot fifteen and twenty years later and might give them a chance now that they were rich and still had all their hair. Or didn't have hair but they had money. Or didn't have money or hair but they were funny. After all the stressors and failures of life they'd discovered wicked senses of humor. Those exes on Facebook. Hot women pundits on Twitter. They lusted after old YouTube clips of 1970s Stevie Nicks, photos of high school girlfriends, actresses, and porn stars. The lust was as mechanical as gears whirling in a tower clock. It chugged on like an engine. It would plow forward until there was nothing left standing.

The stay-at-home dads—there were so few of them—were seen as second-class citizens in the eyes of the traditionally employed.

The stay-at-home dads knew quite a bit more about the traditionally employed dads than vice versa.

With children there were levels and degrees of involvement. They all wanted to be "good dads." They wanted to be better than their dads were. Who doesn't remember, "Cat's in the cradle, and the silver spoon . . . 'When you coming home, dad?'" They changed diapers and swung colicky babies around playrooms full of toys and minefields of Lego that no one was going to clean up, not ever. Whose job was it anyway? Wife was going back to work in two weeks and she had a gut like a trucker and hair that left clumps all around the bathtub— don't even think about touching her, *not now* for God's sake.

The men dreamed of au pairs, of hiring them, of the load of child raising shifting a bit away from themselves. Of gaining back lost ground. Of seducing them or sleeping with them. The men attended birthing classes and the hospital births and home births and held hands and mopped sweaty laboring brows of wives who mooed and lowed and shit on the table or in birthing tubs, sometimes into their hands. It was all natural, was it not all natural? There was no longer a waiting room or storks or cigars or proud papas. They watched babies being pulled from the blood and guts of gaping wide-open abdomens and tried not to pass out or throw up. They were equally happy to receive girls as first children. It was unseemly to seem otherwise. Only fucking Neanderthals wanted boys. They did not want boys. Boys were trouble. Who wanted boys? Not these men.

They went back to work as soon as that newborn was bathed and swaddled. Someone had to pay for diapers and the doula fee. Even when the women worked, let's face it, it was still the husband's paycheck that counted.

What *did* the nonworking wives do all day long?

How would life be for working men if they stayed home all day?

Life would be fucking great, that's what. They certainly wouldn't *whine* about it. They would certainly not insist, after lying around all day getting manicures and attending spin classes, that their *wives* do the dishes. They wouldn't insist on attending fancy seminars and yoga retreats and shrinks' offices and take antidepressants that shrunk their libidos to tiny hard tasteless acorns. They would not ask that grating, infuriating question again and again and again: When are you coming home?

No, sir.

Women worked. Of course women worked. This was the new millennium after all. And then they came home and accepted the dirty house and negotiated who was going to make dinner and who was going to help junior and princess with their homework and then they whined about their jobs. Because of course they did.

No one was happy.

Not sober anyway.

In the very beginning, there was infant rearing, for which the women were required. Nappies, elbow-deep in shit, trying to get the baby down for a nap, breastfeeding, no wine drinking, no anything drinking, stinky cheeses, or sushi. No pot. No Xanax.

Forties were coming so quickly, early forties, midforties, late forties. Fifties. Sixties. Early death and aging parents. There were sculpted bodies and spring tennis. In the winter they played a strange cage game called paddle tennis and they traveled en masse to other cages and played in the snow and cold rain and laughed and it wasn't much of a workout but for that they attended Pilates, yoga, hot yoga, suspended-from-the-ceiling yoga, and ballet barre yoga. They lifted weights and tossed ropes around frantically like hardened Soviet sailors on the deck of a sinking warship, cajoled and humiliated by their cult leader, a lithe former Russian ballerina whose hip bones were a handspan apart and who screamed Russian curses at them as they sweated puddles on the rubberized floor. They spun and spun and spun on their sleek black cycles, caught their reflections in mirrored walls, pumped it out. Shoulders back. Chin up, my darlings.

REMEMBER YOUR CORE.

In the summer the women jogged, hiked, bicycled, rowed, and played tennis. Any time of the year, any time at all, they saw nutritionists and astrologers and therapists. They rolfed. They became yoga teachers, Zumba teachers, Pilates and spin instructors. They discreetly botoxed and juvedermed and micropeeled. They got boob jobs, tummy tucks, microdermabrasions, blood injections. They smoked joints so they could better obsessively clean cupboards and sort toys from playrooms. They smoked joints so they could fuck their husbands without anger. They took Xanax so they could tiptoe around the yawning void. They took Ambien because it was fun and Adderall because they had projects due at work on no sleep, all that coffee was giving them heart palpitations, another fucking marketing presentation, and Adderall made them feel like cocaine, like the whole world was Studio 54, if Studio 54 were an accounting firm, law offices, advertising agencies, and Wall Street. They left for girls-only vacations. They lived the life. They were living their best life. They—those of them in the middle-class to wealthy suburbs surrounding major cities all over America—lived in material leisure and emotional poverty. Sometimes they developed crushes on each other, on their husbands' best friends. They developed crushes and love affairs on themselves, their very own selves who they'd been mocking, deriding, and despising since puberty. Men were superfluous, dogs divine.

DON'T FORGET YOUR KEGELS.

They watched everything that any of them put into their mouths. The skinny ones lived off strange rations of salmon, salad, and green juices and stopped menstruating. Heavier ones ate the same, except late at night when they ate furtive bags of chips, Entenmann's donuts, and pints of ice cream. The regular moms fed their kids cereal for breakfast and pasta with butter for lunch and dinner. The skinny mothers declared gluten and dairy poison and refused to eat it, and then fed their kids cereal for breakfast and pasta with butter for lunch and dinner. And pizza. So much pizza.

There were queen bees and cliques just like in high school, and just like in high school there were popular moms with the good hair and the fashionable clothes and there were the hurting lonely moms at the edges. There were mothers who kept tabs on whose houses hosted the most playdates. They kept tabs on which houses hosted the least. They judged the mothers who refused to volunteer. They judged the mothers who had no life outside of their children and their children's schools. The working mothers were grateful for the nonworking mothers for keeping everything running and judged the nonworking moms for having no life, no financial freedom. The nonworking mothers looked down on the working mothers for their "hobbies," when everyone knew their partners made enough money for them to stay home. On message boards and Facebook pages across America the anger burned with the heat of a thousand rising phoenixes.

They were all rising phoenixes, eating their men like air. They fed the children the ashes.

They watched their gay and lesbian neighbors and noted few differences. Gay marriage at the turn of the century was as banal as straight marriage. Same shit. Same tedium. Same breakdown of responsibilities. Same breakups. Same divorces.

There were books to write. Instruments to learn. Backhands, forehands, slice serves and volleys to master. Languages to speak. Countries to relocate to. Lands to conquer. Cigarettes and flirtations to give up. Bad habits to shed. Bad manners too. Insects to exterminate. Closets of clothing and old sports equipment and skeletons to clear. Grievances and rooms to air.

But there wasn't much time. The wheel of civilization was grinding to a halt if the Mayan prophecies were correct—and who believed that stuff anyway. The Long Count calendar of Mesoamerica. They joked about it, but didn't really believe. If you stayed up late enough with insomniac dread, you could watch the preachers predicting the coming apocalypse and offering prayers for cash or credit. Send money. It couldn't hurt. Someone had to. It certainly felt like the end of the world. It had always, to some, felt like the end of the world. For some in the world, it was the end. For everyone it would be the end someday.

There were breakdowns and depressions. Prepartum and postpartum and one or two affairs with stay-at-home dads, retired men working as teachers' aides, men forced out of their jobs with or without parachutes between mothers. Business trip affairs, office affairs, and office husbands. Infertility. Learning disabilities, affective disorders, seasonal disorders, dyslexia, autism, ADHD, and one boy with Tourette's who barked like a dog at the end of every sentence.

The question they asked themselves: were they as miserable when they were kids as their kids were now?

No, they were happy then and they'd be happy again.

They just needed to work harder.

Chapter Thirteen

An Encounter

THE FLIGHT TO LOUISVILLE to bury her stepmother had gone without incident. Virginia relished the quiet time on the airplane—the first time she'd flown in years. Outside the airport, Virginia rented a tiny economy car and folded herself into it. She drove toward the exit, where she showed her license and rental contract to the woman in the booth. You have a nice visit, y'hear? the woman said kindly, with her warm Southern vowels.

She fiddled with her phone's GPS until she'd punched in the address for the hotel. She'd deal with the funeral home in the morning.

Virginia merged onto the parkway and headed east. She searched the radio stations. She found some twangy old music—the station her mom had liked best—and turned it up, soothed by the familiar drawl of an unfamiliar DJ.

Virginia's mother had died years ago, when Virginia was fifteen. She'd barely even had the thought of teenage rebellion when her mother was diagnosed. But then it began. She'd screamed at her mother, even when her mother's hair had fallen out from chemotherapy, over something as silly as makeup. Or maybe Virginia had wanted to wear high heels or a short skirt. And forever after, Virginia held her own guilt over her mother's death in her hands like a living organ, still warm, still beating, still bleeding. Her father married soon after and they'd lived uneasily until Virginia had gone away to school, across the state.

Her stepmother had died in an assisted living home east of the city off the Hurstbourne Parkway. She'd died in her sleep or maybe that was what they always told surviving relatives. Virginia wondered if there had been any signs of impending mortality. Would she have come sooner if her stepmother had asked for her? Her stepmother had never visited them up in Connecticut. Had not come to Tripp and Virginia's wedding. She'd sent the RSVP card back with regrets and no explanation and had never met Charlotte. Virginia never bothered to visit after that.

After her father's death, Virginia wasn't sentimental and didn't keep contact with anyone if she didn't have to. Rhonda hadn't been part of their lives at all.

Her left breast ached, as it always did before her period. Or maybe it was the damp humid South. Or maybe it was something sinister. As a teenager, she'd overheard her mother say cancer didn't hurt until it had nearly killed you and then, just before her mother had died, Virginia wondered how much pain she'd suffered. Not much, her father had said. They give her medicine through the IV that makes all her pain and fear go away. But when Virginia would go to visit her, she could see the pain and fear on her mother's face. And Virginia never forgot what she'd overheard her mother say: If I survive this, I will never do chemo again. I'd rather die, her mother had said, rather than go through chemotherapy.

She followed the GPS on her phone. She took the Hillsboro exit. Things had changed in the years since she'd last been down there. Hulking over the main drag were new buildings, offices or apartments probably, and in between the new buildings were big hotels. She wondered if the Spotted Hog Cafe was still there or the used bookstore she used to work at when she came home for summers. Later, if she felt up for it, she'd go see what remained. For now, she would head to the hotel room, check in, shower, have a drink, and nap. She hadn't been alone in a hotel room since before Charlotte was born.

The hotel was large and modern and catered toward conferences held year-round in temperate Kentucky. The lobby had a little coffee shop, sofas, a gas fireplace, a little bar. No, she didn't need help with her suitcase. She could find the room herself. She hesitated in the lobby. She only had two days. The lobby was a nice place to have a cup of coffee and pull out her laptop. The hotel bed was tempting so she headed up the elevator and then she keyed into her room. Once inside she pulled off her jeans and her sweater and lay on the bed a minute in her underwear and a camisole. She thought about her book. Her edits had nearly been done for months but she was afraid to turn it in. She thought it was a good book. A little dark. She wondered if she should leave the end the way it was with a small violent act. She wondered what her agent would think of it. In the morning she'd head to the funeral home and make arrangements.

She sat up and pulled back on her jeans and put on a jacket. She gathered up her laptop and a book. She'd just go down and have one drink in the hotel bar.

Virginia saw the cut of his suit before she saw him. There was an aura around a suit as fine as that. And how straight and slim on his shoulders it was. Both these things made up for the fuzz of red hair that was a little too long, maybe California style or European. It shone in the light of the halogen pendant lamps that hung down from the bar. The man turned and appraised her with a pleasant, mild expression. She couldn't quite make out how old he was. He had broad shoulders for his frame. Virginia pried her wedding ring from her finger and dropped it into the pocket of her jacket.

She sat down at the bar next to him. He was bookish and neat. You're a very stylish fellow, aren't you, Virginia thought.

Virginia settled in, ordered a glass of whiskey. She turned and watched the television. Wildcats against Ole Miss. Some guys in a booth shouted behind her. She stared at her phone, conscious of his elbow that rested beside her on the bar. She checked Twitter, the Instagram of her editor, who'd retired to the South of France to start a writing retreat. Beside her, the man had his phone in his hands too. She glanced over at it. He was deleting emails, sliding across the screen with his thumb, long as a finger. She noted one or two emails from the *Chicago Tribune*. Journalist, she thought. She glanced at his rumpled, casual button-down shirt. She noted the dark and current tone of his jeans. His lace-up shoes. A writer. For sure.

I'm Jeremy, he said. He turned toward her and extended his hand.

A Brit, Virginia noted. Virginia, she said and held out her hand. He shook it.

You here for business?

No, she said. A funeral.

I'm sorry, he said.

It was my stepmom. We weren't close.

I see.

Are you a writer, she asked.

Oh, he said. No. I'm in education.

Really?

Sort of. Online education.

Ah, she said. Pearson?

Wiley.

Trips to London?

Occasionally.

Live in Hoboken? Or Jersey City?

Neither, he said. Edgewater.

Well, she said. She looked down at her hands. She didn't know what else to say.

They had some things in common. In fact, he had been a journalist back in London. He liked writing. But, he said. Life, children. My wife. Writing doesn't pay the bills. He waved his hand in front of his face. Occasionally I'll write a book review, you know, for the *Washington Post*.

You're good at what you do, she said. At the business side.

Yeah, he said. I suppose I am. I came up just when the dot-com boom was happening. I sold a start-up and made some money back when that was still possible. Companies poured a lot of money into online education and it's big now. And you? What do you do?

I wrote a book, Virginia said. She blushed. She always blushed when she talked about her book.

Oh really? he said. What's it about?

Oh, you know, she mumbled. A novel.

I'll order it right now. He pulled out his phone. I have internet access. What's the name?

No, she said. You don't have to do that. I don't think it's even in print anymore.

No, he said. I insist.

It's called *The Moral Character*, she said.

He narrowed his eyes and searched his phone. Are you Virginia Powers?

Virginia nodded.

I just ordered it, he said. See. Now you have one more book sold.

Mostly he talked and she listened. It was nice to be talked to. It soothed her not to have to think of things to say or how to say them. She felt a warm glow from his arm that had inched over from his chair and pressed just slightly into hers. His sleeves were pushed up. His arms were ropy, pale, and strong.

Do you travel a lot? Virginia asked.

I do, he said. I'm here now for a convention. Really very boring stuff I'm afraid.

I'm sure your wife loves that. All that travel. Virginia glanced at his left hand. No ring.

She . . . doesn't like it much.

His job paid the bills, and he liked it. Yeah, he said. He mostly liked it. He'd worked so hard over the last twenty years and he'd finally reached a certain level of management and that felt something like success.

One more drink? he asked. Before we call it a night?

I'm not much of a drinker, she answered. They ordered one beer and had it split it into two glasses.

She turned slightly in her chair. Her knee brushed his. Listen, she said. Do you want to pretend like we're in high school and go upstairs to your room and make out?

He shook his head. No, he said sadly. Sorry.

Virginia stared down at her wrists, at the small gold bangle she wore that Tripp had given her and the pattern on the floor of the industrial hotel bar carpet.

Okay, she said.

I just never have, he said. Not in this marriage anyway. In my first marriage, I was married to an Irish girl and I had it annulled. I cheated on her almost constantly. Almost from the very start.

Tell me a secret, Virginia said.

He smiled. That is a secret.

Tell me another, she said.

Okay. He took a breath. I never told anyone, not even my current wife, that I was married before her. In fact, I'm not entirely sure I haven't committed bigamy. I mean, is a church annulment as good as a proper divorce? Is it only good in the UK? We never hired a lawyer or anything. But, there were no children and no property so I suppose no harm, no foul. Now you're the only who knows that too. And you are a perfect stranger. You? Now it's your turn. What's your secret?

Okay, let me think, she said. Virginia stared up at the chandelier of the bar. I have cancer.

He whistled. Is that really a secret?

It is. You and my oncologist are the only ones who know. But I fired my oncologist.

Are you getting treatment?

No.

Will you be all right?

Are any of us?

Fair enough, he said. He finished the rest of the beer with one pull. Feels like a bit of a burden to lay on a near stranger.

I haven't met any men I've actually liked in ages. Think of it as a gift.

Is it . . . in your breast?

Yes. The left one.

Will you have it removed? Like, a mastectomy?

Never.

He whistled again. He sat up. Let me see them, he said. Virginia turned and fully faced him. She let her jacket fall off her shoulders. She wore just the silk camisole and no bra.

You *are* beautiful, he said. It's criminal that a woman should be so beautiful, at your age, I mean. No disrespect. He held his breath and let it out in a rush. Your breasts are worth dying for.

Virginia, stunned, barked a small sound of surprise.

May I touch them?

Virginia looked around. The bar was now empty but for the bartender, who stood with her back to them watching the game.

Yes, she said.

He reached out and caressed her. It felt electric.

Thank you, he said.

You're welcome. Her eyes stung with tears. Thank *you*, she said.

Listen, he said. This is bad timing, but I'm afraid I'll have to shove off—

No, she said. She swallowed hard. It's all right.

It's just that I have such an early meeting in the morning. I've really enjoyed meeting you, Virginia.

Virginia was touched he'd remembered her name. She had forgotten his.

Back in her room, she showered, scrubbed her makeup off with a clean white hotel washcloth and discarded it in a corner of the shower. She washed her hair and added conditioner and then rinsed and stepped out of the shower. A white bathrobe hung in the closet. She turned on the TV in bed and watched the news on mute and held her phone in her hand. A text rattled the phone. She picked it up. It was a text from Richard: I heard about your stepmother, it said. I'm sorry, Ginny. Let me know if you ever want to talk. I'm here.

Dear Petra School Parents: We will be screening the award-winning documentary film *Vaxxed: From Cover-Up to Catastrophe* this coming Tuesday. Please see Nurse Betty Allen for more information. Also, please note that your vaccination exemption forms and letters are due by this Friday.

Chapter Fourteen

THE "G" IS FOR GUNTER

JUST BEFORE VIRGINIA and Tripp's New Year's Party when he'd been too drunk to drive home, Gunter had decided he needed a new car. A big car for a big man in a big land. I'm a tall man, Gunter had said to the dealer. I need a tall car. A tall German wagon is what I require, Gunter told the dealer. I need such a car to navigate the American neighborhood with its large houses.

Gunter, an architect, knew a thing or two about city planning, he told the dealer. Yes, this town had a train directly to Grand Central. Yes, this town was not a town really or a suburb but rather technically a village on the sound. Of course things could be better. There could be better restaurants, Gunter told the dealer. Of course things SHOULD be better! But I have been asked to design a very large building in Dubai for a fair amount of money, and I require a good German car. Such things should be German of course. Cars, education, sweet wines, typewriters, painkillers, train schedules, roads, camps . . . I'm only kidding, he told the salesman, who'd markedly blanched. Of course I'm joking! My wife is Jewish! But only on her father's side. I myself am Swedish of course and not German. But I will admit I like some German ways. And the Swedish have not built a car since the Saab. The Saab was a good car. Do you know the history of the Saab? Originally they made fighter airplanes before World War II. You look surprised! But no, it's true. We built airplanes in order to protect our neutrality. To you, an American, I'm sure it sounds absurd. To fight to be neutral is anathema to the American way! But it is absolutely our way. Indeed, I was in special forces. Well, not special forces. They had not yet become official when I was in the army. Anyway, I thought to buy a Saab but a little birdy back home tells me they are on the verge of bankruptcy. And besides! I have always wanted one of these big luxurious Mercedes. It's grand, no?

Yes, the dealer said. The dealer, short with a mass of black hair who looked down at his watch. Gunter noted it was a small, stainless-steel Rolex. As a rule, Gunter hated status watches of all kinds. Gunter himself wore a microthin Skagen that an ex-girlfriend had given him. It was modest and stylish, like Gunter himself. Gunter loosened his scarf and switched over to price. It was expensive, of course. But Gunter was confident he could be given a good deal. Things were hard since the economic crash and Gunter was well cognizant of the wiggle room of salesmen.

Gunter was asked to step into an office to go over financials. He sat in the chair, his big knees pressing against the desk of the manager. The office was windowless and plain and there was some sort of contraption, some sort of intercom or radio. It looked forty years old. It said MUZAK in faded gold letters. The business manager who sat before him noticed Gunter looking at it. Yes, he said. It's been there forever.

Does it work? Gunter asked.

The man shrugged. I don't know, he said. I've never tried it.

May I? Gunter asked. He reached over with his long, heavy arms and flipped the little switch. The machine burbled a bit and then static like lightning filled the building. People in the showroom looked around fearfully. Some treacly music filled the air. Ah, Gunter said. Elevator music.

Yeah, the business manager said. He flipped the music off. Muzak, he said.

They negotiated.

The car Gunter wanted was a 2013 G-Class, 382 horsepower. It was listed at eleven miles to the gallon but Gunter knew it was more like eight. It tows seven thousand pounds, the dealer said helpfully.

Wonderful, Gunter said. I can tow my house behind me if I like. For that price I could move in.

We can throw in a fridge, if you like.

A "fridge"? There is nothing so charming as the American need to abbreviate. Why abbreviate? Gunter said and threw back his long arms. There is so much space here! Make the word even looooonnnnnger, like the Germans! Gunter stopped and squinted up his eyes and held his chin in his hands. But then again a "fridge" could be very helpful. I could sit in the car and listen to music and have a beer. My wife, sometimes she likes me less than other times. It's difficult being married. Are you married? Gunter nodded absentmindedly, not registering an answer, and continued: The problem, of course, is biblical. As in, if things were as they were in the Bible, we'd have no problems. I'd be a King Solomon with a hundred wives. How many wives could I fit into this car? If they are skinny, I'd say ten! If they are more fat, I'd say five! Skinny or fat makes no difference to me. I'm an equal opportunity lover. But then one must drive the children. Or, you'd put the homeliest wife in a big minivan. She'd drive the children in that. But I have one wife. She herself is of biblical proportions, small, but appropriately stacked . . .

The man wrote on the sales memo a figure and slid it across the table to Gunter. He said, Not including taxes and out-the-door fees, of course.

Gunter waved his hand in front of his face. You know, he said, you have planted your final potato. In other words, I won't pay a penny more than this number. No taxes, not a farthing more. No "out-of-door fees."

The dealer put out his hand, Deal, he said. Gunter waved him away. There is no need, Gunter said. For physical contact. We sign papers like men.

Gunter signed and paid the down payment with his heavy platinum card. In some ways, it was a relief to be in America, where to display wealth was not considered gauche. He would say, if anyone asked him, that it had taken him time to come to terms with this new American way but the truth of the matter was it had taken him money. Now he had it. All of it. His paychecks astonished him. The terribly minor amount of taxes he paid each month was cause for a jig, a dance, a celebration. A party! It was almost criminal, really.

The car was not exactly the model he'd wanted. The color was black—actually Designo Night Black Magno rather than the ultracool gunmetal gray Mojave Silver—or he might have been happy with Obsidian Black, but they had none of those colors on the floor and he wanted to get the G-wagon as soon as he could. Before he changed his mind, before his wife, Rachel, stepped into everything with all the élan and enthusiasm of a wet towel discarded on the bathroom floor. And as he drove it, he thought about how little was rendered to Caesar in this big new country. In this country, he thought, we are all Caesar! He locked up the little Volvo. He'd come back later with Rachel to fetch it. She'd have to learn to drive sooner rather than later.

Gunter climbed in. It was like climbing up a mountain or onto a yacht. The steering wheel gleamed with real leather. The smell of the car intoxicated him. In the back nestled between a window and one of the seats was the refrigerator. Just the right size for a six-pack or maybe some of those cans of Perrier his wife was so fond of.

A 2013 Mercedes-Benz G-Class in Designo Night Black Magno. Gunter mouthed the words to himself. A G-Wagon. The "G" was for Gunter.

He adjusted the mirrors as he drove, adjusted the seat height. He glanced up at the ceiling of the car. He was at the highest seat level and the ceiling was still over two feet above him. He turned on the radio and scrolled through stations, marveling at

the sound booming from the speakers. At stoplights, he glow-
ered down at all the poor people in their cars, so distressingly
close to the pavement, to asphalt, to general filth and humanity.
Then checked himself. He was not raised to be so boorish. He
would work harder to be less so.

He drove the back roads to his house. The old Victorian
reared up from the bushes and trees that surrounded it. It was
painted shades of pink and purple. Rachel loved it, of course,
and Gunter had compromised. If he'd had his way he would
have built a cold steel building of glass and light. But he could
not always have his way, and if he could not have his way, at
least he could have a car big enough for a refrigerator.

Gunter pulled into their driveway. That gleaming hulk of
Designo Night Black Magno reflected and absorbed the streetlights and the low December clouds. He peered into the windows of the parlor, could see shadows lighting and alighting.
Rachel probably cleaned or baked, itching to work, or fit into
the community. The new school of the children where they'd
be attending in a week or two. The New Year's Eve party they'd
be going to later in the week. It touched Gunter really how she
suffered. She suffered like a mother with a mother's woes. He
loved her. He hoped she would be as happy as he was about
the car but he feared she would not be.

She opened the door just as he stepped up to the porch. Her
hair was a wild black mess of curls, her feet stuffed into the
wide shearling boots whose name was short for "ugly." What
the hell is that? she said. Behind her the children wrestled, the
boy lunged at his sister and took her down to the floor. The

girl screamed with the one weapon God had given her—an ear-splitting sound. Rachel turned around. Stop! she said. Anders! Stop at once! She turned back again to Gunter. Please tell me you didn't buy that.

I did!

What on earth for? We can never take that to the city. Are you crazy? I don't think you can even get it into a parking garage.

We're not going back to the city!

Of course we are. To visit! Can you return it?

Gunter turned petulant and his skin blotched with anger. I can't, he said. And I won't.

Rachel turned away from him and back to the children. She pulled Lydia off the floor and spat a word at Anders, who sulked off. Gunter could see that was how the night would go. He had hoped the car would be cheering. It was beautiful how it shone darkly, the very pulse of its hulk was invigorating as a dip in a cold sea. But now, Gunter could see, they'd eat dinner in silence. Anders made furtive glances at his parents, gauging the mood, checking which way the wind would blow. Lydia, oblivious. She watched Anders to interpret the scene for her.

In bed that night, Gunter lay beside Rachel, who beside him fumed. I love the car, he said. I really, really love the car. Do you ever think about how hard it is for me? You hate Stockholm. Okay, I get it. But I didn't want to leave the city. I married you because I thought you of all people would never leave! And here we are. We got the house you wanted. It's a drafty old house with nothing modern about it. So yes, I just want this car. Listen, I don't hate it here. I'm not miserable. Things will get better in the new year.

Rachel pursed her lips and tried to decide how mad she wanted to be. I didn't want to leave the city either! But we had kids! And the city began to feel impossible! And the car has terrible gas mileage, she said. Are you sure you want to drive this car to the Petra School and around town? Around all those, as you say, earthy, crunchy Americans?

As if I care! Gunter said. And anyway, gas is so cheap in America! And do you have any idea how expensive this car is in Europe?

Why would it be expensive in Europe? Rachel said. It's a European car.

Gunter exhaled. Really, he thought, Americans were exhausting when it came to anything outside their own country. No, dear, he said. The taxes make it too expensive. Two hundred thousand dollars at least.

My God, she said. How much did it cost here?

Gunter waved his hand in front of his face. Never mind, he said. But I got it much cheaper.

Okay, Rachel said. The grim line of her mouth loosened. Okay. She turned to him. Will you try? Make an effort to fit in? You made no effort in the city and it was so hard to fit in.

Gunter thought. He realized they were making a deal right then. He thought of the headmistress they'd met with last week. She'd reminded Gunther of someone. He couldn't figure out who. Maybe, he thought, maybe he wouldn't like the school, but he bet he could learn to like the headmistress.

He turned to Rachel and kissed her cheek. I am sure I will love the school, he said. At the very least, I will try.

You can't take the kids to school in that thing!

Of course, I can, Gunter said. And they are already too big for the Volvo. He pouted. There is room enough. There is even a refrigerator!

And then the New Year had come and gone and now it was a few months into school and Rachel had relaxed about the car. She seemed, even, to like it a little. There was another parent with a white Escalade that was certainly more gauche than a large black G-Wagon. (The "G" is for Gunter! Gunter had said to Rachel, who did not laugh. A pity. When they were first together, she might have. But that was back when she found him charming.)

Gunter never felt more American than he felt high up in that wagon. It was like being in a tank or an airplane. It took amazing amounts of very cheap American fuel. There was no car on the road higher than his apart from a semitruck, and Gunter was even eye to eye with many of those on the highway. Sometimes, another G Wagon would pass by as he drove through the towns and they would flash their lights at Gunter and Gunter would flash his lights back. Once, in fact, the car had saved his life. Traveling on the Taconic, driving too fast, as it were, pretending he was on the Autobahn, he'd slammed into a five-point buck. The car barely shuddered. It plowed through that hundred-kilo deer like it was a small rodent. Gunter then had felt, for the first time in his life, immortal.

✳   ✳   ✳

And then later that day of the deer slaying, an email had come from Agnes. It was addressed only to Gunter and suggested he come that night to a meeting. And it was signed: I'd very much like to see you there.

Who had Agnes reminded Gunter of but his very first baby-sitter. The first person he'd jacked off to in fact as a young lad in rural Skåne in the duck blind at the far end of his father's farm. She, like Agnes, had been unwaveringly tall. Like Agnes, she'd had a ferocious spirit and eyes that looked like they'd spit acid when she was angered. In the sauna, as a boy, he'd been enflamed by his babysitter's boyish chest, her long neck, the somewhat comically touching large ears she'd tucked her hair behind.

By the time he pulled into the driveway that night, Gunter made up his mind he would go to whatever it was Agnes had invited him to. It would kill two flies with one swat: One, it would make Rachel happy; she'd held a low-grade grudge with him ever since school started. It appeared Gunter was not properly enthusiastic about the thousands of dollars he was paying for kindergarten and second-grade instruction. And two, of course, there was Agnes and her personal plea to Gunter: I'd very much like to see you there.

After dinner, Gunter told Rachel he would go to the gym. He couldn't explain why he didn't tell her the truth. Something in his gut told him she wouldn't be happy or she'd be happy for the wrong reasons. He couldn't explain what the right reasons were, only that he wanted something for himself. The car was a declaration of independence but after the declaration came action.

He dressed carefully in jeans, a cashmere turtleneck sweater, and a striped wool scarf that years ago had been his father's—that his father had had an affair with the babysitter Gunter had lusted after did not occur to him until much, much later—and he strode down the stairs. Rachel was in the kitchen making a pie or a tarte or a quiche. He wasn't sure which and Rachel did not turn around as he stood at the front door and called out: Heading to the Y! And the truth was, even if she had turned around, she would probably not have noticed the illogical discrepancy between his trip to the gym and his not wearing gym clothing.

When will you be home? she called out.

An hour, he said. Maybe two.

The parking lot of the school was full when Gunter pulled in. It was a sea of Subaru Outbacks, that homeliest of cars, with a few Priuses and a lonely Cherokee. Well, Gunter had never liked to fit in.

Inside there were . . . women. So many women that Gunter's skin began to crawl. There was that plain little plump friend of Rachel's in the corner, but beyond her, Gunter recognized no one.

After ten minutes, during which Gunter refreshed his news app again and again—he did not care he was the only one with his phone out—Agnes strode out into the middle of the room and took a seat on a lone chair.

Good evening, everyone, she said. And she looked pointedly at Gunter. Thank you so very much for coming. She gestured toward Gunter and said, It's so good to see you here.

Agnes asked they all straighten their spines. She asked they sense their feet on the floor. She asked they feel their toes in their shoes, wiggle them around, really sense them. She asked them to start moving through the body. Start with the right hand and move down to the right foot, the left foot. Sense again the toes and the soles of their feet. Gunter had trouble in the beginning. He'd never given much thought to his body apart from how much weight he could lift or how fast he could run a kilometer as a boy. Or how much pleasure he could feel during sex. As Agnes talked, adding body parts, ending at the head, the throat, the chest, and then starting again, Gunter wondered if this was not some sort of character flaw, the fact that he was virtually numb from the head down. He opened his eyes to see Agnes, illuminated by the dimmed lights behind her. She opened her eyes and locked his with hers and said, Don't think. Let go of the thoughts, she said. And return to the sensation of your body. This is the true meaning of "be here now." Be in your body now. It is the only present. By extending your mind into your body you become mindful.

Gunter closed his eyes again and the school around him, shabby and dim, began to dissolve. Her words were a rhythm he found he could follow. It wasn't a matter of concentrating but something more akin to surrender. After a while, Gunter lost track of time. His phone buzzed in his pocket, but it had no pull or attraction for him. He was only conscious of the lulling quality of Agnes's voice and his body. The tension in his shoulders and his low back flared and then by some strange and divine power melted away.

Time passed but Gunter wasn't sure how long and then Agnes rang a small bell and everyone began to wiggle and rustle around Gunter. He opened his eyes and watched Agnes. When he stood, he felt as though he had begun to float. She walked right up to him.

I'm so glad you are here, Gunter, she said. I thought you might come. I had a feeling.

Gunter felt words clog in his trachea, not a feeling he was used to. He didn't know what to say. Agnes reached out and touched his arm. She seemed very tender to Gunter and it felt like the first time in a long time since a woman had been very tender to him. It turned him on.

I wonder, she said, if you wouldn't mind coming by the school one day next week. There are some projects I'm thinking about and we could use an architect's knowledge.

He nodded without much consideration and mumbled in the affirmative.

He did not stay for the apple juice and organic packaged cookies set up at a table in the back but instead left right away. The shabbiness of the school no longer fazed him quite as much. He saw it with new eyes. Perhaps he could jazz it up a little. Why not? Great men adapt to their circumstances and make them their own. There was his G-wagon in the parking lot, rising like a phoenix above them all. Gunter unlocked it using his key fob. The beep the car made was a form of music. He climbed into the car and his eyes adjusted to this new reality. The power of the car combined with the power of whatever he'd just experienced was intoxicating. Stars glittered through the windshield and through the moonroof and a feeling of peace seemed to enter his body through his wrists as though intravenously.

Chapter Fifteen

Richard's Pot Chapter

I T WAS A PERFECT mid March day. There was the smell of early spring in the air. Richard drove Aiden and Teddy to their soccer games. The season had just begun. The tulips had popped out of the ground, and that morning Margot had pointed out the first robin, something that Richard truly got excited for. At the great soccer facility, newly built by the town, soccer fields stretched in every direction. Smiling parents everywhere. A sea of earnest, friendly, mostly white faces turned toward the bright spring sunshine. They cheered on their children. Smaller children hung around the playground near the concession stands and ate hot dogs precariously balanced in their buns. The younger children made slow rotations around the slide and kicked playground wood chips. There were twelve hundred parents and kids stretched over twenty soccer fields.

Richard located the boys' teams, grateful that for once they had games at the same time. He walked over to the concession stand and bought himself a cup of coffee and a cream cheese bagel. No matter what it looked like now, in five minutes it would be delicious. He carried the bagel and coffee back to the minivan and drove slowly, careful to avoid the tiny erratic children and distracted moms, out of the complex.

The soccer complex had been built partly on the grounds of what had been the old county psychiatric hospital. There were old wooden buildings with peeling paint and ivy-covered brick ones, certainly haunted. The green grass lawns were mowed and the brick drives were tidy. The old abandoned homes on large lots that lined the grounds around the hospital were nearly swallowed up by long grass and snaky, thick vines. Inside the hospital, there had once been a bowling alley, Richard knew, and a children's wing with cheery figures from popular animated series of the last century painted on the walls. Attached to the children's wing were classrooms and a gymnasium. Great trees now climbed the lower half of the walls of the buildings and covered up the doors. The building was nearly inaccessible.

He pulled up beside one of the buildings now and felt the old shiver he'd felt since he had first come to the hospital as a teenager, already abandoned twenty years by then. His father once told him that his mother had spent a few weeks there when she was young but Richard couldn't imagine it, had nearly forgotten it. His mother was born in Belgium and had been smuggled out during the war as a small child, and his father had told Richard she'd borne the scars ever since, but Richard never saw them. He'd come with Tripp and their friends after baseball practice to smoke and drink and fuck on the old wooden lawn chair pulled behind the hedges. He liked to imagine the inmates. He thought of his mother. He'd even written little poems there that he'd kept hidden.

Now, he packed his bowl and lit it with the lighter he fished out of the compartment between the seats. He inhaled and coughed violently, disrupting the coffee wedged between his thighs. Coffee shot up and spattered all over his bright-red Patagonia. He wiped at the jacket with his hand and then wiped his hands on his jeans. It was not unpleasant, the smell of coffee and the fabric of his coat and the funny fungal odors of their old minivan. He ate his bagel and sipped the hot, bitter coffee. He tongued the ridge of hard plastic lid. He sat back in the seat, reclined a little, and exhaled. The clouds were white and the sky as blue as a gem. He swirled around the coffee to dislodge the few granules of sugar to sweeten it. He thought about the words they'd used for getting high when they were teenagers: pot, Mary Jane, chronic, indica, sativa, I'm so baked, I scored today. Surely the words had changed. Richard checked his watch. Fifteen minutes until the end of the boys' games. He'd have to leave a little early to watch the boys play or Margot would be angry. And he wanted to be good.

In the bushes, he saw something large and brown. Gray-brown like a wolf, not the familiar red-brown of a deer. Perhaps it was a rabbit or a groundhog. But no. It loped out. Its great mouth hung open. It was a coyote, alone, and it was stark against the green ivy of the hospital walls. Richard held his breath and watched it. He imagined that it lived in the collapsed hallways of the asylum, maybe had pups there. He thought of his very proper mother with her helmet of blonde hair now in Boca trucking off to yoga retreats and jaunts to the library for reading lectures and temple on the holidays. He imagined her once living in those ivy-covered buildings. She never talked about her childhood. It was unimaginable and he'd never been able to ask her about it. He thought about the coyote and he thought about his mother. Something wild in his mother she'd never let him see. He started up the car. He pulled out his phone. A message from a girl. He tapped in a few words and then backtracked over them. Richard tried to be good. So far, at least, he'd mostly succeeded.

And he thought about Virginia.

He'd harbored a secret crush on Virginia since the moment he met her. It wasn't that she was beautiful, though she was. It was some deeper unknowable quality—the emotions just beneath the surface of Virginia that no one ever acknowledged. Or maybe it really was just that she was beautiful.

The parking lot was nearly full when he returned. By luck he found a spot near Teddy's game. In the distance he could see Aiden's bright-red hair playing two fields west. A group of parents clustered on each side of the field. The soccer field on a Saturday was the only place you'd see equal numbers of moms and dads. He nodded at them; they nodded back. His game plan—drop the kids, get stoned at the abandoned psych hospital, what he did every Saturday—didn't leave much room for meeting other parents. He could never remember a face when he was high, never remember which kid belonged to what parent. The town had changed so much since Richard was a child. People had more money and trickled in from the city. A lot of classmates had never returned, heading south or west, pushed out by high taxes, lured by better jobs.

Aiden's game finished first and Richard walked over to fetch him. Good job, bro, Richard called out to Aiden, who loped toward him on legs adolescent and too long. He held out his fist to Aiden, who ignored him. Dad, Aiden said. You reek.

I what? Richard asked.

You reek, Dad. You smell like *weed*. You baked or what?

Richard held his coat to his nose and took a big silly sniff. I don't, he said.

Aiden rolled his eyes and pulled out his phone. You do, Dad. I'll get Teddy okay? Just please go back to the car.

No, no, Richard said. I'll hang around. Mom would want me to watch.

It's not a good idea, but, what*ever*, Dad. And then under his breath: *Cringey*.

Teddy's game ended. Richard didn't know if they'd won or lost. Aiden slung his arm around Teddy's shoulder and said, Better luck next time, asshole. Richard, paranoid now, started toward the car but not before he saw Aiden whisper to Teddy.

You know, Dad, Teddy said, in our DARE class, Officer Fred said marijuana leads to crystal meth.

God bless old Irish Officer Fred, Richard said. With the thick, reddened skin and bulbous nose of late-stage liver disease.

Dad, Aiden hissed. The coaches talked about you. You *reek* of weed.

Richard stepped carefully through the grass and pits of mud toward the car. The boys followed far behind. He knew what would happen. Someone would tell Margot. There'd be a reckoning at home and he'd be in the doghouse. He gulped air and held it and then let it out in a rush. He could take heat. He'd survive. They'd survive. He could make up for it. He could deal. He could be the fall guy for whatever it was that was unsaid and unnamed in their house. He climbed into the car and exhaled. He was strong like that.

Later that night, Richard shot grateful, pleading looks at Aiden and Teddy as he fussed around and made dinner. Margot was on the sofa with a blanket over her knees. She'd thrown out her back cleaning under the beds. George was at Tripp's for the day to hang out with Charlotte and George and Charlotte had forged a friendship. Virginia had gone to Louisville for a funeral. What have you done all day? Richard asked.

I shaved Buster, Margot said. He did not like that!

He still looks pretty fluffy to me, Richard said. Aiden shot Richard a look of disgust and shoved his earbuds in his ears.

I shaved his hindquarters.

I'm sorry? Richard said.

I shaved his hindquarters. His rear end.

You shaved his asshole.

Richard! Margot sat up and set the book on the coffee table. Buster hopped back down to the floor. Language.

Richard grated the cheddar and sprinkled it over the just-boiled pasta in the casserole dish, then added salt and pepper and parmesan and bread crumbs.

You putting hard cheese in? Margot asked. Margot believed she could not digest hard cheeses.

Nope, Richard lied.

Put out some cut fruit, Margot said. She headed up to the bedroom. Otherwise the kids won't get any vitamins at all.

The pot wore off. Richard grabbed a beer from the fridge and cracked it open. George had a playdate at Tripp's house— Virginia was down in Kentucky—and he thought about texting Tripp to see if he wanted to bring Charlotte and George back over and have dinner at their house. There was more than enough food. But then he remembered Tripp was getting himself lean for the apocalypse or whatever and had given up bread and pasta and beer. All the things that made life bearable. That was exactly like Tripp, who would go from nothing but brown rice and broccoli to bacon and raw hamburger meat. He'd been like that since high school. Constant reinvention and yet exactly the same. Same old Tripp.

The beer warmed Richard's sternum, burned in his throat, and he decided—yes, no—he *knew*. He was happy.

In spite of everything, he loved his life.

* * *

But later after dinner, after Richard had cleaned up all the dishes, he understood something was up. He got the boys to finish their homework, got their teeth brushed. He climbed into bed with his laptop opened to some reports he needed to finish before morning. Margot showered and stood a moment by the bed, still damp and fragrant. He noted she'd gained some weight. It looked good on her. Her breasts and hips were full and her face pretty and healthy. She climbed into bed with him and she had that sarcastic wide smile on her face that she did when she was crazy. When she was about to lose her shit or freak out or have a breakdown. Richard snapped shut his laptop and closed his eyes and remembered the times he'd opened drawers and found the boys' pared fingernails and hair trimmings in labeled plastic baggies filed in alphabetical order, by age. Or the saved Q-tips from all the kids in baggies, arranged by date. He'd thrown it all away in a kind of fit of terror, and she'd cried, inconsolable. I just want something of them to keep forever, she'd said. It's such a small thing to ask.

But something was up. She'd heard. She'd heard something about him smoking pot. Or the porn he watched online. Or the websites he visited promising girls who would love him like they meant it. That was it. Did he not deserve any fun in his life? Was there nothing, for the love of everything that was holy, to look forward to anymore? Recreation? Relaxation?

And then she stood over him looking down at him with hot limpid eyes. Baby, she said, unbuttoning the top of her nightgown with her long fine fingers. She climbed on top of him, and straddled him. She her hands on his shoulders. Let's have sex.

The next day, Monday, the kids were off from school for superintendents' day. Margot begged and Richard relented and called in to work. It was a beautiful day filled with sunlight and Richard had cajoled the boys into taking a walk down to the beach along the creek outside of town. They brought Buster, who promptly threw himself in the river and then walked back out full of sand and brackish water. Aiden eyed Richard and said, Now Mom's *really* going to kill you.

Come on, guys, Richard said. The boys were bored, settled on a bench staring at their own devices. George, who had yet to get a phone, leaned over Teddy in a way that annoyed Teddy. Get off me! he said and shrugged hard, pushed George off.

Come on, Richard said again. Let's go home and get some lunch. Mom must be done with her nap by now.

Can we go to Massey's? they asked as they did daily now, the new diner in town. No. Richard shook his head. Your mom would prefer you eat at home I'm sure.

They walked up the steep hill from the river to their house. Buster got tired and Richard carried the small, muddy body of the dog in his arms. The dog rested his chin on Richard's shoulder and let out a tiny spurt of noxious gas and Richard got so mad he dumped him on the street and half dragged him another block until George—the tenderhearted they called him—felt sorry for Buster and carried him the rest of the way home.

Richard was hungry when he walked in the front door. He'd hoped all the way home it would be warm and full of cooking smells. He opened the front door and the house was dead quiet and sterile.

Margot appeared from the bedroom and stalked down the stairs with her lips pressed so tight they'd lost their color. She was plainly furious. It took her two whole minutes before she could spit the words out. Teddy's coach had called Margot while they were down at the creek and told her that all the kids had smelled marijuana on Richard and the parents were pretty mad. There had even been discussion of banning Richard from the soccer fields.

The boys scattered for their rooms like animals that sensed a storm. Margot was surprisingly calm. She had some thoughts about the boys, after all, about their education. About soccer games and the endless succession of soccer practices. This seemed as good a time as any to bring those thoughts up. Which is how Richard agreed they could send all three boys to the Petra School. She was so grateful and good that Richard went to bed that night believing he'd gotten off easy. And then he lay in bed with Margot, who snored softly beside him. In his head he counted and recounted how much it would cost to send all the boys to private school. He'd have to ask Tripp what the tuition cost was. He still had four more years until Aiden was out of the house and six more years until Teddy and so on. They'd have to cut back on dinners out. He'd have to ask his parents for help.

Between the Petra School and college tuitions there was no doubt: He would work until he dropped dead.

Dear Petra School Parents: Competitive sports are inappropriate for Petra School children. Ours is a school of cooperation. Chess, however, is encouraged.

Chapter Sixteen

MARGOT ON THE ROAD

MARGOT FLOATED HOME from the Petra School Wednesday night meditation. Around her wrist was a blue thread tied by Agnes herself, who told her: When you see this, try to be present. The thread, Agnes told Margot, represented her initiation into presence. Each participant in the meditation circle received one and they'd stood around with their wrists held awkwardly at their sides and beamed at one another. Every time Margot saw it she felt the small jolt of belonging and she tried to sense her feet and to be present, just as Agnes told her she should. And she thought of Agnes. Tall, confident, strong, straight-back Agnes, and she pulled herself a little more upright and held her chin a little higher.

Her van hummed its solid safety around her quietly. It transported Margot through the clouds of dense fog off the sound. She would be home in five minutes. She could have walked from her house and would as soon as the weather was a little warmer. And maybe she'd get a Fitbit and some new shoes and some athletic wear and a black Velcro strap so that she could wear her phone on her arm and a pair of headphones that wouldn't fall off if she decided to do a little jogging. She had never liked to run. Or to exercise at all really but maybe that would change. Agnes promised change. The radio played, quietly, Mozart. She felt armored, uniquely so, to the demands of the children who would be fed—pasta—but not bathed. Their homework would not be finished. Their all-but-useless babysitter would be sitting on the sofa pouring her youthful soul and energy into a tiny chirping, buzzing device. A screen. Margot could see, as she pulled into her driveway, the glow of the girl's phone screen through the window, a beacon of all that was wrong with the world. She'd have to have a talk with her about that.

Or else! Margot sat bolt upright in the van and threw it into park. She felt a rush of optimism: or else she wouldn't need the sitter anymore. After all, she didn't work, hadn't worked in a while. Aiden could watch them. He couldn't drive of course but he was old enough to watch the younger two. What did Margot have to do anyway besides be with her children? Other than meetings at Petra, what could possibly be more important to Margot? Anyway, Richard resented the twenty dollars an hour the babysitters charged. The money they saved could go to Petra tuition. She'd for a time thought maybe she'd go back to work. Or get back to volunteering, but for now her children needed her. They needed her to show them the way, to walk the walk with them on the Road.

Hello, Melissa, Margot said. Margot handed the girl a wad of cash, twice as much as she was owed, and thought good riddance.

Will you need me tomorrow? the girl asked.

No! Margot said, her voice clipped and strained. That won't be necessary! I will be sure to ring you just as soon as I know our schedule.

The girl nodded. She shoved the money into her schoolbag and fled the house.

But now that she was on the Road—she looked down at the little blue string around her wrist—activities seemed utterly ridiculous if not actually reprehensible. Margot marched into the family room so purposefully that the older two looked up, their eyes wide.

Children! Margot chirped. Come and gather round. Off your devices! Teddy, turn off the video game. Teddy? Turn off the video game. Teddy. Teddy! Okay, *thank you*. I've mentioned this to you before but I've had more time to think and this time I'm very, very serious. Margot lowered her voice. We will have changes.

Aiden rolled his eyes. He went back to his texts.

Aiden! Aiden, off your phone now please. Listen. Children, Margot said. I'm asking you to take a ride with me on a Road.

George stood up and shouted, Where we going? I want Target! Target! Target!

No, no! she said. Not a real road—the child slumped in her arms—a proverbial road. The boys looked up at her uncomprehending. A road metaphorical.

A *virtual* road, explained Aiden.

Yes! said Margot. A virtual road. A magical road. More important than a real road. Even more important than Target! A life-changing road.

She ignored Aiden, who rolled his eyes. George and Teddy began to wrestle on the floor.

Kids, she said. Kids! George stop hitting Teddy! Listen to me. Things will be changing around here. For one thing, we will no longer be playing Xbox.

Who's "we"? asked Teddy. He slouched against the wall and tossed his Xbox controller onto the sofa with disgust.

I beg your pardon?

Who is this "we"? You say "we" as though you also play Xbox. Even if it's a royal "we," it's still us and not you since you don't play. Be more specific, Mother.

If I'm royal, George said, if I'm a king, then I can play Xbox. Kings do what they like, he said and crossed his arms definitively over his chest.

Margot moved him off her legs and settled him on the floor beside her. She could feel a tension snake down the back of her head and into her neck and her left shoulder.

Okay then. You will not play Xbox, PS4, Nintendo, or any other sort of video game. We have a healthy library full of books that I enjoyed as a child, books your father enjoyed as a boy—she stopped for a moment and massaged her temples—he was once a great reader, your father! Well, she thought. She'd start reading too. There were books she wanted to read. Things were going to change. Things have gone entirely too far in the other direction, Margot said out loud. The wrong direction. Aiden slouched against the wall and gave her a knowing look. A look she feared as much as she admired. He had her number or at least a good part of her number. And she knew that as each of them grew up, they'd know her more and more. "Mom" would cease to be a sufficient disguise. You will leave your phones, she said.

The kids grumbled and groaned.

I'm not getting rid of my phone, Aiden said. How will I get in touch with my friends? How will anyone get a hold of me? Do you want me to be a social pariah?

No, Margot said. She thought a moment. She was definitely getting another muscle spasm. You can leave your phone on the kitchen island and check it periodically.

Aiden groaned loudly and tossed his phone beside Teddy's Xbox controller.

Also, she said. We will be moving *away from* soccer practices and tournaments and basketball. We will be having a more—what was the expression they'd used on the Road?—a more easeful existence. Less competition. More simplicity. At Petra School—

Aiden said, No way, Mom. That sounds *horrible*.

Teddy stood up. I know a kid who just transferred to our school from Petra, he said. He had never even seen *Star Wars*.

He totally pretended like he did and he totally knew nothing about it. He didn't even know what a light saber was. He called it, like, a *light wand*. He wasn't even allowed to read Harry Potter there! He took a math test and he didn't know a single answer to a single question. He couldn't eat Halloween candy and when Mr. Brandon showed *The Nightmare Before Christmas*, he asked to leave before the movie had even started! He said his goldfish died from brain cancer because the bowl was too close to the television. Mom, Teddy said seriously. Please do not send us to that school.

Yeah, Mom, Aiden said. You don't want to get mixed up in that.

I don't want to go there! George said, siding with his big brothers.

But listen, guys, Margot said. You've already seen *Star Wars!* And Petra School kids LOVE school! I heard they don't even like summer vacation because school is so much fun! Anyway, it wouldn't be so bad to do less activities! We'll still watch movies. In the theater! *Fantasia* is playing on Main Street this week. Maybe we can all go—

Fantasia? What's that? George asked.

It's a movie made a long time ago. A classic!

No way, Teddy said. Forget it. Remember the time you made us watch *The Sound of Music?* I'm not wasting my time on a movie old people like!

Later while bringing in the trashcans she saw a herd of deer in the meadow across the street. Their eyes shone in the dark night as they lifted their heads to peer at her. George leapt out of the car and ran toward them. Margot panicked, imagining he'd be kicked or mauled—she really couldn't imagine what—but first one and then another and then all of them turned and ran, leapt over the wooden fence into their neighbor's yard. It was beautiful to watch them. Even the smallest of the deer cleared the fence. Margot felt an acute envy for the deer. How sure they were. They'd raised their babies exactly the same for millions of generations of deer. How intelligent they were. How mixed up were humans in the end, really.

Chapter Seventeen

TRIPP AND CHARLOTTE

TRIPP PULLED INTO THE HOUSE just as the school bus pulled up. Across the street someone started up a lawn mower. The gardeners had descended on the neighbor's property. Their machines roared to life, bullying the landscape into submission. Tripp got out of his car and watched the men ride their machines. The bus squealed to a stop and the doors opened with a rush of compressed air. Charlotte was deposited across the street. The bus fired off in fumes and Charlotte cautiously looked both ways and walked toward Tripp and the house.

Hey, Char! Tripp called. He felt his heart sink. He felt certain Charlotte's heart was sinking too.

She walked up shyly beside him. They didn't spend much time together. They had before, when she was a toddler, when she was out of diapers, when she started to speak. Virginia had charged him with teaching her how to swim after Charlotte had once fallen into the pool as a toddler and Virginia had had to jump in and fish her out. Tripp signed her up for swimming lessons at the Y. I'll take her, he'd said. And he had.

He found he enjoyed that time in the pool with his daughter. He liked how she felt in his hands, slippery and solid. A little bony. The teacher said Charlotte was a sinker—no body fat, all muscle—and Tripp had felt proud. He was the same way. All leanness and heavy bones. An athlete. After six months of lessons when she was three and a half, she'd been able to jump off the diving board into his arms. Virginia had watched and clapped and that night after they'd put Charlotte to sleep Tripp had said they should have another baby, a boy, and Virginia had winced and said no. No, she'd said. I don't think so.

Now Charlotte stood awkwardly beside Tripp. You want to go into town? Tripp asked. We could get a snack. Maybe an ice-cream cone? Charlotte shrugged. Tripp, annoyed, said, Cat got your tongue?

She looked up and scowled at him. What? she said. And Tripp could see then the teenager she'd soon be. The gangly arms, her legs pencil thin in stretchy denim, a kind of half shirt and through the fabric Tripp noted Charlotte wore a bra, which made him uncomfortable. Wasn't she too young? he'd asked Virginia when he'd first noticed. Virginia had said all the girls did it. It was no big deal.

Well? How about it? Tripp said. Ice-cream cone?

Charlotte half rolled her eyes and then caught herself. Yeah, she said. Sure.

Tripp got into the car and Charlotte got in the back and buckled her seat belt. He'd regretted buying the Mustang almost the same day he brought it home. It was loud and cost a fortune to fill the gas tank. It was the car he'd always wanted as a kid but it didn't translate well into adulthood. Especially in their neighborhood. At the tennis club, some of the guys had teased him. Richard asked him seriously if the car was a loaner or a rental. Fuck them, he thought. Only he said it out loud. He looked up in the rearview mirror. Charlotte watched him.

It was an unusually warm day in the upper fifties. Should I put the top down? Tripp asked.

Charlotte shrugged in a way that made Tripp think the answer was no. He pressed the button on the dash and the roof shuddered open, slowly. They waited.

You miss Mom? Tripp said.

Charlotte shrugged. She just left this morning.

The man on the lawn mower waved as they passed and Charlotte from the back seat gave a little wave and a smile back to him. She looked so sweet. He remembered when she looked at him that way. When she was little. When she was jumping off the diving board into his arms. Now she was waving at strangers. You know him? Tripp asked.

Charlotte turned to him. He does our lawn, Daddy. His name is John.

John, eh? You sure it isn't Juan?

Charlotte got very quiet and still.

They drove in silence.

Tripp found parking on the street. He fed the meter and they headed to the Double Dip. The Double Dip had been around since Tripp was a kid. His first girlfriend worked there after school and she used to give him free cones. Except that she hadn't been his girlfriend exactly. She'd been a kind of a girlfriend. For one thing they'd never had sex. Tripp blamed himself for that. She'd put up the usual resistance that all his friends talked about with their girlfriends. None of them wanted it but they did. Deep down inside they all wanted it. Or maybe they didn't want it but come on, their boyfriends took them out on dates and drove them around in their cars and listened to them whine about their PMS. They just needed some cajoling, some wheedling, some prodding. A guilt trip, subtle threats to leave. That was half of what teenage boys discussed. But instead, Tripp had just kind of let it go. He wondered where she'd gone. Lori Carmichael. She'd probably gone to the city or San Francisco. She was daring. Maybe she'd gone to Paris. She had always wanted to live in Paris.

Hey, Tripp said. He turned to Charlotte, who followed behind him. You and me should go to Paris, he said. But as soon as he said it, he realized he didn't mean it. Charlotte's eyes lit up.

Really? she said.

Sure, he said. He opened the door. Someday.

The truth was, he hated to travel. He hadn't enjoyed it as a kid. He hated strange food, he hated not knowing what people said around him, he hated not knowing what the pillows were going to be like. Too hard or too soft. He hated flying. He got motion sickness. Once on an airplane, he'd thrown up in the little paper bag. So that's what they're for, his mother had said ruefully. His father had looked away. He hated to feel unsafe and unmoored.

He ordered mint chocolate chip on a cone. Charlotte ordered pink bubblegum flavor over chocolate raspberry and Tripp made a face. Don't knock it 'til you try it, she said and held out the cone to him. He realized they'd spent so little time together that he didn't really know her that well. Girls had always scared him. He never thought he'd be afraid of his own daughter but her very femaleness, the fact she grew more and more female every day, terrified him. He'd never admit it to anyone but it was true. He took a bite of the ice cream, vaguely mortified to share such intimacy with another person even if it was his daughter, mortified to wipe some of the pink from his chin. She handed him a napkin. Well? she said.

It's not bad, he said. Yum.

Would you order it? she asked.

No, he said. Of course not.

They'd had enough conversation he decided, and he started back out the door. Want to sit on a bench outside? Charlotte asked. But Tripp didn't want to. Less and less did he want to interact with the town. They thought everything would go on exactly as it always had and Tripp would always be Tripp and they were wrong. Lately he'd stopped going into town at all. When he went to the Home Depot, he traveled a few towns over to get what he needed. Or better yet, he ordered online.

Out of the corner of his eye he saw an old neighbor of his parents', Mrs. Anderson. He averted his eyes just in time and climbed into the car, unlocking the passenger side, starting the engine, putting the car in reverse—

Dad!

Charlotte shouted: You going to leave me here?

Charlotte banged on the window, her cone in her hand. She climbed into the car and said, Dad, what are you doing?

His heart was racing. It was like ordinary life was causing him to panic—

Dad, you okay?

Oh, he said. Ha. Sorry about that. I got distracted.

You afraid of Mrs. Anderson or something?

No, he said. Of course not.

Tripp shifted into drive. The trees were budding. Charlotte fiddled with the car radio. You don't have any stations pro-grammed, she said. You don't listen to music in the car?

No, he said.

Really?

Yeah. I don't. So what.

You just drive in silence?

Sometimes I listen to books on tape.

He glanced over at Charlotte, whose eyes bulged slightly agog.

You read books?

Yes, he said. He wondered who he could fob Charlotte off on. Maybe Richard and Margot would take her for the afternoon. A headache brewed in the very center of his skull.

Well, let's hear it.

Charlotte pressed play and Tripp froze. It was John Monroe and he was talking about Grandmother's Prophecies. John Monroe droned in his nasal accent: *The children of the earth will be pushed deep inside it but those who know will run for the forests—*

They listened a few minutes more and Tripp pressed Stop. They pulled into their driveway. You want to go to Margot's house? Maybe George is around?

Ew, Charlotte said. No.

I thought you liked him!

I do, she said. I just don't want to see him today.

Okay, Tripp said. Well, I got to do some work in the basement.

Sure, Dad, Charlotte said. I'll find something to do.

The light was different in the house this time of day. He almost didn't recognize it. He'd made it a habit to come home as late as possible, avoiding Virginia, avoiding Charlotte. Avoiding even Richard, who texted often wondering if he wanted to grab a beer or catch the game. More and more Tripp felt a certain anxiety around people. A kind of misanthropy. He was claustrophobic and hated to be bound by four walls. He was agoraphobic and hated to be outside in the wider world.

Tripp walked into the kitchen. There were still breakfast dishes in the sink. Tripp felt a flash of rage. When he was a kid he washed dishes. Didn't kids do anything these days?

Charlotte! he called. Why don't you come and wash these dishes up from breakfast!

There was no answer.

Tripp, fuming, bounded up the stairs and pushed open her bedroom door. It was a riot of pink and clothing everywhere. Charlotte sat atop a mound of clothing on her bed with big pink headphones clamped over her ears bobbing her head to music. She pulled them off. Hey, Daddy, she said.

Your mom has you do dishes?

No, she said.

You know how to do dishes?

No.

Well, why don't you come downstairs right now and learn how?

Charlotte pulled a sullen face but followed him down the stairs. Tripp stood at the sink. There was the pan he'd made scrambled eggs in and their two plates and two glasses and two forks and a knife with a smear of butter that clung to it. She looked up at him. He looked down at her. How old are you again?

I'm eleven.

By ten, I was cleaning the entire house, Tripp said. He was exaggerating, he realized. You ever vacuum before? You ever dust? You ever clean out a toilet or a shower? No? The girl shook her head. That's not right! What do you and Mommy do all day anyway?

Charlotte shrugged. Her eyes filled with tears.

This touched Tripp. Finally. Some tension was released. He put his hand on her shoulder. I'm sorry, sweetie, he said. How about if I wash and you dry?

Charlotte nodded her head. Okay, she said.

Tripp got out the sponge and dish soap. He scrubbed out the pan and handed it to her, and she sagged slightly under its iron weight. Her arms were so thin. That touched Tripp too. But she dried the pan thoroughly. You know where to put that? She nodded. Tripp washed the rest of the dishes and Charlotte dried them, even handing back the knife, telling him: It's not quite clean, Daddy. There's butter still on it. Tripp nodded and gave the knife another swipe with the sponge, rinsed it, and handed it back to her.

What should we eat for dinner? Tripp asked. Charlotte shrugged. Don't be afraid of me! Tripp longed to say, but he knew that was not how you win anyone's trust. And anyway, shouldn't fathers be a little scary? Well, he said gently. What would you like to eat?

Pizza? Jelly sandwiches?

No, Tripp said. No way. Charlotte winced. I mean, that's what you eat all the time, right? I guess Mommy is too busy to make you a proper dinner. How about we make something together? Would you like that?

Charlotte looked down.

Char?

She shook her head. Not really, she said.

Tripp sighed. Okay. Fine. Go on upstairs and I'll figure something out.

In the end, Tripp ordered Thai. Making dinner was too daunting. He didn't understand what was in the fridge. Pickles, mustards, mayonnaises, barbecue sauces, eggs, jams, a jar of yogurt. Some sticks of butter. Some moldy cucumbers and wilted lettuce. He tried to remember what his mother made for him when he was a kid. Campbell's soup casseroles, mac and cheese, Salisbury steak, a big ham for special occasions. He figured Virginia hadn't fared much better in the food department as a kid. She always seemed sort of neglected, half feral, what with her mom sick for most of her childhood. And now here they were, surrounded by the finest grocery stores and farmers' markets but moored in a kind of suburban food desert of their own making.

Tripp made the call then shouted up to Charlotte: Food will be here in forty-five minutes. She didn't respond. Headphones again, surely. Tripp stood uneasily in the kitchen and then headed down the basement stairs to his little room. He let himself in, bolting the room behind him. Behind the plywood walls there were concrete blocks he'd laid himself one by one over the last six months.

An hour later the doorbell rang. Tripp ran upstairs and paid the sullen teenager with acne. He was Seth Gordon's kid. Tripp and Seth had played baseball against one another. Seth had grown up one town over and never left. Not even for college. Tripp nodded at the kid and gave him an extra few dollars. He carried the box up to the dining room table.

Charlotte came down and made a face. I don't like pad thai, she said.

Then what do you like? Tripp said.

I like the noodles, she said. But I don't like the chicken and I don't like the green things. I'll get napkins, Charlotte said.

That would be very helpful, Tripp said.

They ate in silence. Tripp tried to think of things to ask Charlotte but she answered with just a word or two and Tripp remembered what it was like when a parent was talking too much, how his mother would jabber on asking him this, that, and the other and how he'd wished she'd just leave him alone already. Silence wasn't so bad, was it? When they were done eating, Tripp said he would clean up and Charlotte said she'd maybe go watch TV if that was all right.

Don't you have homework? Tripp asked.

Charlotte shook her head.

Maybe you should read something. Weren't you enjoying those Harry Potter books?

Charlotte shook her head again. My teacher says it's too grown-up and it doesn't have a good message.

What do you mean it doesn't have a good message? Tripp said, though he'd only seen the movies. It's about fighting fascism! What could be a better message than that?

I don't know, Daddy. I don't know what that is.

Are you sure you're learning anything at that school? I mean, it costs a lot of money. Tripp thought of the phone messages from Agnes.

I don't know, she said. I guess so. I mean, I'm only in sixth grade. Today we learned how to make oatmeal and tomorrow we are going to learn to make a salve for poison ivy. Which is pretty cool, right? You could take it on your camping trips.

Tripp closed his eyes. His headache suddenly worsened. This would be Charlotte's last year at Petra. That was for sure.

Okay, he said. But are you sure you're allowed to watch TV? Thought they were strict about that kind of thing.

They won't know, Charlotte said. Will they.

Tripp shook his head.

Don't tell Mommy either.

I swear.

At eight o'clock Tripp told Charlotte to shut off the TV and take a shower and get into her pajamas. Charlotte took a long shower, singing. Tripp was surprised by her voice. It was a good voice. A good clear, high voice. Again, he was touched. A wave of feeling rushed to his sternum. His eyes smarted a bit and watered. Charlotte came bounding down wrapped in a towel and headed into the laundry room, where she pulled a pair of pajamas from the dryer. You okay? Tripp asked. I'm going to shower too. Hope you left me some hot water!

Sure, Daddy.

Tripp took a long shower, running the soap over his body, gauging, as he always did, the size of his muscles, the flatness of his stomach. He'd need to up the protein if he wanted any mass on him. He'd canceled the club membership Virginia never used and his monthly unlimited Krav Maga classes—they couldn't afford it—but he thought he might join the Y or maybe go down to his little room in the basement and power-lift some of the big cans of beans he'd squirreled away. He stepped out and had half-dried himself when he heard a scream from downstairs. From the basement.

Holding his towel around his waist, Tripp made his way, careful not to slip with his wet feet. The door to the basement was open. He ran down the rough stairs. Charlotte stood in the middle of the room, the single bulb illuminating her like a saint. The string of the bulb still in her hand. Her eyes were wide. He took in what she saw—guns mounted on the wall, boxes of ammo stacked up from the dirt floor.

Daddy! she said. What is this?

Tripp swept her out of the room. He closed and locked the door. He gripped the little key in his hand so tightly it cut his palm. He dragged her up the stairs and then leaned over her. What were you doing in there?

I dropped my book down the basement stairs. I swear! The door was open and I was curious. I'm sorry, Daddy. I'm sorry!

This room is a secret, he said. He closed his eyes. His thoughts were wild. He couldn't believe he'd left the door open. You can't tell Mommy about it.

Why? she said, her eyes wild. Is it bad?

No! Tripp said. It isn't bad at all! It's good. We're the good guys. We want to protect ourselves from the bad guys, right?

The bad guys, she said. Like Nazis?

Yes, he said. Just like Nazis.

I thought the Nazis all were dead.

They are! I mean. Kind of. But there are other bad guys and we always want to be protected. Do you understand? Tripp said.

Why can't we tell Mom?

I don't think she'd understand, Tripp said. I think she would be upset.

Charlotte nodded. Tripp's heart sank. She'd seemed like such a grown-up girl just a few hours ago. Rolling her eyes and almost talking back. But now she was a little girl again.

Mommy has a secret too.

What?

I don't know if I should tell you. She didn't tell me not to tell you.

What is it? Tripp squeezed his eyes tightly shut then opened them.

Charlotte stood very silent and pursed her lips. Tripp could see her mother in that gesture. The stubbornness. Virginia's touching independence and how she didn't need anyone. I don't think I should say, Charlotte said. I don't think Mommy wants us to know.

It's okay, Tripp said, imagining the worst. Other men. Divorce. *Richard.* Maybe she knew they were broke. You can tell me, he said.

Mommy's sick, Charlotte said.

What do you mean?

She's sick. Her doctor sends her text messages begging for her to come in. I saw them once before Mommy deleted them.

Oh no! Tripp said. I'm sure she's fine. Your mother is strong as an ox. Don't worry about your mother.

Charlotte looked relieved. I won't tell anyone about the room, Charlotte said, mature again. She held up her pinky. I pinky-promise swear, she said.

Tripp held up his pinky and hooked it into hers. Well, he said. Our secret.

Charlotte went up to brush her teeth. Tripp kissed her goodnight.

You know, Daddy. You're not so bad.

Really?

No. You're okay.

Well, you're okay too. Love you, Char. Tripp shut off the overhead light.

Leave the light on in the bathroom, she said.

Tripp lay on the sofa downstairs a long time before he trudged upstairs to bed. She was a good girl, Charlotte was. And there was some of Tripp in her after all.

Chapter Eighteen

The Viewing

VIRGINIA WOKE EARLY and flung open the heavy hotel blackout curtain. She made herself coffee from the pod machine. It took her a minute to get it to work but when it did it made a pleasant smell, like a diner. She considered ordering breakfast but decided against it.

She dialed Tripp's cell, though she knew he was on the train and wouldn't pick up. I'm here in the hotel, she said. I'm about to head to the funeral home now. I'll call you when I get a chance. Give Charlotte a kiss for me. Don't forget to be home before the bus. Call Margot if you can't get there in time. She can pick up Charlotte before the boys come home.

Virginia showered and pulled on a dress, deemed it too low-cut, and pulled it off. She didn't really know what to wear. She'd forgotten about the South, about how it made her feel. The humidity made her itchy.

Her phone began to ring. She snatched it up. Tripp, maybe. No, it was the hospital. Edward. She sighed and let it go to voice mail. A moment later the phone buzzed with a text message. She was ready to ignore it and saw the name. Richard again. Hey, she read. How are you doing? Are you okay?

It was odd he was texting her. It was a breach but a welcome one. She put her phone in her bag along with her key card and walked out into the frigid hallway of the hotel.

The funeral director was as oily as a used car salesman but it wasn't his fault he sold boxes for the dead and fixed up corpses for a living. Outside his office window, behind him, Virginia could see the Sizzler steak house where her stepmother and father had taken her on her sixteenth birthday. It must have been six months after her mother had died. They'd ordered her an ice-cream sundae and told Virginia they were getting married.

In his quiet voice, the funeral director pushed a paper with her options across the table. There were a lot of options. Would you like me to show you our caskets?

No, Virginia said. I'm not going to buy a casket.

I'm sorry?

What are my options here? What are my real options?

I'm afraid I don't understand.

Virginia spoke carefully, trying not to dip into the Southern drawl that she'd lost years ago. I want to know how I can spend the least amount of money. I'd like to know what your cheapest option is.

The man stared at her. He opened his mouth and shut it. Well, I.

I didn't know her well. I don't really mean to be crass or unchristian but what's the cheapest way I can dispose of her body?

The director, in that moment, dropped his oily salesman quiet-to-the-mourners voice. You can have her cremated and put in a cardboard box. You will be able to pick it up in a week.

I won't be here in a week.

Well, I'm sure we can arrange for shipping.

That will be fine, Virginia said. Can I see the body?

Oh no, no, no, he said. She has not been embalmed.

I'd like to see her anyway.

He winced. I'm afraid there will be a charge. We would still have to prepare the body.

How much?

Fifty dollars.

I'll give you forty. Can you roll her out now?

Fine. Forty for the viewing. Two fifty for the cremation. Cremation is nonnegotiable, he said. We contract out.

Virginia walked back out into the lobby, where she sat very straight and calm. *Put your best Baptist face on now, Ginny,* she remembered her mother would say. If only she'd had her mother all these years she thought, and she felt real sadness then. Real grief. She handed the man her Amex, but he stared at it on the desk and said, I'm SO sorry but we don't take Amex. We take Discover card though.

I don't have another card right now, Virginia said, irritated. I'll call my husband.

That's quite all right, the man said. You take your time.

In the little waiting room, Virginia texted Tripp. They don't take Amex, she wrote. Please call me with another credit card. She leafed through *Better Homes and Gardens* magazines and *Today's Christian*. A woman walked out. She looked so kind and sympathetic that Virginia couldn't muster any anger for her. Come with me, dear, she said, and she held Virginia's arm. Virginia longed to sag into the woman who held her arm with a strong, firm grip.

Virginia began to cry. I don't know why I feel this way, she said. I didn't even like her. I barely knew her. I haven't seen her in years.

It's okay, the woman said in a calm, kind voice. Grief is different for different people. If you need me, she said, I'll be right outside.

The room was empty except for a couple of metal folding chairs and her stepmother laid out on a hospital gurney. Her stepmother wore a hospital gown. A sheet was pulled up to her waist and her hands rested beside her over the sheet. She looked a good deal older, a bit fatter. Her hair was high and blonde (the higher the hair, the closer to God) and her lipstick was that same Maybelline cherry red. Virginia could close her eyes and smell that lipstick. Red Revival. She could feel it, cold and waxy on her cheek after her stepmother kissed her goodnight. Virginia raised her hand to her own cheek now.

Virginia walked up to the gurney looking around first to make sure she was alone. She stood a long while and felt her heart pound in her chest. The woman was not in the room, nor in the hallway. Virginia remembered a long ago moment and leaned in close to her stepmother's liver-spotted ear. She whispered: I'm going to tell you something. I was not, nor have I ever been, a whore. You took nothing away from me when you called me that.

Virginia took a breath and three steps backward until she was seated on one of the metal chairs. The metal was cool on her backside. She remembered the guy from the night before and his hand on her breasts and she felt hot with embarrassment. Jeremy, she thought. That's what his name was.

She bowed her head to look as though she was praying, leaning forward slightly. It was so cold in the room Virginia would not have been surprised to see her breath.

I'm supposed to be dying too, Virginia whispered to her stepmother's cold body. That was what she wanted to say to her. That was why Virginia had come. But I'm not afraid. I bet you were afraid, Virginia said. But I'm not.

The air-conditioning kicked on and Virginia jumped. She looked behind her. She could see the shadow of the woman just outside the door. Virginia bowed her head again and said a prayer. She couldn't remember any from when she was young so she said the pilgrim's prayer from a book she'd read as a child again and again: Lord Have Mercy. Lord Have Mercy. Lord Have Mercy. Dear Lord, she whispered. Have mercy on all of us.

On her way out, the undertaker stood quietly and respect-fully beside the front door. Send me a bill, Virginia said. I have no money to give you. She turned up her palms at him as she strode by to show him she had nothing. Really nothing.

Back at the hotel, she had two glasses of white wine at the hotel bar, hoping the man she'd met the night before would come back. When he didn't, she went up to her room and watched the news. Just before she turned off the TV, she texted Richard back. I'm not great, she wrote. I'm not doing all that great at all. And then she turned her phone off and very quickly fell asleep.

Dear Petra School Parents: Please remind children that backpacks are never to be worn while climbing the front entrance stairs. There have been two documented cases of spinal injuries from children falling backward due to heavy backpacks combined with stair climbing.

Chapter Nineteen

AGNES AND GUNTER

AGNES USHERED GUNTER into her office and shut the door. So glad you could come, she said. I'm so grateful you took the time.

Gunter looked around the shabby little office. He noted the low ceilings full of asbestos and windows with plastic overlaid to look like casement windows. They were probably relatively recent and a sad monstrosity. The floors were vinyl and peeling around the edges. The room was an afront to his senses and in his big coat he felt too hot and itchy. But he didn't want to take it off because he already regretted his decision to come to the school. He thought he'd just get up and leave. Make an excuse and exit. Agnes sat down and looked at him warmly. She seemed to anticipate his discomfort. Rachel had begun to sour on the school and Gunter felt disloyal. But also irritated with his wife. To sour so quickly on something they would pay, by the end of the year, thousands of dollars for. It was so like Rachel to change her mind in that way.

Agnes up close was not quite the same Agnes he remembered from the meeting last week. She was smaller somehow, shrunken and vulnerable and also a bit older than he'd realized. Closer to Gunter's age. Maybe even older. He felt heavy and deflated. Whatever was he doing there? He didn't have time for these sorts of things.

You know, she said, Anders is doing so much better recently. We really think that he will adjust eventually. Do you remember yourself at his age? I bet you were a firecracker.

Gunter nodded. Yes, he said. That's true. I was a "firecracker."

Agnes nodded. She held Gunter's gaze and said, The other day he helped to build a new tree house. He was extremely methodical about it. We had Miss Hensel help him draw up plans and we talked to him about inches and how they could translate into feet. He took to it right away. Everyone was quite impressed.

Is that so?

We were so happy with the boy, she said. Once we gave him the hammer and nails, it was like a duck in water. We have also given him some "tools" to come back to himself. Much like the tools we gave you, to be present, to sense your feet.

Gunter felt his feet in his shoes. They were a hair too narrow and caused him discomfort. Yes, he said. I am sure that's helpful.

Shall we walk around the grounds? she asked. I can show you what we are thinking about.

Gunter stayed seated while she pressed past him, felt her arm press into his side and linger there a half beat before she was out in the hallway. Gunter lumbered to his feet—Oh his knees. Oh his feet in these infernal Italian shoes. He followed after her. She strode down the hallways of the school. She stopped to peer into classrooms. Hello, children, she said as she walked, ducking her long neck. Hello, my dear teachers.

And it seemed to Gunter that there was genuine affection for Agnes in the school. Lydia played with the dolls when they stopped in front of her room. She shouted when she saw Gunter. Papa! Look. This is Finn the Giant. He has no heart in his body. And this is Holda the witch who lures children into the forest so that she may eat them!

Ha! Gunter said, amazed. These are Swedish fairy tales!

Yes, Agnes said. Of course. We want to honor the girl's roots. Lydia hugged Agnes around her knees and buried her face in Agnes's skirt.

I love you, Miss Agnes, Lydia said.

I love you too, my dear Lydia, Agnes said.

After they left the classroom, Gunter turned to Agnes and said, Can you please just explain to me the dolls with no faces?

But you see, Mr. Olson. Lydia has made up her own tale about the dolls. In her imagination, she has likely given them faces as well.

They walked out into the backyard where children sat on the cold ground nailing planks together.

Anders was deep in concentration as he carefully set up his nail and pounded it into a board.

Gunter walked closer. The plans were crude, not quite to scale, the lines wavy. But if he squinted and looked at them just so, he could make out a tree house. Well, that's wonderful, he said at last. Really. That's quite wonderful.

Anders beamed at him with pride. He held up his hands, and they were filthy dirty. Look, Papa, he said. We at Petra are not afraid to get our hands dirty.

So I see! But tell me something. Is it true, as your mother tells me, that you can't sit still in choir or art?

Anders screwed up his face. Those things are boring. They are boring to me and I bet they were boring to you too. But you had to sit through them. I don't.

That's true! But we are working on it, aren't we Anders?

Anders was already back to pounding at his boards.

Gunter remembered the school of his childhood. It had been dreadful of course. Impossible to sit still. He'd look out at the school grounds and watch the birds outside the school window with envy. How bored he'd been. He hadn't questioned it. It was simply what one did for years and years upon years until finally you were set free.

Gunter? Agnes said. She placed her hand on his wrist. For a moment there you drifted off.

Ah, he said. I was just remembering how I felt about school. I did hate it.

They walked toward the back door.

I hated school too, Agnes said. I was miserable. I wanted to be outdoors. I couldn't understand why I was forced to learn all these abstract concepts at such a young age. I was a bad student. And then my great-aunt took me in and I attended this school, and for the first time I felt happy and at peace. Here we strive to reach the whole child where they are, not where we want them to be but where *they* want to be. Our kids take a little while, yes, but by the end of their experience here they go on to great things. Good colleges, fulfilling careers. It's a kind of magic, really.

Inside the school, Agnes led Gunter to the former vestry.

Ah, he said. Good bones here.

Yes! Her face was girlish and bright. I have some ideas about what we could do here but perhaps you have better ones.

Oh yes, he said. I can think of a few things we could do, to open this place up, to modernize it.

Great! Agnes said. That's wonderful. We are just getting the funds together. I can show you a budget very soon.

All right, he said. That would be helpful of course.

The great room of the vestry was cool and smelled of sweet pine. There were only a few windows of colored glass in abstract patterns. It was a lovely place, Gunter had to concede. Almost magical.

Well then, Agnes said. I guess we will spend a lot of time together.

Chapter Twenty

TOMPKINS SQUARE

T HE WEEKEND FOLLOWING Rachel's last visit to the
school, she drove down into the city with Lydia to
visit their old neighborhood. She missed it down there.
She missed the park. She missed walking over to Veselka for
pierogi or the Bagel Zone for whitefish or Lavagna for their
sausage and peas pasta. She missed running into friends she'd
known since their kids were babies. Like her, so many of them
had moved away. To New Jersey and Long Island and Los
Angeles and Toronto.

It felt already like spring and was nearly sixty degrees when
they got downtown. A wet warm wind brushed the debris up the
avenues and swung the sycamore branches back and forth. They
drove down and parked at the lot on Eleventh Street between
Avenues A and B and then walked the two blocks to the park.
There had been no traffic into the city and they were forty-five

minutes early. Rachel pushed the heavy gate and held it open for Lydia, who zipped off to the play structure. Rachel closed the gate behind her and found a bench that faced the sun, where she nursed a cup of coffee she'd bought at her favorite kiosk, pleased that the girl had recognized her and asked where they'd been. She half wondered if she'd see an ex-boyfriend, David. They had a rapport that barely disguised their disgust for one another. She scanned the park. She hoped to see him and she hoped he wasn't there. And then he sauntered up. He was, as usual, unkempt. His wooly hair a cloud around his unshaven face. His two little girls ran around him and then off for the swings. His wife worked high tech on Wall Street and Rachel had never met her.

Hey, Rachel, he said. How's my cold Wasp friend? Still doing the dead-fish act in the sack?

Half, Rachel said. Half-Wasp you mean. What's new with you, David? she asked. Been polishing up your horns?

Oh, I see. Wasp when it counts, Jewish when you want to make anti-Semitic jokes. He took a bite of an apple. Still chewing, he said, I hate the pretentious names you gave your kids.

I hate the cliché of a Jew marrying an Asian woman. Rachel reached down and scratched an itch on her ankle bone. Still trying to pee on girls in bed?

Cunt.

Asshole.

David sat down on the bench beside her. He said, Remember that time I sold your underwear on eBay? You were so mad.

Remember that time I fucked your best friend.

David sat back. You did not.

No, Rachel said. I didn't.

They sat a while in silence and watched the girls play. The sun was warm on her black wool coat. Dust in shafts caught the sunlight.

Rachel thought about how fun illicit sex used to be. Stakes were low, of course. Who cared about some boyfriend one kind of liked but was never going to marry? Back then, best friends of boyfriends were always more seductive than boyfriends. Boyfriends stopped trying to seduce just about the moment one went to bed with them.

Rachel had actually fucked David's best friend half a dozen times but had forgotten his name. She sat for a moment running through the gamut of American male names: Alfred, Frank, Alan, Vinny, Michael, Manfred, Mort, Miguel, Manuel.

What was the name of your best friend? Rachel asked.

Nat, he said. He's married with three kids out on Long Island. David kept his eyes averted and wouldn't look at Rachel. In a flat voice he said, Nice talking to you. He stood up and walked over to extricate his girls from a tangle of swings and chains.

Rachel remained on the bench. She tried to decide whether to get another cup of coffee or not. She thought she might leave Lydia for just a moment to run across the street and grab one but decided it wasn't worth it. Mothers had been arrested for less. She thought she might ask David to watch Lydia for a minute but decided against that too. She thought about David. She regretted they weren't friends. She remembered when they'd dated and how he'd asked her to wear pantyhose when they had sex. The cheap kind out of an egg that made her legs orange and how kinky and rock and roll that had felt. Sometimes, he'd rip them off her. And sometimes she'd wear them ripped after sex on their way out to a club. Back when they'd walk over to the Bowery to see Bikini Kill at CBGB. Or maybe it was 1020 Bar. It had all been so long ago. She remembered Nat, David's best friend. He'd been so cute, so much cuter than David but so bad in bed. The only thing fun about it was the secrecy. Rachel stood and squinted her eyes, scanning the playground. She'd get a coffee and something for Lydia. But first she had to find her.

Where was Lydia? She was just there. She was just over by the swings playing with David's girls. She was just here. Lydia? she called.

Rachel stood up and shoved her feet into her clogs. She looked around and called out, Lydia? Lydia? Her heart raced as she lapped the playground, twisting an ankle on the uneven stones. Her panic grew and she barely noticed the sharp pain.

There were two entrances. One was kept chained up. The fence around the park was fortress-high and she'd sat on the bench beside the gate that was open. Some parents didn't shut the gate all the way. She always did. Sometimes she'd even get up to shut it when an errant kid or parent leaving the playground forgot. She shuddered to imagine a kid disappearing. Like Etan Patz, years ago. Rachel had been the same age and in the city when he disappeared. Rachel wasn't one to worry about homicidal maniacs, not really, not like some of the moms she knew. But just now, with Lydia gone, anything seemed possible.

For five or six minutes, Rachel ran frantically from one side of the park to the other. She searched all the hidey-holes, the swings, the sandboxes, the tires. She tapped a nanny on the arm, who wrenched her arm away and gave Rachel a murderous look. Rachel said, Have you seen my baby? Have you seen my girl?

What was she wearing? the nanny asked. What does she look like? How old is she? You got to keep an eye on kids here!

A group of mothers and nannies gathered around. In her panic, Rachel forgot what Lydia was wearing. Rachel forgot everything. She pulled out her phone to call—who? Gunter? The police? She called Lydia's name again and again and again. The park rallied. Parents and children raced around the park calling Lydia's name.

Rachel headed for the unlocked gate. It was unthinkable that Lydia had left. It terrified Rachel to think of her somewhere in the wider world. And then, Lydia appeared in front of Rachel with her serious eyes and cut-glass cheekbones. She was very, very grave. Rachel wondered when she'd grown so serious and so quiet. She said, What, Mommy? What is it? She said, I was hiding but I'm right here, Mommy.

Rachel couldn't help herself. A mother wrung her hands and said, Praise the Lord. Rachel held her arm with one hand and raised the other and gave Lydia a slap on her rear—just once. Lydia began to cry, Rachel picked her up and held her, and Rachel also began to cry.

Yael arrived, heard the story, and hugged Rachel a long time. Yael's son Shai ran off with Lydia toward the swings. I miss you, Rachel said. I miss the city. I don't think I can do it anymore up there. I don't know what it is but I don't think I can stay there. It's not for me. I don't know who it's for but it's not for me.

But what are you talking about! Yael said. You told me you loved it there. You tried to get me to move there.

Will you? Rachel asked.

Well not now! No way, Yael said. Move back. It's an option.

Rachel shook her head. No, she said. Gunter will say we made our bed. And he's right. Besides, Gunter loves it up there now. He has embraced suburbia, the school, everything.

That's wonderful!

No, Rachel said. It's not.

Dear Petra School Parents: Please be aware that the Connecticut State Board of Health has passed a new ordinance disallowing titers to take the place of vaccinations. Donald Levine has agreed to file a lawsuit on behalf of the school in order to fight this new ruling.

Chapter Twenty-One

GUNTER ON THE ROAD

GUNTER AND RACHEL lay in bed and Gunter coughed. Rachel looked over at him. The rims of his eyes had filled with tears. What's wrong? Rachel asked.

I don't know, he said. I don't know what's wrong. My chest is tight. When I am home I feel like something stands on my chest. Am I dying?

I don't think so, Gunter. You're young.

I am older than you, he said.

No one would know it, she said. Rachel drifted to sleep but Gunter propped up on his elbow. He placed his hand on her chest and shook her gently.

He said, What if our third eye was a kind of like . . . Wi-Fi hotspot. I could generate energy and others could link up to it. Wouldn't that be amazing? Sometimes I feel like I can do this. Like I'm capable of mysterious things no one has dreamed of.

Since when do you talk like this? Rachel snapped awake. She sat up in bed, propping herself against the headboard. You are a Swedish architect. Stop it. She felt her heart begin to beat fast. I've never heard you talk like this, Rachel said. She wondered if Gunter were having some kind of psychotic break with reality or night terrors. She wondered if this was what happened in Gunter's first marriage. Did he simply wake up a different person? She thought of her stepchildren, of seeing them once a year, and she suddenly felt afraid. Would Gunter leave them too? Would he move across the country and see Anders and Lydia just once a year?

I feel an energy now, he said. Do you feel it? Lie quietly. Maybe you can feel it too.

What are you talking about? Rachel's body filled with dread. Where are you getting these ideas? Oh wait. No. She sat up and leaned against the headboard. She pulled her knees up to her chest. You joined that group, that group of nutty women at the school. On Wednesdays.

Gunter rolled onto his back and stared up at the ceiling. There are men there too!

Who leads it? Rachel asked.

No one! It's strictly egalitarian.

Who leads it, Gunter?

Well, Agnes does most of the talking.

Of course she does.

They sent a notice home, to everyone, Gunter said. They wanted someone from each family to join. Why wouldn't it be me? I can grow, can't I? he asked. He sat up and his eyes shone with a fervor that was entirely un-Gunter-like. In fact, I feel more and more American every day.

Rachel sat up and massaged her temples. She was fully awake now.

I'm changing, Gunter said. I know it sounds odd. I was so against that place. It rubbed me the wrong way but I've been going to those meditation groups and it has transformed me. Agnes had said it would and of course I only went for you and for the boy. I hoped to help him, to understand him better, but I'm changing. I've changed. I think they could change Anders too. Make him calmer. I think they can do that. I've been like this for so long, Gunter said. But maybe I can be different. I want to be a better father than I've been. I want to do it right this time!

Rachel said, I just don't understand why you didn't tell me what has been going on with you. I didn't know you were going there. I didn't know you were attending those meetings. Why wouldn't you have told me.

I know! I'm sorry, Gunter said. It's weird. It's like we are swapping our places and now it's I who thinks that place has something to offer and I am afraid now you disagree.

I don't . . . disagree. If you are happier. I'm just not sure Anders can be happy there.

I think he can, Gunter said. I believe he will be, Gunter said. His strange earnestness an afront to Rachel.

In the morning, Gunter was gone before Rachel got up and Rachel took Anders to school. Agnes stood in the doorway as usual. Anders ran into the school with his classmates and Agnes said, Would you like to come in for tea?

Rachel followed Agnes to her closet office and perched on a wooden stool. One of the upper-grade girls made them tea. It was a weedy green tea. She set the cup on Agnes's desk. Rachel looked up and saw Easter eggs, dozens of them. They hung from wires all over the room. Everywhere she looked there were Easter decorations of rabbits and brightly painted eggs.

No decorations for Passover? Rachel asked.

Agnes shook her head. None of the teachers here are of the Jewish faith, she said.

I don't follow your logic, Rachel said tightly. Some of the kids are.

You are welcome to send something in, if you like. Or come lead a Passover workshop! Agnes leaned back her chair. You know, Ms. Olson. We've noticed you don't really participate in the goings-on at Petra School. You don't come to the work days, you don't come to the seminars or parenting classes. You know they are very popular! Sometimes it's difficult to get a seat. People come from all over, not just our Petra School community. You don't come to the attachment or the simplicity parenting meetings. We haven't seen you at the Soul Creatures parenting meetings Lydia loved so much. Are you not interested in the Road? Your husband has come to meetings but we know these things are more effective when the mother participates. The mother tongue, so to speak. Are you not interested in being more social with the other parents? The other mothers at least?

Rachel nodded and thought about the parents at Petra she'd come to know in the few months they'd been there. There was Alison, who ran around dispensing nutritional advice while apparently she starved to death. There was Julia, Sage's mother, who seemed at every moment to imagine that Rachel or Gunter or Anders or maybe even Lydia was out to molest her children. And Bruce, who splashed his Facebook pages with articles about how work was unnecessary and the world could be completely mechanized. Then there was the single mom Alice, who was a socialist and posted screeds against capitalism but who also apparently to Rachel lived off a large trust fund or perhaps a good divorce settlement and didn't otherwise work. There were the hovering helicopters of moms. The moms who walked like zombies because each night their beds were full of children. The moms who discussed ad nauseam the amount of sacrifices they were capable of as they still breastfed their four-year-olds, spoon-fed their eight-year-olds, tied the shoes of capable ten-year-olds, and cut the meat of their tweens. And never ever let their kids out of their sights not even for a moment. The ones whose kids had never watched television, had never seen such cretinous fare as *The Lion King* or *Finding Nemo*. Parents who didn't believe in using the word "no."

No, Rachel said. You're right. I don't.

Do you not think that's to Anders's detriment? Are you a good role model for Lydia? As a mother she will look to you to model social behavior.

Is this really your jurisdiction? Rachel asked.

But as a Jewish woman, I would think you *believed* more in community—

Well, she said. I'm not sure what you are getting at.

Strange, Agnes said. Usually the Jewish mothers are so warm.

At home, Gunter and Rachel argued about the school. Gunter said, It could be terrible for his self-esteem to move him again. You cannot be serious.

Since when do you care about these things? Rachel said. You said once high self-esteem was the very character flaw that filled American prisons!

This was before the Road helped me to understand my own feelings of inferiority!

You don't have feelings of inferiority, Rachel said. You're Scandinavian!

Gunter pouted a bit. I don't think you realize, Gunter said, how hurtful you are being right now.

Rachel woke in the middle of the night to find Gunter sleeping on the couch.

Days passed in a kind of holding pattern and at breakfast one morning Rachel noticed a blue string around his wrist. It came from Petra, Rachel knew. More than half the parents at drop-off and pickup had the string around their wrists.

During the day, he didn't answer Rachel's phone calls.

At school, one rainy afternoon when Rachel had gone to pick up the kids, Angela, the woman she'd met at the first parent-teacher meeting, cornered her.

They've got him, Angela said to Rachel. Her bony fingers held fast to her wrist. They've got your husband. She pushed her other finger into her chest.

What are you talking about? Rachel asked her.

Your husband!

That's ridiculous, Rachel said, though her hands had begun to tremble. You don't even know my husband! He's a Swede! He doesn't believe in nonsense.

Okay, Angela said, backing up. But you watch and see. They got him! You'll see. Agnes has her hooks in Gunter! I'm right though. I can see I'm right, aren't I. Not just the school but Agnes. Agnes and your husband. Don't say I didn't warn you, she said. Don't make the same mistake I did, she said. Get out while you can.

When Gunter was home, he was different. Sometimes she'd see him sitting quietly in a chair early in the morning with his eyes closed, apparently meditating. And then Gunter began to push for therapy for Anders. Therapy that Petra endorsed, he told her pointedly as though that would make Rachel happy. But it didn't make her happy. It made her uneasy. What can it hurt? Gunter said. Just to see. Agnes suggests a therapist. She says there are very few therapists she likes but that she likes this one. Agnes thinks—

I don't care what *Agnes* thinks.

I think it might be a good idea, Gunter said. I am the boy's father, Gunter said. After all. And I'm coming around to the school finally. Isn't that what you wanted? You were always going on about it and I thought it would make you happy if I were more involved.

The school's not normal. It was founded by a Nazi, Rachel said, remembering Angela with her frowzy white hair, their conversation earlier that day and what she'd said what seemed like a lifetime ago at that first parent-teacher conference. The founder of the school.

Wife of a Nazi, Gunter said. Back home we had a saying: Not everyone was playing pinochle in the war.

Rachel felt white-hot rage. That's not even a saying! she said.

Gunter sniffed. It sounds better in Swedish.

Dear Petra School Parents: Due to the fact that there are no teachers of the Jewish faith in the school, we will not be celebrating or discussing Jewish holidays. We apologize for the inconvenience.

Chapter Twenty-Two

THE DINNER PARTY

MARGOT SAID she'd host the dinner. Virginia, who'd just come back from Kentucky, said they would be happy to come. Please bring Charlotte, Margot said. George would love to see her. Virginia said she would. Virginia asked Margot what she thought about inviting the Olsons. Margot hesitated. Are you sure? Margot said. I thought it would be just us and the kids. But no, Virginia was sure. Virginia had known Rachel for years, back when they both lived in the city, and she'd reached out to Virginia and Virginia hadn't had the energy recently to meet up with her.

Margot wanted to be the kind of person who liked to host, but she wasn't, not really. She didn't have Virginia's way of floating through the guests. Virginia would talk to everyone, and make everyone feel special. Virginia could let dishes pile up with a shrug. And Virginia didn't care when Margot's boys had once put a window out with a basketball. She didn't notice the rings of wine left from wineglasses on her coffee table or the crumbs ground into the hardwood floors. Or mud tracked in at their Fourth of July parties and snow tracked in at New Year's. It was pathological to Margot, the things Virginia didn't care about. Virginia could throw open her doors with a bottle of cheap red wine and some plastic glasses and it would feel like a party.

Margot was good at being a guest at parties. She would wipe up the wine rings on the table and pull out the bottle of Resolve to squirt on the spills in the good Oriental rug. She'd make sure someone put on a pot of coffee or turned off the stove. Margot policed the house as though it were her own. And since Richard and Tripp always barbecued something, steaks or burgers or salmon or kebabs or lamb chops, meal preparation was never much of a consideration.

She wrote down in her little notebook: buy gas for grill.

She thought a moment and wrote down: paper plates and plastic forks and knives. She'd get a bottle of bourbon maybe in case the men wanted to really drink. She went back and forth about wine. She didn't mind boxed wine, actually. In fact, she almost preferred it. Not a drop ever went to waste in a box. You could even take the bag out of the box (for it was really in a plastic bag, only encased in a box) and squeeze out the very last drops and it never went bad. At least not that she could tell. But she wasn't sure. Rachel and Gunter were transplants from the city and Gunter was a European of some sort or another. Margot closed her eyes.

Margot would go to the wine shop and buy a couple of proper bottles of wine. And she'd spring for a good bottle of vodka and the bourbon. She would go to the store herself. She would get everything she needed by herself.

She'd also decided she was tired of the men who always wanted to barbecue. She'd make a proper meal herself. Why not? She had time. Perhaps she'd make a duck the way her mother used to. It was difficult to know where to get a duck. There was Whole Foods in Stamford. Perhaps the Fairway would have duck. She thought she'd make a lasagna, but then so many people had gluten issues. No one ate pasta anymore. She racked her brain until she came up with it—chicken! Two chickens roasted in the oven. What could be more delicious? She'd add some potatoes and carrots, salt and pepper, and call it a day. There were chickens in the freezer she'd bought ages ago from Costco. Easy-peasy.

Virginia called to tell Margot that Gunter and Rachel were in and that they would bring their kids. That was okay, right?

Well of course, Margot said. Why not?

Their boy is a little wild, Virginia said.

Wilder than my three?

Yes, Virginia said. From the sound of it. I've heard things about him from the school. I've seen him in action. He's . . . something.

Well, Margot said. The father seems like something of a handful himself. Remember how drunk he was at New Year's? Although I've seen him recently at Agnes's classes. Maybe he will redeem himself.

He's not so bad, Virginia said. Hide the hard stuff. Stick to wine.

It's been so long! It will be really great to see you, Ginny, Margot said.

There was a small silence. You too, Margot.

That Friday afternoon, the chickens were still frozen and Margot had no idea how to quickly thaw them. They were too big to stuff into a microwave. It was late March but a freak snowstorm was forecast and the kids were sent home early. They came home in dribbles according to their bus schedule and entered the kitchen with their dirty boots and grubby hands while Buster the dog barked and jumped, happy for company. Out! she shouted. Out! And Aiden, Teddy, and George scattered from the kitchen and tromped up the stairs to their bedrooms.

Margot barreled out of the kitchen and stood in the hallway in the center of the house, and bellowed: SHOES OFF! HOW MANY TIMES MUST I TELL YOU NO SHOES IN THE HOUSE.

Margot returned to the kitchen and the chickens had not thawed even a little bit. They were as cold and hard as they had been this morning when she'd pulled them out of the basement freezer. The settings on her refrigerator must be too cold. Well, what to do.

Margot chopped carrots and potatoes, sprayed them with a fat-free olive oil—alternative spray and added salt and pepper and set them to the side in a bowl. She sprayed the chicken with the same fat-free olive oil—alternative and added salt and pepper. She tried to shove some of the carrots and potatoes into the depths of the chicken but the chicken was still too frozen. She preset the oven. Chopped lettuce and tomatoes for a salad. She stood a moment and thought about the wine. How much should a proper bottle of wine cost? Maybe she should ask Rachel and Gunter to bring a bottle. But surely, they'd know to.

Margot waited for the oven to heat. She looked around her kitchen and thought of things she could clean. There was, for instance, the cabinet below the sink. She crouched down and opened it. The hinge on the door was a little loose but it wasn't difficult to fix. In the kitchen junk drawer there was a screwdriver. She peeked into the rooms. All the boys were quietly on their devices. Only George was animated. He jumped and down as his little character on the screen in Aiden's room hopped up and down. Pow, pow, pow! he shouted. Teddy did homework. Of course he did. Aiden lay on his bed on his back and stared at the phone in his hands and occasionally tapped out words with his thumbs. Margot sighed and wondered how they'd adjust next year at Petra, if she got her way.

Back in the kitchen, Margot fixed the cabinet door, pulled everything out of the cabinet, the Resolve, the Clorox, the Bon Ami, the Pine-Sol, the vinegar, the Windex, the Endust, the Pledge, the extra bottles of dish soap and hand soap and dishwasher soap. She lined them up beside her on the tile floor and went to work cleaning. She'd just get as much done as she could in the time she had.

Mom.

Margot jumped, hitting her head on a sink pipe and pulled out of the cabinet.

Aiden! she said. You hungry?

I'm fine, he said.

You sure?

Mom, he said. You know you just cleaned this cabinet a couple of days ago.

I did not!

You did. You cleaned it. Aiden looked up at the ceiling. You cleaned it on Wednesday right before your Petra meeting. Are you okay?

Of course I'm okay! Well, she said. There was a leak. And one of the Bon Amis was ruined and dissolved into powder and rust, she lied. It was really disgusting. I had to get to it right away. And we're having people over for dinner today!

Aiden looked away, not really listening. He said, You're not really going to send us to Petra are you? I heard you talk to Dad about Petra.

Less homework, she said. Doesn't that sound good?

No, Aiden said. Nothing about Petra sounds good. I want to get into a good college. Teddy wants to go to Harvard and he wants to get on varsity soccer next year. George will just get weirder if we don't keep him in regular school.

Margot sighed. Can we talk about it later? I know you say you're not hungry but I'm putting a frozen pizza in the oven. Set the timer on the microwave for ten minutes and I'll call you when it dings.

Aiden shrugged and Margot turned back to her task. She stifled the urge to ask him what exactly it was he thought was wrong with her.

She went upstairs and called Richard to see if he could come home early and if he would get the wine and maybe some cheese and crackers. The crackers they had at home were just a tad stale, not up to par for guests.

Margot took a moment to check herself out in the mirror. It was true. She'd put on some pounds. Not that much really. She took her dark hair that was piled on her head down and fluffed it around her shoulders. She wondered if that was why Richard had avoided her in the bedroom and instead watched basketball games until late into the night. No, she decided. He was just tired, stressed. She applied lipstick, then wiped if off with a tissue so that just a bare stain remained. She swiped on some mascara and pinched her cheeks to make them rosy. She swept up her hair back on top of her head and pinned it. Thought she might cut it short. Simplicity. But then she thought of Agnes with her long, straight black hair. Maybe she'd just stop cutting it. After all, that was simpler, wasn't it. Severe, plain Agnes. How fiercely she wanted to be like her. Cold and unexpressive and always in control.

Margot had a new "task" from Agnes and the task was not to lean on anything. Every week they were given a new one. For her first task she'd sensed her feet. The next week she'd brushed her teeth with her left hand. Now, Margot's task was to notice how she constantly leaned: on the counters, against walls, to one side. The mundane tasks she was given were weirdly magical. She felt peppier, lighter, and clearer. Just as Agnes had promised. She pulled up her shoulders and straightened her spine and tried to feel a sense of gratitude.

His boss had just stepped out of Richard's office when Margot called. Richard watched the phone vibrate on his desk. It went on a long time. When it stopped, he exhaled loudly and turned back to his computer screen. He had reports to prepare for the upcoming quarter. A whole spreadsheet to go through. He glanced down at his phone and waited for the inevitable text message when the phone lit up again and danced its vibratory dance against the formica. Margot again. He picked it up. Hey hon, he said.

Richard! I'm glad I caught you. I have a house full of kids and an entire bottle of Bon Ami disintegrated under the sink from a leak and I had to clean that up and fix the cabinet door and the chicken has yet to thaw for dinner tonight, she said. What a day!

Richard pressed his fingers to his temples. Wait, he said. I'm sorry. Did you say there was a leak?

Oh, just a little one, Margot said. Don't worry. I fixed it.

You fixed the pipe?

Never mind! What time do you think you'll be home today?

I'll be home tonight, Richard said.

Could you maybe come a little earlier? Did you remember we have a dinner party tonight? Tripp and Virginia and it looks like the Olsons too.

Who are the Olsons again?

Richard! You met them at New Year's!

I thought tonight it was just us, just the four of us, the old gang.

Can you be home early? Can you bring wine and cheese and crackers?

How early is "early"?

She hesitated. Can you be home by five?

That means I have to leave practically now. With Friday traffic. The snow. I don't know.

Margot was quiet for a few long audible breaths and Richard could feel his insides cramp. Okay, he said. I'll leave soon. I'll have to get some work done this weekend though, you understand?

Weekends should be for family, she said. Agnes likes to say—

Richard sighed. I'll do the best I can.

Richard set the phone down. He closed his eyes and thought of Virginia. She'd said she wasn't doing well. He wondered what was wrong.

Rachel was pleased to have been invited. Gunter was less enthused. Why should we go eat at this woman's house? We don't really know them.

Rachel was exasperated. Yes, well, that's the point. We don't really know anyone.

Will Virginia be there?

Rachel rolled her eyes.

What about her awful husband?

Tripp? Of course. He's not awful.

He is, Gunter said. He is awful. He reminds me of someone. I can't think of who.

Is it—

Hush, Gunter said. He snapped his finger. I remember now! He reminds me of that man who shot up those kids. In Norway.

Rachel stopped. He does not!

No, Gunter said. I'm right. You Americans never look beneath the surface. There's something not right about him. Start with his name. Tripp, Gunter sneered. Treeeep.

I'm sure it's short for something or a nickname.

Gunter made a face. *Nickname.* What a stupid word for an even stupider concept. I tell you something else. No, Gunter shook his head. I cannot tell you.

What? Rachel said. What is it?

He has a closet full of guns. In the basement.

Oh, come on, Rachel said.

I saw them at New Year's.

You were so drunk on New Year's. You were hallucinating. Should we bring a bottle of wine? Rachel asked.

Gunter made a face. Yes, of course. I'm not drinking whatever dreck they offer.

You're being terrible, Rachel said.

I'm not! Gunter said. I am just not full of fairy tales about dinner parties. Gunter reached for Rachel. I'm sorry, he said. Sometimes I think I just miss home. It's not so easy to live so far from one's country. Gunter scowled and said, I will put on a good face. I promise.

But as Gunter dressed he was annoyed. AIK played Hammarby. He could catch it live. And then he remembered the women. The plain but pleasingly plump Margot. Well, there was something about her. Something sexy. And the Venus: Virginia. Yes, he'd dress extra special of course. He'd wear a jaunty scarf around his neck. American women loved that kind of thing.

They made small talk around the table. Richard mentioned to Virginia and Margot that an old high school friend of theirs who'd never married was dating someone new.

I saw that! Margot said. She's pretty.

Yes, I saw, Virginia said. She's lovely.

Rachel set down her wineglass. Every time I see that a young couple has gotten married I want to tell them: Please, whatever you do, don't have children!

Hear, hear, Richard said. I'll drink to that.

Margot pursed her lips. How can you say that? I love my children.

Oh, Rachel said. I wasn't saying you didn't. I mean, of course we do!

They all looked at Gunter, waiting for a ribald comment but he was only staring blankly at his wineglass lost in a thought.

233

He looked up and said, I have children. Two of them that I haven't seen in over six months. Both in Sweden. Both in college. Lovely children, he said. Really.

Virginia exclaimed, So Rachel, you are a stepmom! I guess I'd forgotten that.

Yes, Rachel said. I barely know them. They are almost grown.

Richard asked Gunter why he'd left Sweden. Gunter's eyes flashed: Do you know the tax rate in Sweden? Ack! Almost seventy percent! It's a crime.

That's unbelievable, Tripp said.

Yes, Gunter said. I know.

Virginia said, Yes, but that includes health care and college. I would imagine that's why your kids are in college there rather than here. And child care! Imagine if we factored those costs into our tax rate.

Rachel drained the wine in her glass. It's true. And it's unfair, of course, here in the US where you pay two hundred grand for college regardless of your income.

Well, Gunter scoffed. That's not entirely true. You have many grants and scholarships. You have very cheap money by way of student loans. Your cars are cheap. Your clothing is cheap. Even your Lego costs half as much as our Lego!

It's just amazing what Obama has managed to do in just a few years, Tripp said. Worst president ever.

Everyone looked around awkwardly. Rachel's eyes widened at Virginia, who looked down.

Well, Richard said. I mean, come on. He's not that bad.

The table sat silently for a minute until Richard, wanting to smooth everything over, said to Tripp and Virginia: Don't you have an anniversary coming up? Didn't you marry in March?

What's today? Virginia asked. I think our anniversary is in a couple days? The thirtieth, right?

I was a witness, Richard told the table. We drove down to Maryland because you guys didn't want to wait for a blood test. You were wearing some kind of silk dress, sort of like a wedding dress, I guess, more casual of course. Very Carolyn Bessette. But then you were wearing sneakers because you'd forgotten to take other shoes.

That's right, Virginia said. I can't believe you remembered that!

Margot said, But that could be a look! Sneakers with a dress. That could be cute.

Virginia shook her head. These were big old running sneakers. Not cute. Not cute at all.

But still, Richard said. You still looked good, Virginia. Richard looked at Virginia with a little crooked smirk. The table became unnaturally quiet. Margot stared down at her hands. Rachel glanced shyly all around. Virginia squirmed imperceptibly under Richard's gaze. Tripp's face settled into something grim and unreadable. And then Gunter boomed something about the wine. Delicious wine! But it's all finished. Let's open another! he said. Gunter grabbed his own. Richard opened it and Gunter splashed it into everyone's glasses, mixing it in with glasses still unfinished. Margot took a sip. It was sweet. Of course it was sweet.

What is this survival course you were talking about, Tripp? Gunter said. I've never heard of such a thing!

It's his hobby, Virginia said dryly. Isn't that right, Tripp?

Tripp nodded. Things aren't looking so great in the world, he said. If you have eyes to see. The way I see it, Hurricane Sandy was a wake-up call. A few more days without electricity or food on the shelves and I believe we would have seen bloodshed. It isn't entirely unreasonable to imagine everyone needs to arm themselves—

You people, Gunter shouted. You think your own demise is the center of the universe! America might end but I assure you the world will go on! Let me tell you about Europe and about the Bosnian War! I was in a unit that . . .

Gunter went on. Rachel tried to interrupt but Gunter talked over her. Finally, he quieted. He looked around the table and settled on Tripp and Virginia. Tell me, he said. Do you like the Petra School?

We love it, Virginia said. The teachers are wonderful. The students all go off to do great things. The play structure and the goat's pen were built by Tripp and some of the other dads. I love that the parents are so involved.

I am starting to like it, Gunter said. I didn't at first but now I do. I started to do these meditations. I feel like a different man. I go every Wednesday.

Yes, Margot said. I see you there.

Gunter peered down his nose at Margot. You are there? Ah yes. I remember now.

Margot stared down at her hands offended. I sit in the back, she said.

A pulse began to quicken around the table. The wine they passed around sang a song. The night coalesced. They came together. They loosened. Even Tripp opened up.

They sat an hour together. And they were like a group, a crowd, the building of something between them. They riffed off one another, ribbed one another. Gossiped. Virginia said, Did you hear about Craig and Gabriel? They quit the tennis club! I guess they were upset because they wouldn't let the baby in the big pool with a swim diaper on—only the baby pool. They decided Jordan was bored with the baby pool so they quit.

No! Margot said. That's outrageous. I can't tell you how many swim diaper fails I've suffered through.

Margot asked Virginia how her next book was going.

It's going, Virginia said. I haven't worked on it in ages but I think I'm going to just turn it in. Get it off my desk. Send it to my agent next month. I don't even care anymore. Not really. It just doesn't feel important anymore. She smiled weakly and looked down at her plate.

Oh, you can't turn it in next month! Rachel said. Next month is an eclipse. In ancient days no one did anything during eclipses. Kings were toppled! States fell.

I have been toppled, Virginia said. I am falling. Virginia looked at her hands. That's how I feel anyway.

I know what you mean, Rachel said kindly.

For a moment Margot looked out at all of them and felt that the evening was a wild success and she was happy. Virginia seemed like her old self. She didn't look so tight and pinched. They stood from the table and Tripp, drunk, hugged everyone, holding on a beat too long. Even Virginia. He hugged her and kissed her on the mouth and said, You look beautiful tonight, Ginny.

The men went out to smoke cigars. Margot cleared the dishes. Virginia began to wash up. Rachel helped out, drying and stacking dishes on the counter. Margot tried to help but the two women wouldn't let her. No, no, they said. You did all the cooking. Margot was pleased. She listened to the two of them talk about the Petra School and for a moment she disappeared into a fugue state, plotting how she'd get her boys there. She would get them there. She would, eventually.

Virginia disappeared to the hall bathroom where she splashed her face with water, swiped mascara from under eyes. She stared at herself for a beat or two in the mirror. She looked tired, maybe, but otherwise no different. She took a deep breath and sighed loudly. There was a tap at the door. Hang on! she called. She flushed the toilet, washed her hands, and wiped them on Margot's pristine monogrammed hand towel and opened the door. Richard stood against the wall with his arms crossed. His eyes were soft and kind. Are you okay?

Yes, she said. I'm fine. Do I look unwell?

Maybe, he said. Maybe a little. Your text from Kentucky worried me and you look a little dispersed.

Dispersed?

Like there are pieces of you scattered everywhere.

Virginia nodded. Yes, she said. Or maybe I've just had too much wine.

I had too much to drink too. He put his hand on her wrist, circled in his fingers. She looked down, not able to meet his eyes, and noted his neat cuticles and the weight of the flesh of his hand, and felt an ache behind her navel.

You sure you're okay?

She smiled and nodded. I'm not fine, she said. I'm dying.

I know, he said. And smiled. I'm dying too. And then he kissed her.

He walked her back into the dining room, his fingers rested lightly on the small of her back, as though to steady and propel her. And when she sat down again, she could still feel the weight of them. The weight of what she'd tried to say.

Outside, the older boys taught Anders how to play basketball. George led Charlotte to the spare room to show her pictures of his baby sister. You don't have a baby sister, Charlotte said. You only have brothers. George showed Charlotte a pink album with "Lily Pea" embossed on the front. Inside were photos of a perfect tiny baby. This was my sister, George told Charlotte. But she died before I was born, George said. I think it still makes my mom really sad.

After everyone had gone, Margot sat on her sofa with a cup of coffee while Richard wrangled the kids to bed. She felt a satisfaction, an earned exhaustion. She leaned her head against the sofa. The evening conversation flashed around her in bursts behind her closed eyelids.

There had been a moment when Gunter, quite drunk, loudly asked if Virginia had actually been a prostitute. It was in your book, he said. So vivid and real. And Virginia—wickedly!—said yes and Gunter had gone white as a sheet. Speechless. Margot laughed out loud. Of course the brashest men are at their hearts absolute prudes.

And Rachel, a dear, who had been rather quiet all night put her hand over Gunter's hand and said, She's joking, of course. Virginia was more of a . . . dinner whore. She went out with any- one who would buy her dinner. Remember those days, Virginia?

Richard watched her with half a smile. Virginia watched him, trying to read his expression. Tripp, unnoticed by all, watched them both.

Gunter recovered and turned to Virginia, and said, Well, my dear. You are ravishing. I would not have paid for your services but I'm certain I would have bought you dinner.

Everyone, it seemed to Margot, left contented if not happy. Margot resolved she'd host monthly. Maybe they'd revolve from house to house. Friday night dinners. A new tradition. Community.

The following week was spring break. Margot had no camps scheduled, no activities planned. She had no idea what the kids would do. It exhausted her just to think about it.

Dear Petra School Parents: Let your Petra School student introduce you to our latest addition, the Petra School computer! Thanks to the Roscoes for the cardboard box contributions and the Layles for the chalkboard. The children are very excited about their new "computer"!

Chapter Twenty-Three

THE PLAYDATE

RICHARD ANSWERED the door wearing shorts and a T-shirt.

Where's Margot? Virginia asked.

She's out, Richard said. What are you doing here?

I'm coming to pick up Charlotte. Are you sick?

No.

Laid off?

No!

So where's your wife?

She went out. There's some women's work day thing at Petra, I think. She's taking the day. So I decided to take the day off too. Why aren't you at the work day? You want to come in for a bit? Charlotte and George are playing really well together.

Virginia hesitated, shy, remembering that sudden kiss at Margot's.

Come on, he said. I don't bite.

All right, Virginia said.

I'm making myself a gin and tonic. Want one?

Truth serum, Virginia said.

I'm sorry?

In college we used to call gin and tonics truth serum, Virginia said. She walked through the door. She kicked off her shoes in the foyer, and noted the children's shoes in neat rows on small wooden shelves. Virginia thought Margot must feel good. When Margot was depressed, the house fell apart. Virginia left her shoes in the middle of the floor and walked into the living room. I'll have one. I completely forgot about that work day thing. I'm out of the loop, I guess.

Richard shook his head. She really needed some time off, I think. Usually the kids are in sports camps but this year she didn't schedule any. She claims Petra helps her. She gets a little nuts sometimes.

Well, she can't be that bad, Virginia said. Virginia poked her head into the kitchen. The kitchen cabinets had been painted a kind of dark yellow. Did you guys just paint? Virginia asked.

Margot did. You don't like it?

No! I do! It's lovely what you guys did.

Richard smirked. Liar. He handed her the drink in a cold, sweating glass. It's awful. It looks like a McDonald's in here. Have a sip and then tell me what you really think.

Okay, Virginia said. I don't even need to drink this to tell you I think it's hideous.

Richard winced.

Okay, not hideous. But I mean . . . dated. Kind of, you know, dark but . . . shiny.

Doesn't show fingerprints, Richard said. But yeah, I know. You pick your battles.

I get that, Virginia said. She sipped her drink. Mmm. Very nice. Perfect on a spring day.

How was Kentucky? You didn't mention anything about it at the dinner party.

Virginia took a gulp. She blushed. It was nice.

Nice? It was a funeral for your stepmother, right?

Wasn't really a funeral, Virginia said. I had a kind of private viewing and then she was cremated. She didn't really have anyone.

And you didn't see any friends or family?

No, Virginia said. I guess I don't really have any out there anymore. No one I care to see.

Virginia could hear the kids shout in the backyard; the boys were involved in some kind of soccer match. Richard stood up. Virginia looked at him through lowered eyes. Something was in the air. Something was up. He grabbed her glass and walked back into the kitchen. You drank that pretty fast, he said. You want another?

Why not?

Richard called out from the kitchen: How's Tripp?

Tripp is, you know. He's Tripp.

Right. Still into all that survivalist crap?

He's at John Monroe a lot, I think, down in Pennsylvania.

Richard nodded. He doesn't talk to you about it?

Not really, Virginia said flatly. And I don't want to know.

Richard walked back into the living room and handed her a new drink, then sat down heavily on the sofa, his big knees just a couple of inches from hers. So tell me, now that you've had some truth serum—

Virginia took a sip. Strong, she said.

Indeed, Richard said. What was all that blushing about?

Virginia blushed again. I don't know what you're talking about.

Come on, Richard said. I think you do. What happens in Louisville stays in Louisville, isn't that how it goes? You seem . . . different.

Hang on, Virginia said, conscious of a slight slur in her voice. She thought of the man in the hotel bar. Winced, embarrassed of how she'd propositioned him. I don't know what you're suggesting, Virginia said. I mean, you of all people. I see you getting texts constantly. Let me guess. Big blonde hair, right? Sends videos?

Richard gaped at her.

I'm a snoop. Virginia shrugged. What can I tell you? And you're not that careful. You don't even try to hide your screen.

That's what Margot thinks?

She never talks to me about anything personal. I can only tell how she's doing by the state of the house and how much weight she's lost or gained.

Nothing happened, Richard said. It's just videos. Flirting.

Virginia nodded. Okay, she said and scooted to the edge of the sofa. Listen, I got to get going. I have to get Charlotte home and try and get something like dinner ready.

Richard set his glass down. I loved your book, he said.

You did? Virginia sat back on the sofa. Really?

I did.

I'm sorry but, I mean, do you even read?

I read all the time, Richard said.

I'm surprised.

Yeah? Richard said. His expression soured. You think I'm dumb? Big dumb jock?

No! Virginia said. It's just that Tripp never told me. You never talked about it.

He used to smack books out of my hand when we were in high school. He can be such a prick, you know. But yeah, I read all the time. I read before bed and in the mornings on weekends, if I can. I have a degree in modernist poetry. I used to think maybe I'd be a professor. I'm sure that's funny to you.

Virginia stared at him. I'm shocked.

Richard's eyes narrowed. He picked at a thread from the seam of his jeans and rubbed at his beard. You think I'm just like Tripp, huh? Tell me something. If you think I'm so bad, why'd you marry Tripp?

I don't think you're bad.

Yeah you do. Richard started to pick dog hair off the sofa. Thing is, Richard said, marriage is fucking hard. And I love Margot but she's . . . hard.

She's a mess, Virginia said. But I am too. We all are.

Yeah, exactly. I mean, but Margot can barely function sometimes.

Virginia nodded. Why did you have three kids? Three *boys*.

She wanted a girl, Richard said. After, you know . . . and I thought it would make her happy. I can't tell you how it happened. Plus, she's better when she's pregnant. She said when we married that she wanted a dozen kids. It seemed selfish for her not to have that.

Yes, well. It didn't happen by itself, Virginia said.

No, Richard said. Of course not. She locks herself in the bathroom. She threatens to leave. One day she did leave! That day I had you pick up George? Remember? She went to a hotel somewhere in New Haven. I had to make excuses to my boss and rush home. I mean. She loses it with the kids. Three boys. It's not easy.

That's one reason I don't think you're an asshole, Virginia said. You're always with them.

Richard started to say something and then stopped himself. He didn't want to throw Margot under the bus.

Maybe she needs therapy or medication, Virginia said.

After she lost that girl, she changed. We never knew what happened. It made her want to hang on to things, to control things.

I'm sorry, Virginia said. She never talks about it. We weren't really close when it happened. I should have tried to talk about it with her but it felt somehow private.

She thinks Petra will save her. She walks around "sensing her feet" and counting backward to calm down.

Petra might help, Virginia said. It's a good place. Charlotte is really happy there.

Yeah, Richard said. We might send the boys there next year. They'll be miserable if we force them to leave the public schools. And we can't afford it and I'll never retire.

The girl? Virginia asked. That's your steam valve?

What girl?

You know. The girl. The blonde.

Richard blushed. She's a GFE.

A what?

Girlfriend experience.

Virginia was very quiet. Okay, she said. I get it. I understand.

You don't think it's awful?

Well, yeah. Isn't it? But I feel like most women don't want to know the truth. Most men too. Once a man has a sexual proclivity, whores, chicks with dicks, jailbait, whatever, they can never change it.

You saying I can't help it?

Virginia shook her head slightly. Probably not.

Tripp doesn't cheat on you. At least I don't think so.

No, Virginia admitted. That's true. Perhaps he'd be nicer if he did. Sometimes I think Tripp is in love with you.

Richard nodded. Yeah.

Virginia's eyes widened. Wait, really?

I don't know, Richard said. When he gets drunk he gets . . . weird. He gets grabby, affectionate, really personal.

Virginia put her head in her hands. You're not serious.

Richard shrugged. Guys get weird when they're drunk.

Well, Tripp isn't all that interested in me these days. We haven't had sex in months. He sleeps in the guest room most nights. She sipped her drink. It's weird. You and I have known one another all these years and never really talked.

Richard rattled the ice in his glass. Well, you know Tripp. He's jealous.

But he's not! Virginia said. Not at all. He's the opposite.

Richard said. I don't know. I get a vibe. Or maybe it's my own guilt because, the thing is, I guess I always had a crush on you. And I was afraid Tripp would figure it out. And I shouldn't have kissed you the other night but it seemed so natural somehow. And listen, there's something, about Tripp. Something I should tell you about him. He's doing this prep thing, for the end of the world. And in the basement—

Virginia let go a ferocious breath of air. Oh please, she said. The day is so pleasant. Let's not talk about Tripp.

I really should tell you—

She gave a shake of her head and sipped her drink. Please no, she said.

They finished their drinks. Something physical was moving through the air. It changed the atoms and molecules and arranged and rearranged the chemical composition of the room. It was a hot wind or a spirit. The kids played happily, harmoniously. No one fought or yelled or ran screaming into the house with bloody limbs or tears or hurt feelings. No one came to ask for a snack. No one came to complain they were bored or too hot or asked to play video games or watch TV. Virginia could hear Charlotte's quiet, happy voice on the other side of the house. Richard drained his drink and held the sweating glass in his hands. Virginia pulled her legs up under her and sat cross-legged on the sofa, happy, buzzed, content.

Virginia's phone vibrated with a message and she noted the time. I should take Charlotte, she said. Pull some supper together.

Yeah, Richard said. Me too.

Virginia stood up from the sofa. Charlotte? she called.

Richard slid to the edge of his seat and grabbed Virginia's wrist. There are two kinds of people in this world, he said. There are those that come to the edge of a cliff and are afraid they'll fall. And then there are those who are afraid they'll jump. Which one are you, Virginia?

Virginia wrenched her arm away and gave Richard a hard look. Neither, she said. I'm already free-falling.

And then Virginia stood up and said, I think it's time we go. Richard lurched closer to Virginia and kissed her again. Virginia sank into his hands and allowed it.

He backed her into the spare bedroom down the hallway from the powder room and then he held her and then he lifted up her shirt and kissed her breasts while he caressed her. His hands were sure and deft. You have good hands, she told him. Is that from baseball?

It's from knitting. I have three sisters. I'm the baby. They mostly tortured me but also taught me valuable things: knitting, how to entertain myself, how to soothe crabby women.

He eased her down on the day bed and kissed her neck and smoothed her hair from her forehead, entangled his fingers in her soft curls and then untangled them with a flick of his wrist.

This is a really bad idea, she said.

I'm ready to blow up my life, Richard said.

When he pulled her up on top of him, she noted that she was shaking. There was a vibration and the vibration was love or something like it. Love, Virginia thought, was just the ability to harness something that was everywhere. Like extracting water from clouds.

I'm shaking, she said.

I like it. It just means you are moved and I am moving you.

You're not moving me, she said. But I'm glad you are here.

I think I've always been in love with you, Richard said.

Have you?

Yes.

I'm glad I never knew that.

Why is that?

Virginia paused a minute. She drew her arm over her breasts. Because expectation is ugly.

Richard laughed and kissed her again.

Virginia gathered Charlotte, her bag. Shaky on her feet, giddy. On the way to the car, Virginia's phone rang and she answered it. It was Edward. Hi, Edward, Virginia said.

Virginia! I've tried to get a hold of you for weeks. Do you have a minute? I think I have good news! I got you into a study, a protocol. It wasn't easy given your . . . financial situation. But it's free. This is good news, Virginia. This is really good news.

Edward was excited. He was happy. Virginia was excited. She was happy too. But she did not want to talk to Edward.

Great! she said. Can I call you back tomorrow?

Virginia hung up.

Who was that? Charlotte asked. She clicked shut her seat belt.

Virginia climbed behind the steering wheel and turned the key. No one, she said. The dentist. Dr. Meyers. He says I don't have any cavities.

Dear Petra School Parents: Our film *Dyslexia as a Dairy-Related Condition* will be aired in the library Thursday night at 7:00 p.m. Proceeds from tickets will go toward our spring fundraising drive. For tickets, please call the school office during school hours. Tickets are tax-deductible.

Chapter Twenty-Four

GONE GUNTER

GUNTER CAME HOME later and later from work. Those evenings alone, Rachel, Lydia, and Anders watched endless hours of Noggin cartoons. Lydia dropped off to sleep but Anders stayed awake. His dark eyes burned into the night.

Rachel thought how she'd loved Gunter when they met. How intelligent he was with his black-framed architect glasses and the way he slid between languages and cultures. He was older than her, more wise and knowledgeable and worldly. Love was something Rachel had never anticipated. Why didn't the need for love die away after forty? Why did it continue, an unnecessary organ like the appendix or the gallbladder? The need for romantic love should atrophy with age.

And then the next morning after Rachel had walked the kids to school, Gunter texted her, somewhat contrite, somewhat apologetic, and then an hour later she met him at Starbucks in their village. Starbucks—a place Gunter loathed—and he was telling Rachel something, but Rachel wasn't listening. It seemed so many things had changed and Rachel had not paid attention. They nursed their cups of black coffee, gripped in their seats by something strong that did not allow them to add the requisite sugar packets. A dollop of half-and-half or almond milk. Gunter was explaining what it was all about: his life, their life, the children. He'd gone to those meetings and he'd done those meditations and the exercises he'd been given and it had changed him. He'd transformed. Well, didn't Rachel think it was possible? That Gunter could transform? He'd been spending some time with Agnes and he had learned a few things he said. Rachel nodded and sipped at the bitter coffee but all she could think of was Agnes. Rachel could see her long, rangy limbs. Arms like flat, long bits of fettuccini. Flattened hearts. Rachel flattened on the street. After they finished school Lydia or Anders would come and peel her off the pavement. They'd brush Rachel off and Anders would put her under his arm and carry her away, out of sight forever.

Gunter explained what it was all about and why it was so irresistible. I'm different! he said, scowling. It's like you don't notice, he said. I feel I've been living a lie and now I'm finally becoming myself.

Tell me, Gunter, is that what happened with your first marriage? With Heike?

Gunter did not respond. Agnes, he told her, had plied him with irresistible ideas. The Road. He had been powerless to her ideas.

I have ideas too, Rachel mumbled.

Gunter ignored her. He was excited and plowed on with words, with syllables and vowels, with *ideas*. He fingered his watch. Rachel was getting a headache. Gunter kept talking. It's like Aristotle, he said. And the three laws of good ethos—

Yes, Rachel said. I know them: You cannot win. You cannot break even. You cannot get out of the game.

He gaped at her. Are you joking? That's . . . *thermodynamics*.

Rachel said, That's exactly what you're *supposed* to be interested in—

Good ethos, he said. Good moral character, good sense, goodwill. Agnes says—

What's such great moral character about sleeping with Agnes? Rachel asked. Headmistress of the children's school?

He sucked the air in.

Rachel leaned over the table. Why do you tell people you were a soldier? That you were in the Gulf War? Why don't you tell people you got crazy right after basic training and drove your tank into a pond and got thrown out of the army? Why don't you say that? During the Gulf War you worked in a phone bank—

With his right hand he swiped off his thick, black architect's glasses and with his left he gripped the table. He bent slightly and rose to tower over Rachel. He said, I'd like you to know I don't have the same problem with Agnes I had with you.

Which problem is that? Rachel asked. I can think of so many.

The sex problem. With Agnes I could last hours. I could literally fuck her for hours. I wouldn't even need pills.

Rachel felt a pressure collapse her throat then and a stab of pain down the left side of her neck. She stared at his face. His handsome face and fair hair. Still blond with only flecks of white though he was nearly sixty. He'd gelled it today, straight up off his forehead, so that he had the permanently surprised look of someone who'd just been dropped out of an airplane. Anders had the fine, blond goyish hair of his father. His father's mouth and eyes. His father's provocative spirit. Lydia was dark, like Rachel. Easygoing, like Rachel. Rachel thought of her father, giving his blessing with a caveat: They were a mismatch. Rachel and Gunter were a mismatch. *Like you took a salt shaker from one set and a pepper shaker from another.* And he was right! Rachel's father had been right! And it was all so very unfair. No one would fuck him—no one at all—if it weren't for that hair and his stupid accent, his blameless Scandinavian-ness, those glasses, that watch that cost as much as a compact car, his *architecture degree.* The gas guzzling G-wagon!

Rachel stood too. In the beginning, Rachel said. In the beginning I could fuck you for hours. But after about eight months it grew stale. And then I couldn't wait for you to finish. And then, I didn't even want you to start. After eight months I fantasized about everyone and their brother. Everyone and *your* brother. Your brother especially.

I don't have a brother! he shouted, but Rachel had gotten up, hurried around the tables, and run from the Starbucks onto the village streets.

* * *

At the ShopRite the next day, Rachel saw Julie out of the corner of her eye. Julie scurried down the cereal aisle. Rachel stood still and gripped the shopping cart. She'd fought a migraine since Starbucks the day before. The migraine was a pike in her brain. It activated courage in her. It activated the part of the brain that no longer had anything to lose. No fucks to give. She turned around and sprinted with stealthy steps up the snack aisle, where she grabbed a bag of Terra Chips and tossed them in her cart. She'd wondered when she would run into Julie and she'd dreaded it. But now, slowing as she rounded the corner, her eye on the ground beef, she realized she'd been waiting for this day for weeks. Preparing for it like an athlete.

Hi, Julie! Rachel said.

Julie, just as falsely, said, Hey, Rachel!

It's been a long time, Rachel said smiling. So long.

Yes, it has. Julie started to push off but Rachel grabbed hold of her cart.

Tell me why, Rachel said. The smile emblazoned on her face like a declaration of war.

I'm sorry?

Are you?

Wait, Julie said. I don't know what you mean. I can't think what I should be sorry for. The speaker droned above them: *Cashier needed on five. Cashier needed on five.*

You broke Anders's heart. I know Sage wanted playdates—he told me himself at drop-off. And he told Anders you wouldn't let them see each other.

257

Julie winced. I should have said something. Agnes just mentioned—

Agnes, Rachel said. She looked up at the fluorescent lights. The loudspeaker squawked: *Cashier on five, please! Cashier on five!*

Yes, Julie said. Agnes mentioned the boys were at different stages in their development and that they should take a break from their friendship—

Agnes told you that.

Yes, she said the boys needed some time apart from one another. Agnes felt—

Did you know that Agnes is fucking Gunter?

Julie looked down. Rachel put her hand to her temple. The lights of the grocery store were unrelentingly bright, like the sun in a desert of white sand. The migraine squeezed with its strength and the tile floor beneath her feet tilted.

They're not . . . having sex, Julie said. They are only very close. That's what I heard. They are just very good friends. Agnes just likes to have men around, you know, as helpers. For a few years it was Tripp Powers. Before that it was, oh, let me think. Julie put her hand on Rachel's arm. Rachel jerked it away. It's really for the best, Rachel. You'll see. Gunter will get such a beautiful education from Agnes. Anders will benefit too. Everything happens for a reason.

Rachel turned her cart down the aisle toward the front door. She was nauseous now and the floor tilted and lurched and only the frigid air of the market soothed her. She remembered what Joan Didion had once said about migraines. The blessing of them. The aura that erased all concerns. The immediacy of pain and how everything else that existed receded into the background, into a space on the other side of the aura. Okay fine, Rachel thought. I'll wait here on the other side with the pain.

She could hear Julie behind her, Rachel? Rachel? Rachel? Rachel thought, Once you fall, human nature is on you.

Dear Petra School Parents: Please see the following attachment regarding the Connecticut State Department of Education's guidelines for the regulation of private schools. While we understand Connecticut State's desire to regulate unaccredited schools, this proposal reaches far beyond that stated goal. Our school already meets the requirements for substantial equivalency and should be exempt from the proposed regulations.

Rachel read the email and pressed Reply. She typed: What if you are wrong. What if the Petra School is teaching our kids nothing at all? Her cursor hovered over Send. She deleted it instead.

Chapter Twenty-Five

RICHARD'S DREAM

SHE CAME TO RICHARD in a dream. She wore all white like it was her wedding day but scarlet slippers like Dorothy in *The Wizard of Oz*. They sparkled bright and blinding and her golden hair spilled all around her cleavage. Of course, he said in the dream. Of course I'll marry you. They walked down the aisle. The long aisle that led to that great death's head, Oz, disembodied. It hung over the church aisle. The most frightening thing Richard had seen as a child. Their friends and family seated in pews, cordoned off and separate, watched them walk down the aisle with looks of horror on their faces. There was Tripp on one side of the aisle and on the other side of the aisle was Margot.

He'd wanted to be someone different in the dream, someone braver, not so obedient, but instead he was running in the opposite direction. He turned his head to see her look back at him with disgust, and when he woke up Margot lay beside him with her head propped up on her hand. Hey, she said. You had a dream.

Ha, Richard said. I did.

What was it about?

Richard closed his eyes. He could still see the red slippers and Virginia in that white gown. Virginia, who he'd seen just a handful of times since that kiss in his guest room. I can't remember, he said. You know I never remember my dreams.

Margot kissed him on the forehead and pulled the covers over her head. Do you mind getting the boys ready for school today? I barely slept at all last night.

In the afternoon, Margot sent Richard a text at work. He was in the middle of gathering up numbers for his quarterly report. His boss had been breathing down his neck all day, sending his minions into Richard's office asking when it would be ready. He knew he wasn't going to make it to softball practice at McCarren Field and his teammates were going to be pissed.

He was tempted to mute the texts from Margot. If there was ever a time he couldn't deal with her shit, it was now. He swiveled around to the cabinet where his phone beeped and rattled against the metal. Maybe it was Virginia. That dress she wore in the dream and those crazy shoes. But somehow, he knew it wasn't from Virginia and the truth was he didn't have time to deal with her either. And what the fuck had he done anyway?

Call me, the phone read.

Goddamnit, he muttered. There was no time to deal with Margot's shit. He clenched his teeth and muttered to himself, Can't you just hold it together for one fucking day without bothering me?

The assistant stood in the doorway. Richard? You okay?

Richard rested his chin in his cupped hands. I'm drowning here. The fucking printer is jammed. I'm waiting for IT to come and they're taking forever.

The assistant was actually sweet, pretty even, slender in her cheap black pants and a low-cut striped shirt. She'd studied poetry at Dartmouth. That was partly why Richard hired her. She probably hated her job. That makes two of us, Richard thought. There was a little lipstick on her teeth. It endeared her to him. So young, nothing had ever happened to her. Nothing more than the usual unlikable parents, college alcoholism, pregnancy scares. An eating disorder that would work itself out with marriage, family life, babies. That was the nice thing about the Girlfriend Experience, you never had to hear all that shit. That's what he should have done. Not Virginia. A girl he paid. A girl he never had to see again. Nothing complex. No entanglements. Richard watched the assistant pull at the printer in the hallway just outside his office. She ripped paper out as though her life depended on it. Perhaps her life did depend on it. He remembered the apartments of all the broke girls he'd gone to bed with before Margot. Maybe they saw their poverty as romantic; Richard hoped for their sake that one day they would.

Richard turned back to the numbers. His wife would survive for one day, surely, without communication from him.

The assistant brought him in a cup of coffee. Want me to get you something to eat? she asked.

Richard waved his hand in front of his face. I'm not even hungry, Richard said. But I really appreciate you asking.

No problem! she said brightly and Richard noticed her freshly applied lipstick, none of it now on her teeth. He wondered if the lipstick was for him.

An hour later, Richard printed out the reports and the assistant walked into his office with a haunted look on her face. Listen, she said. Your wife just called reception. She wanted to know why you didn't pick up your cell. Do you want me to put her through?

Richard sighed. Sure, he said. Go ahead.

The phone on his desk rang. He so rarely used it he wasn't even sure what button to push. He pushed several and heard her voice.

Richard? Richard?

Yeah, babe. What's up? I'm right in the middle of this budget thing and my boss is on my ass—

I have news.

Richard opened his mouth, sucked in air, and held it.

I'm pregnant!

But—

I know, she said. I don't know what happened. I was on the pill.

Richard sat back in his chair and exhaled. He could see the assistant peer at him through the glass window of his door. He replayed back her words: *I was on the pill. I was on the pill.*

263

Which is it, Margot. You were or you weren't?

I was, she said. And then I wasn't.

Richard swiveled in his chair. He turned to face the window. His view was an airshaft. Before, back when you could open the windows, he'd crack it open and throw paper clips out just to see how long it took for them to hit the ground below. But the noise from the HVAC units and the general hum of the buildings had obscured that final sound. He thought of those paper clips. He thought he'd wrench the window open and throw himself out of it. He thought maybe he'd at least throw his chair down.

Richard?

Yeah.

Aren't you happy?

I mean . . . I'm in shock.

But Richard, this is the one. This is the girl. I know it.

Richard made vaguely excited noises while Margot prattled on. He imagined her pregnant again. She was stable when she was pregnant. Happy and excited, active, attentive and full of love to the boys. Try and come home early, Margot said before she hung up. I'm going to make a big dinner and we can announce it to the boys.

I'll try, Richard said. He still had to proof the docs, run the numbers. Maybe he could get the assistant to help him—

What time do you think you'll be home?

I don't know, Margot. I'm swamped here. Richard tried to sound jocular. He tried to sound happy.

I'm sorry, Margot said. I know you hate when I ask when you're coming home.

Richard calculated traffic. It's just that I have so many things going on here. I know you need help at home but I have so much on my plate at work right now.

It's fine, she said. Be home when you can, okay? I mean, as early as you can.

Richard thought of Virginia in the white gown and red shoes. When he opened his eyes, the assistant cracked the door of his office open. Are you okay? she asked. Is everything all right?

Richard groaned. Yeah, he said. Everything's fine. Everything is great.

Dear Prospective Petra School Parents: We will be holding the workshop "Funding Your Prospective Child's Alternative Education" in the Petra School multipurpose room on August 12th. Tips include approaching family members, withdrawing from IRAs, and how to become a Petra School teacher to offset the cost of your child's education.

Chapter Twenty-Six

VIRGINIA AND CHARLOTTE

S HE WAS HAPPY. She was happy for Margot. A girl, finally. Yes, she had hand-me-downs from Charlotte, and yes, she was sure Charlotte would love to babysit. No, she hadn't noticed Margot's bump. Six months was not a long time to wait. An autumn baby. How wonderful.

Virginia hung up the phone. She held her breath and counted to twelve. Charlotte came down the stairs. Virginia tried to calm herself. She breathed like she had when she was in labor, long, slow, calming breaths. She tried to stop her tears. It was hard even to know why she was crying. Everything she'd held in threatened to rush out. It wasn't Richard; it had never been him. Not really. A missed connection maybe but not much more. Charlotte looked so alarmed, so frightened. Her expression hit Virginia like ice water.

I'm sorry, Virginia said. I'm sorry, baby. I'm okay. What should we do? Should we order something? Should we go out to dinner?

Charlotte watched her mother. No, you're not, she said. You're not fine. Virginia hugged Charlotte and then pulled away, looking hard at her face.

No, I am. I really am.

Did someone die?

Virginia sucked in her breath. Kind of, she said. Charlotte eyes widened. No, Virginia said. She pulled Charlotte to her and smoothed Charlotte's hair with one hand and wiped at her face with another. No, no. It's actually very exciting news. Margot will have another baby! Virginia squeezed her eyes shut. Do you want to watch a movie? There's a new anime on Netflix. I think it's called *The Red Turtle*.

Charlotte nodded. I heard it's very sad.

Oh, Virginia said. I'm sure it will be fine.

There was no dialogue in *The Red Turtle*. A man washes up on an island and tries to escape multiple times. Always thwarted by a giant turtle, who smashes all his attempts at rafts. Finally, the man, in a fury, smashes the turtle's shell and out from the shell crawls a beautiful woman. Together they have a small boy but the boy grows up and soon it's his time to leave and he is sent off into the surf on his own small raft.

Charlotte sat wide-eyed while Virginia sniveled and wept beside her, wiping at her face with her sleeve.

Mom, Charlotte said. She turned and placed her two small hands on Virginia's wet cheeks. Mommy, are you okay?

267

Sweetheart, Virginia said. I'm okay. I'm really mostly fine. The words "motherless," "loveless," "health," and "illness" marched through her mind. Remembering her mother, shrunken in her bed, so ill.

Charlotte nodded gravely and said, Mama, what would make you feel better right now?

Virginia thought a moment. I think I'll take a shower. I think I'll feel better after a nice long shower.

Virginia passed through the kitchen, where she pulled down a bottle of Tripp's whiskey from the liquor cabinet and poured it into a small tumbler. She drank a shot and poured a second. She felt the cut glass with her fingers, noticing the soft pliant tissue of her finger pads.

I am love, she said out loud.

She leaned over the counter now and felt the warmth of whiskey and her eyes filled with moisture. She climbed the stairs to her bathroom, where she opened the faucets, set the temperature to almost unbearably hot, stripped, and stood in the mirror naked.

She ran her hands along her face. The basic structure was still there. A few lines. Some blotchiness. Brown spots along the left side of her cheek. A red rough spot on the end of her nose that she could not make go away no matter what products or exfoliation she tried. She was burned slightly on her décolletage and freckled on her shoulders. He's not mine, she thought. Richard. He never was. They never are. And I belong only to myself and to Charlotte. She thought how she'd finally reached the place she'd aimed for all her life. Nothing was hers except her. She belonged only to herself. Not even Charlotte was hers. And she thought in a rush of words: in that moment it didn't matter where she was, who she was, who she loved, who loved her. It didn't make any difference at all. And she knew that Charlotte would be okay no matter if Virginia was there, no matter what happened to Tripp. Charlotte was loved and that Charlotte was also love.

She was not okay to vanish. She was not okay at all. She wanted to live forever. Edward had left another message and she needed to call him back—

Virginia stepped into the shower and the water sluiced over her body.

Mom? Charlotte stood at the door. Virginia could see her through the steamed glass of the shower. Mommy, do you feel better?

Virginia felt her throat close. The soap glided over her body. She rinsed it off. I'm fine, baby.

She watched Charlotte slink into the bedroom. Resilient child. Virginia sighed loudly. She ran her hands over her flesh. Her belly, the early stage saddlebags growing on each side of her hips. The thighs that rubbed together when she wore shorts in the summer. She soaped between her legs. No point to shave there now. The dark blonde hair would grow wooly and unmanageable and silver. Or else it wouldn't. She'd find the money. She'd find out what was going on with the credit card. She'd call Edward. She'd make an appointment. Her hair would fall out. Her breasts would be gone. Her hand swept over first her right breast and then her left. There was the lump. No, that wasn't it. It had been closer to her armpit. Hard and immobile. Where was it? Where had it gone? Was it ever there?

She heard Margot's excited voice in her head, replaying their earlier conversation. *Ginny, this could be my girl at last.*

Oh, Richard, Virginia thought.

And Virginia was no one's. That was okay, Virginia thought. More and more that was okay.

It wasn't the worst thing.

It was the best.

Later that night Virginia heard the front door open. She could hear the familiar rustle of Tripp making his way from the hall closet to his study, where he kicked off his shoes. Virginia heard them hit the floor. She heard him walk into the bathroom and turn on the fan to disguise the sound of his stream of piss and the grunt he always made when he finished.

He washed his hands. He turned the fan off.

He tramped into the kitchen and poured himself a glass of water. The glass hit the counter with a sharp sound. She couldn't hear anything for a long while and she imagined he stood in front of the empty fridge. She and Charlotte had eaten cheese sandwiches with cold glasses of milk. She'd cleaned up the evidence quickly. He wouldn't complain about the lack of a hot meal for him, but she could feel his displeasure that she'd fed Charlotte yet another cheese sandwich. Yet another frozen pizza or Chinese takeout. You knew when we married I hated to cook! she'd teased him. I'll learn to cook, he'd said. But he was only kidding. He had a job in the city and would make piles of money and she would stay home and have a brood of babies and write books and maybe teach college one day. He didn't say but she knew she was supposed to learn to cook, to tend house, to be a good wife and a good mother. To keep a happy healthy hearth. His mother had stayed home, after all. And made the same meals night after night. A chart on the fridge that listed them. Mondays were macaroni and cheese and Wednesdays were pork chops and Fridays there was something called river stew made from a can of Veg-All and a pound of ground beef. If it was green and in the kitchen, Tripp used to joke, it's probably mold. They used to joke around, Tripp and Virginia. They used to like one another.

Tripp might ask her what she'd done all day. He might make a half-hearted effort sometimes to keep the accusations out of his voice. Try to be kind, to be supportive, to be a good husband. And other times beyond caring. He might remind her how much her first book had actually cost him when all was said and done. And I let you stay home and write it! he'd said. *And I let you.* Just to let Virginia know who was in charge.

And just the other day, Agnes had cornered Virginia to ask her if she'd like to teach something at Petra. She'd offer a significant break in tuition. If that would help, Agnes had said. Agnes didn't want to lose one of her favorite Petra School families. And Virginia, who was so preoccupied, had barely paid attention to Agnes. Had thought, What do you mean "lose" us? Charlotte was a good student. An easy student. They were a model Petra family. She'd never had any problems with

Charlotte. Charlotte was one of those windup children. You wind them up and they go.

Not like other kids who required work. Who required effort.

Virginia thought about Richard. That was done now.

She wanted to see Tripp. She wanted to go to him and talk to him. Maybe she'd tell him about Edward. Maybe he'd be kind to her and ease her burden. He'd been kind to her once. He'd been her only family. Her rock. Her base. Her person. Her man.

She wondered suddenly how she could be so obtuse. There were bills unpaid. There was the insurance that covered nothing. Agnes asking her if she needed a break in tuition. The credit cards declined with no explanation from Tripp. And there was Tripp, running off to prepare for an apocalypse to come when maybe the apocalypse was already here. Maybe this time they were really and truly broke and Virginia had been too distracted to see.

But now, at the top of the stairs outside Charlotte's door she was okay. She was better than okay. She could start again. She could find her way to Tripp again. She could teach at Petra. She could write a new book. Perhaps teach creative writing at a university. She closed her eyes. A rush of adrenaline and joy shot through her spine. She crossed her arms around her breasts, rooting around with her fingers for the empty spot where the lump had been. Feeling it again and again like a child feels the space where a tooth has been with his tongue. It was gone. Was it? Could it really be gone? No, it was there. Was it? She wasn't sure anymore. Perhaps she wanted it gone so much it had disappeared or perhaps she wanted it gone so much she'd tricked her fingers into believing it wasn't there.

The basement door creaked open and Virginia heard Tripp take the stairs down. She had the sense he was walking lightly so the stairs didn't creak. Virginia stood up and pulled a robe around her. She shoved her feet into soft felt slippers and inched out of the bedroom and down the stairs.

She pulled the string that turned on the single light bulb that hung above the basement stairs but the bulb was out. The floor was still dirt. They'd once thought they'd finish the basement or at least pour a concrete floor. Back when they'd been happier and thought about having more children. She felt her breast again. Nothing there. Could it be? No, it was there. Her body flushed with panic. *It was still there.* She thought of Edward. She was ashamed she hadn't called him. Was it too late? He'd left her so many messages and text messages over the last couple of months. It was touching, really. She wanted to tell Tripp, to find him where he was. To engage. Where had Tripp been all these months? She'd find him. She'd go now and tell him about Edward, about the lump. She'd hold his hand and lead them into their bedroom. She wasn't that old. They could have another baby.

She tiptoed down the stairs. Determined to surprise him. Oh, Tripp, she thought. Once we shone like the sun. She crouched on the landing. After a few minutes her eyes adjusted. Tripp was feeling around in some antechamber. There was a door made from the wall creaking open. A chamber she didn't know existed. Virginia's skin goose-pimpled with excitement. A funny secret room. She crept down a few more steps.

Except she wasn't prepared. Tripp in a small room carved from the basement. Tripp stood surrounded by guns of all shapes and sizes that she'd never seen before. He had his back to her and she noted then a kind of elderly stoop to his shoulders. Ah, she thought. Tripp too is getting old. Tripp is getting old and these guns, Virginia thought, for now she was thinking wildly, are a kind of exoskeleton. Something to prop him up, shield or blind him from old age, from death, somehow, maybe even from her. Fragile Tripp.

The stair creaked. What did she care if Tripp saw her? This was her house too. Tripp whipped around. His eyes were wild and he had a gun of some sort in his hand and it was pointing at her, and Virginia noted, even as he squeezed, that his finger was on the trigger.

Is this death? said the air. My blood is the color of lack. Love is time slowing, said the specks dancing in the bare bulb that hung from the basement ceiling. There is joy now too. No one would imagine that. Now she was on the floor of pressed dirt but before, weeks ago, she'd woken up weeping into her daughter's hair and Virginia hadn't wanted to know, no Virginia hadn't wanted to see that Charlotte was awake and murmuring: Mommy? Are you okay, Mommy? Are you going to be okay, Mommy? Yes, baby. Yes, she'd said. Or maybe she'd said no. Or her dead stepmother lying on a gurney dressed in a hospital gown with her mouth made up with bright-red lipstick. She'd told her stepmother she had cancer and her stepmother had said nothing. Well, what had Virginia expected? She was dead. Had her stepmother also known this exquisite joy? Or how Richard had followed her to the bathroom at Margot's dinner party and asked her if she was okay and she'd asked, Do I look unwell? And she'd said she was dying but he hadn't heard her. Love is truth, but love is also lying. Love is mostly lying.

The human organism was so complex it was impossible to know how not to damage it.

I'm not in love with you anymore, Tripp had once said in a fight they'd had when there was still enough between them to incite anger. But I feel love for you sometimes, he'd said. It is a kind of love, still. Now he wasn't saying anything of the sort. In fact, now Tripp was crying, leaning over her and cradling her head in the crook of his arm and punching at the screen of his cell phone. Virginia lowered her eyes and scanned her body and saw shining ribbons of red like a dying actor in a Shakespeare play she'd seen at Stratford-upon-Avon. She'd taken Charlotte, and Charlotte had been too young but so easy to travel with, like a backpack. So young, like maybe three or four, that people had tsked at them when they'd taken their seats and Virginia had leaned over and whispered into Charlotte's ear: We can go whenever you want. If you get bored, we'll go, okay? But Charlotte hadn't been bored. She'd been very quiet and well behaved and only when Mercutio was stabbed and the ribbons of blood had exploded from his chest had Charlotte cried out with excitement and fear and clapped her hands and Virginia looked around apologetically but also with joy and pride.

To see a person is to love them.

Virginia looked down at her chest and saw the blood that welled around her shirt and soaked her. She could feel Tripp's hard strong knee pressed into her back and could feel his arm hold up her head. She'd married him for his arms she remembered. He was so strong and tall and sure.

Tripp had his phone in his hand and he talked to someone. He'd taken off his T-shirt and shoved it into the space in her shoulder where the bloody ribbons had flown from and Virginia smiled up at him.

Love is the present tense.

Thank you, Virginia said to Tripp, who stared back at her, his eyes wild with terror and adrenaline. Take all my loves, my love, yeah, take them all. Virginia heard the calm, tinny voice of a woman from his cell phone. Sir? Sir? Virginia smiled weakly and said to Tripp, Thank you so very much. I feel love for you too.

And then, a stream of fog and light that slipped under the basement door. It entered and filled and warmed the damp fecund under the ground air. Virginia was dying and Virginia was thinking: *When this is all over I'll call Edward after all.*

Chapter Twenty-Seven

TEXTS AND EMAILS

Text Messages from Dr. Edward Bang:

Hi, Virginia. I've left you countless phone messages and emails. Listen. I know you're scared. And I don't really know your financial situation but it seems maybe not great but I want to help you. I found a program—in Baltimore actually—and it's free. I could still be your MD. Please call me. I know you have a little girl and I know she wants you to be her mom for as long as possible. I cared for you once and I know it didn't go so well in the end, but I can care for you a different way.

Hello, Mr. Travis Powers: My name is Dr. Edward Bang and I'm an oncologist here at Sloane Kettering. I have been trying to get hold of your wife, Virginia Powers, about some medical concerns I have. You're listed as her emergency contact and since I haven't been able to get in contact with her, I'm contacting you. There's some issue with your insurance and I don't know if you are aware. You can change your insurance to cover Virginia's condition. There's also emergency Medicaid. I'm happy to walk you through the process and answer any questions you might have. I'd like to discuss this with either you or Virginia as soon as you or she are able.

Hey Ginny . . . I've been calling around to oncologists and hospitals. It appears you're not seeking treatment anywhere. I know you. Remember? I know the things you've struggled with but if you just get back to me I can help you. I know I can. Please call me. —Edward

Ginny, I heard what happened. I am so glad to know you are okay. Please send me a message when you are able and let me know how you're doing and if I can help you in any way. If I don't hear from you, know I'm thinking of you. I'm rooting for you. —XO, Ed

Emails:

Dear Petra School Parents:

The school would like to thank our wonderful parents and students for the turnout last night at our fundraiser dinner for the Powers family. Thanks to the Erez family for the quinoa spaghetti dinner and the Landesmans for the vegan paella and Gunter Olson for the Swedish meatballs! Better than Ikea! We wish the Olsons well on their new adventures. Thanks to all of you, we raised $800 for the Powers family! We are sure Charlotte Powers felt wrapped in love during this difficult time. Please watch out for a follow-up email from our newest incoming family member, Margot Cohen. She will arrange meals for Virginia Powers while Virginia recovers from her surgeries and will be need lots of donations. She will send around a Meal Train link shortly.

We are also pleased to report that in a few months, once he is released, Travis Powers will join the school as our chief custodian. He will run workshops to teach children woodworking and masonry skills. Please welcome him with open arms. We at the Petra School believe in second chances.

Chapter Twenty-Eight

RACHEL AND GUNTER

IT WAS EXCITING to move. Rachel enjoyed the nitpickiness of carefully packing every box, bubble-wrapping fragile items. She had the kids separate newspaper sections, fold clothing, and assemble cardboard boxes. Anders was excited and Lydia was weepy. Will there be Soul Creatures in Dubai? Lydia had asked in a near sob. Rachel shook her head no, trying to hide her delight. No Soul Creatures in Dubai.

Out the window, Rachel could see the trees full of leaves as they shook in the late spring wind. Everything was in bloom and flowering. It was beautiful at last, there in the village not far from the sound. A train's horn. Small birds outside that Rachel could not identify chattered to one another. A fawn followed her mother in the neighbor's backyard. Gunter ordered pizza from Two Boots and they sat around the table surrounded by packing boxes and ate slices on paper plates. Rachel and Gunter locked eyes across the table. They were on to brighter adventures.

Gunter had signed on for a project in the UAE. They would stay six months at a five-star hotel that boasted a mall and a ski mountain and Rachel had decided she'd take it easy for a couple of years until they returned. There was more than enough money. The kids would attend American schools. They were flying out in a couple of days.

Margot called to see if Lydia wanted to come over and bake a cake with her. I don't want to send extra work, Rachel said.

It's all right, Margot said. I'm sure you guys have plenty to do. Richard took the boys to the Y to swim and you know I'll miss my Lydia time. Bring Anders too. He could pile in with my boys. I'm sure Richard won't mind. Virginia will be there too. With Charlotte.

But you are so pregnant. You should rest while you can!

Bring them over, Margot sang happily. I'm doing fine. Pregnancy gives me enormous energy. I feel like Superwoman.

Gunter drove the kids to the Cohens and returned. Nothing to do but take a nap, he said. His thick eyebrows waggled.

He had been so much more involved since the crisis had happened, and he'd begged to return. So involved and apologetic. At first Rachel had been pleased and by the time she'd felt annoyed by his cloying obsequious apologies, he'd mostly returned to his old Gunter ways. She liked him that way, truthfully. He wasn't for everyone but he was for her.

Gunter would do anything to avoid another divorce.

Did you? she'd asked him in the middle of their last 3:00 a.m. fight, worn out. She wanted the truth finally. Did you fuck her?

No, Gunter had said. He hung his head. But I wanted to. He stopped for a moment, gulped air, and stood quiet.

What? Rachel said. What were you going to say?

Would you like to know the weirdest thing about Agnes?

Yes, Rachel said. I really would.

I was at her house just one time. It was quite grand actually, right on the sound. She'd inherited it from her great-aunt and in a spare bedroom was a portrait of her great uncle in full Nazi uniform. I was quite shocked.

And that was when you knew it wouldn't work out?

Well . . . to be honest I was kind of fascinated. But yes, soon after.

Upstairs on the stripped-down bed, Gunter took his tiny blue pill. Rachel found the small discreet vibrator she could wear nestled against her and it didn't get in the way or make much sound.

Rachel checked her email one last time. An email had come in from the Petra School. Rachel scrolled to the bottom and clicked the Unsubscribe button.

Chapter Twenty-Nine

CHARLOTTE

CHARLOTTE WAS CAREFUL not to hug her mother too hard, but sometimes in the night she'd find herself with her arms wrapped tightly around her mother's middle and her mother lying on the bed with her eyes wide open in the dark and wincing. I'm sorry, Mama, Charlotte would say. Her mother would nod and tell her it was okay. Everything was okay. That was what Charlotte needed to hear.

Charlotte had asked when her father would come home. Her mother told her she wasn't sure. Did Charlotte want to see him? Charlotte didn't know. She remembered the few days she'd spent with him when her mother had gone to Kentucky. How shy she'd felt with him at first. She'd always been a little afraid of him but in those few days he was different with her. He'd promised to take her to a camp in the woods where she'd learn about nature and wilderness and how to live off the land.

She'd read a book like that, *My Side of the Mountain*, about a boy who lives in a hollowed-out tree and befriends animals. She'd asked if he'd ever read it and he said he hadn't. She wanted to tell him about the book but could see he was bored and didn't really listen. It was okay, she'd thought to herself. Dads were often distracted.

The night of the accident, George's mom had woken Charlotte from her bed and taken her back to George's house. Your mother will be okay, she'd told Charlotte. I promise you. She's going to be fine, and in a couple of days we will take you to see her. Charlotte had been too stunned to cry the first few nights and George's mom apologized. She didn't feel that well but was there anything Charlotte needed? There were so many things Charlotte needed, but she didn't know how to ask and later at night she'd heard Margot throw up in the bathroom down the hall. Charlotte understood something. George's mom was pregnant. Charlotte didn't know how she understood it. She thought that maybe because she was close to being a teenager. She finally understood things now. Grown-up things.

It was George who'd finally explained everything to Charlotte. He'd overheard his brothers. Her father had shot her mother in the basement stairwell. It wasn't on purpose, George told her to comfort her. But the police had had to take him away.

Charlotte knew all of that too. She'd already figured it out.

After her mother had come home bandaged and groggy, Charlotte couldn't figure out why her father was in a place called a halfway house if he hadn't done anything wrong. Hadn't her mother and everyone said the shooting was an accident? And once back in school, Charlotte didn't believe Forrest—a kid in her grade who had Tourette's or something—who'd shouted that her father had been charged with attempted murder. It bothered Charlotte so much that Agnes brought Charlotte into her little office and rubbed her back while she cried. Your father is a good man, Agnes had said. He made a mistake. But he is a good man.

But still, Charlotte wasn't ready to see him.

Meanwhile, parents and teachers from Petra brought food to the house and others drove Charlotte to and from school. George's mom came over and cleaned the house top to bottom. She did the laundry and showed Charlotte a new way to fold her clothing, which Charlotte promptly forgot. And then, a week after Virginia came back from the hospital, Virginia gave Charlotte a phone. It was brand-new and still in the box. You can call me anytime, her mother had said. Even at Petra? Charlotte asked. Even at Petra, her mother replied.

Charlotte knew the phone was some kind of compensation and it didn't help with the nightmares Charlotte had, but still. Snapchat was fun. She enjoyed scrolling through Instagram. It turned out a lot of the older kids at Petra had secret phones too. It was fun to connect with the kids from the public school and see the kind of clothing they wore and the filters they used. When Virginia was better, she took Charlotte shopping. She let Charlotte know on the drive to the mall that she'd sold her book, not for much, but enough that Charlotte could get some new things. Charlotte bought all the things she saw fashionable girls wear on social media. She bought skinny jeans and little cropped T-shirts and hoodies and a pair of cool sneakers.

That night as she carried the bags from the car to the house, Charlotte had a realization. She wanted to go to public school.

Okay, her mother had said. Of course. Whatever you want. I'll enroll you for fall.

No, Charlotte had said. I want to go now. As soon as possible.

You don't have friends in public school! her mom said. Besides, you love the Petra School. Every kid loves the Petra School! Do you want to deal with testing and bullies and everyone on their phones and, like, *eating disorders*?

Yeah, Charlotte had said. I do. She laughed. Even the eating disorders, Mom. She jutted out her front lip. She felt strong, stronger and bigger than her mom for the first time in her life. Yeah, she said again. I do.

She didn't go to the public school, not right away at least. Instead, Virginia decided they would move to Kentucky outside of Louisville to the house Virginia inherited from her stepmother. The house Virginia had grown up in. Virginia decided a clean break was good for the both of them. Charlotte was more reluctant to leave. She'd never lived anywhere else. And she realized she was sad to leave her father behind. Will Dad come with us? she'd asked her mom. He might, Virginia had said, but her eyes darted around in a way that made Charlotte feel uncertain and nervous.

Charlotte did see her father once before they moved. She met him at Starbucks not far from school. He seemed kind of out of it and didn't talk much. Charlotte felt the adult strain of having to make conversation. Would you want me to come with you to Kentucky, he'd asked. When I get out of here?

Charlotte didn't know what to say. She sipped at her frappuccino. It was so sweet it made her teeth ache. I guess so, she said finally.

Movers came the following week while Charlotte was at school, and when she returned, the house was empty. Charlotte and Virginia drove down together. As they passed the exits and mile markers, Charlotte felt a great tension unravel in her chest. She wouldn't have to pass the basement stairs ever again. She could become something completely new. She could become a cheerleader or an actress or a poet or a Goth. She could get into anime and K-pop or hip-hop. Maybe she could be a model or a singer or an actress or maybe just a basic girl, get good grades, live her life.

Charlotte liked the big public school. She didn't mind feeling lost in the corridors or crowd that pushed through the hallways. She grew two inches the first few weeks in Kentucky. She tried out for volleyball and she fell into a crowd of athletic, smart girls. Virginia started treatment, warning Charlotte that her hair would fall out and that she might be tired a lot of the time but that she'd be okay.

One day after volleyball practice, Charlotte sat alone in her room. The room had been her mother's bedroom, and the vanity where she sat had also belonged to her mother. She stared at her reflection in the mirror and scraped her hair off her face. She imagined herself without hair. Maybe she would shave her head in solidarity with her mom. With her hair back, she realized she looked more like her dad than her mom. It surprised her. She'd never thought she looked like either of her parents. She'd always just been Charlotte. Downstairs her mother puttered around in the kitchen making dinner, loading the dishwasher, and Charlotte felt a sense of warmth and well-being thinking they'd be all right. They would go to the mall. Virginia would buy Charlotte a new sweatshirt. Everything was going to be okay.

Acknowledgments

S PECIAL THANKS to the amazing Katie Raissian, Elisabeth Schmitz, Deb Seager, Justina Batchelor, Julia Berner-Tobin, and Paula Cooper. Love and gratitude to agent extraordinaire Duvall Osteen for everything. Much gratitude to Yvette Sims, FNP, Michael Radziemski, Michelle Goodman, and Anthony Keene for their knowledge and expertise. And to dear friends Steven Wagner, Abi Keene, Sara Weiss, Ophira Edut, and Anna Shalom for reading drafts. Thanks to David Means, Lauren Acampora, Kim Brooks, and Jonathan Vatner for moral support and writerly conversation. Very special thanks to Bill Hutchison, dear friend and reader for twenty-five years. All my love to my family for putting up with me.

Planning for the End of the World (Or: Hopelessness as Superstition)

First published on *Literary Hub*

The night Hurricane Sandy hit my community—upriver in the Hudson Valley—I spent the night with a group of friends at a neighbor's house. The children were nestled safely in the basement. As the storm grew stronger, one friend headed down to join the kids. I stayed upstairs by the sliding glass doors that led to the back porch. The house was surrounded by enormous old oak trees that had been there for a couple of centuries. They probably weren't going anywhere. But smaller trees around the perimeter of the property crashed down at regular intervals, taking out first the fence, and then an old shed.

We opened a bottle of mezcal and laughed with drunken nerves each time we heard a crash or when the wind really started screaming. The power had gone out, as it usually did at the first gust of wind, and the living room was lit with candles. It was eerie, vaguely romantic, and oddly exciting.

I vanished into the kitchen to get a glass of water and when I returned, some of our group had run out into the blackness. I stood on the back patio gripped with anxiety until they came back a minute later to tell me what they'd surveyed: lines down, cars smashed, road impassable by felled trees. Power was out for millions up and down the eastern seaboard. All around us we heard small gas generators powering up. Three hundred people died in the storm. We had no power for ten days and spent hours idling in lines stretching miles to the one gas station that was still open. The gas station only took cash and charged five dollars a gallon. Days passed and the grocery stores emptied. Target shelves emptied. It was junior varsity doomsday.

When Sandy hit in October of 2012, I'd already been thinking a lot about the end of the world. While Y2K had come and gone without incident, 2012 was the year the ancient Mayans had predicted would herald the end times. I, newly stable both financially and emotionally, finally happy, with a town I really loved and two small children, was somehow susceptible to this idea. It had wormed into my head during that whole year. Though I joked about it, and laughed it off, there was something in me that was becoming a true believer. 2012 would be the end, I decided, and Sandy cemented it.

I've always been superstitious, curious about the occult, astrology, prognostication. I will never turn down a tarot reading. Something about all of it still makes me shiver the way a good ghost story did at camp, or a Ouija board pulled out at a sleepover. If it was late in the evening and I was feeling vaguely mystical or apocalyptic or just bored with the Mayan predictions, I would instead watch Howard Camping, the evangelical, predicting the world's end. I would read all about Nostradamus and his predictions on the internet. It was like looking for WebMD symptoms, but instead of a fatal illness, I was watching for complete and universal devastation.

Unlike the Boomers, who didn't know what to do with excess, the Gen X midlife crisis is about preparing for and dealing with decline. The decline of our planet, our political systems, salaries, soaring housing and education and health costs. But for the first time, we were prospering and I was stunned by my good luck and believed it would all end in the most devastating and global way. To imagine the end times will happen in one's lifetime is fairly egotistical. The end times have been prophesied for centuries. And besides, already all over the globe disasters were occurring, people's worlds destroyed. Wars, flooding, tsunamis, fires—it was already happening somewhere to someone. Even here.

After Sandy, one of my fellow hurricane watchers attended a week-long tracking course for people who wanted to learn to track animals and live off the land. He has a PhD in math from an Ivy League school and attended the tracking course with men who had done time, urban commandos, special forces, corporate executives, and academics like him. There was no dominant political affiliation. All they had in common was a belief that living off the land—starting fires from scratch, hunting animals, and building lean-to structures out of brush and branches would be useful when the end of the world happened.

The world-famous tracker advertised his pedigree. He said he'd learned everything he knew from a native prophet, and he'd been working with law enforcement for several decades. The prophet had taught him world-class tracking skills and he'd also prophesied horrific events—massive catastrophes that would necessitate all knowledgeable people to scurry off into the woods until the coast was clear. My friend, the professor, came home breathless telling us all he knew, planning to attend future courses.

In spite of my staid village existence, preparing for the end times seemed fairly doable. As a child, my mother had taken me camping in a broken-down Chevette. By the time I was nine, I could jump out and push it while my mother popped the clutch to get it started again. We camped all over the country in all months of the year. February in Michigan? No problem. We had sleeping bags, a small leaky backpacking tent, a tiny stove, and wool long johns. We had backpacked all across the Presidential Range in New Hampshire and camped through the Adirondacks.

By age ten I could put up a tent by myself in the dark in the middle of a thunderstorm and I could start a fire and even light the tiny butane stove. And later I'd used those roughing-it skills in New York City when I'd lost my apartment and found myself penniless in an abandoned building in Harlem, squatting there alone for months until I could save enough money on my publishing salary to move to a proper room. I'd come from pioneers and sharecroppers, making do with almost nothing as they trekked across the country in covered wagons, stealing the land of the people who'd lived there for thousands of years. "Cleared the snow off the stove," my great great great grandmother had written in her journal around the 1880s somewhere in Iowa with her seven children, "and made breakfast."

If necessary, and for survival, I could live off anything. I could live anywhere.

One weekend my friends and our families trooped upstate to visit a doomsday compound. The compound was hours north in the Catskills, several acres with a small pond and a large garden. There were four or five large houses in various stages of construction and one older house already kitted out with solar panels and a stove so efficient that a cord of wood could heat it for three days and leave behind just a cup of ash. We saw the food storages below. Large bags of shrink-wrapped rice and beans. The guy who ran the place was a professional homeopath.

He tried selling us his homeopathic remedies by telling us what was wrong with our kids—my son had pulled my daughter off a top bunk bed—and the homeopath had just the remedy for him. He tried to sell us a stake in the community, and as we sat around his table in the one finished house in the community, eating his homemade chili, while we endured his annoyance at our dogs and kids, and ordinary messy family lives, he shared his theories for what would end the world.

The first problem, at least for me, was that all his ideas were different. He talked about shifting poles and solar flares knocking out the power grid worldwide. Maybe for days, maybe forever. He spoke of climate change and widespread flooding and hurricanes. Each would be equally as devastating as the last and they would all happen simultaneously. It was so over the top that at the time, I found myself wanting to laugh. And he wanted to know if we wanted to buy a $30,000 room in his apocalypse Airbnb. For an extra grand, he'd throw in a yearly family plan for homeopathy.

"*Your* kids," he said, staring right at me, "could really use it." I looked around at the dowdy furniture, and outside at the houses in various stages of construction, and the rough beginnings of a garden we'd be expected to toil at for our sustenance. I thought about the rice and beans stashed under the house, and I thought about living in someone else's property—with *this* guy in charge and I thought, No way would I live here. Even if fire was raining from the sky.

And the second problem I had was all the people this kind of plan left behind.

So we walked away. We walked away from all of it. From survivalist training and from the compound upstate and from the end of the world. We look back now a little bewildered. What were we thinking? If the end of the world actually happened, my professor friend said, I realized I'd rather just hold hands with my loved ones and jump